THE LEAGUE OF FREAKS

and the secret key

ALBERTO HAZAN, M.D.

ISBN: 1451519168
ISBN-13: 9781451519167
Library of Congress Control Number: 2010903011

When we internalize our senses,
we gain unlimited power;
[That is] how children become Gods.

–Shreeveda Gurumandvi,
Hindu Goddess, 5th Century B.C.

What's Inside

Prologue ix
One: Leaving the Bronx 1
Two: Lost In Salem 7
Three: A Path In Motion 13
Four: The Demon Twins 21
Five: The Myth Of The Secret Key 29
Six: Hindu Gods 37
Seven: Shree, Shree, The Bumblebee 47
Eight: Regarding The Treasure 57
Nine: Back To School 63
Ten: A Close Call 71
Eleven: Target Practice 77
Twelve: The Best Laid Plan 89
Thirteen: Changes 95
Fourteen: The Transformation 101
Fifteen: All About Bees 109
Sixteen: Not Alone 117
Seventeen: Ellie Espagueti 123

Eighteen:	A Field Trip To Harvard Yard	129
Nineteen:	Inside The Statue	141
Twenty:	Pinocchio's Lair	147
Twenty-One:	First Flight	155
Twenty-Two:	Girls Just Want To Have Fun	163
Twenty-Three:	The Other Freak	169
Twenty-Four:	Discovering Ralph	179
Twenty-Five:	Halloween Night	185
Twenty-Six:	An Uninvited Guest	191
Twenty-Seven:	The League Is Formed	199
Twenty-Eight:	The Secret Key	207
Twenty-Nine:	Defeat Of The Freaks	217
Thirty:	A Common Dilemma	223
Thirty-One:	A Word Of Advice	231
Thirty-Two:	Stealing It Back	239
Thirty-Three:	At The Twins' House	247
Thirty-Four:	Resolution 101	251
Thirty-Five:	Making Amends	255
Thirty-Six:	A Sixth Sense	261
Thirty-Seven:	Treasure Hunt	265
Thirty-Eight:	The Boathouse	271
Thirty-Nine:	A Shaky Foundation	275
Forty:	A Subterranean World	283
Forty-One:	Unlocking Doors	287
Forty-Two:	Water	293
Forty-Three:	Wind	299
Forty-Four:	Fire	303
Forty-Five:	Earth	307
Forty-Six:	Gold, Silver and Jewels	313
Forty-Seven:	A Celebration's End	317
Forty-Eight:	Hear No Evil	319

Forty-Nine: Showdown At The Boathouse 323
Fifty: Saying Goodbye 331
Fifty-One: Massachusetts General 339
Epilogue.. 345

Prologue

Shree struggled to free herself from the tight rope around her wrists. With each attempt, the rope cut deeper into her skin. Blood trickled from an open wound on her face, but the drops never reached the floor.

Instead, they were lost in the sea of water that submerged part of the chamber where Shree and her friends were imprisoned. The dark blue stream coming from the tunnel's entrance below them was now gushing in at an alarming rate. There was water up to Shree's knees. The room was filling up fast; soon she'd drown.

But Shree wasn't thinking about herself. Her friends around her were also in danger. One lay unconscious next to Shree. Another attempted to free her hands from a barbwire cage. A third was wrapped in rope and struggled as the cold water inched up her body.

The only one of her friends who could help them was nowhere to be found. Shree was afraid he was beaten up and left for dead somewhere in the deep recesses of the underground labyrinth.

Shree heard the Demons transferring the treasure from the side of the collapsing building. They had ambushed Shree and her friends, stolen the treasure, then tied them up and left them to drown.

The boathouse creaked and moaned, its foundation shaking from the rushing water that filled the room. Tiny pieces of debris and wood floated all around Shree. Large sections of the ceiling were now falling from overhead.

Shree thought about her parents and regretted not having told them about the treasure. She had snuck out with her friends. Nobody knew where they were. Nobody could help them. They were going to die alone, without their families. They'd drown inside the boathouse, steps away from the Harvard University campus where the search for the treasure had begun a few months back.

What frustrated Shree the most was that each one of them had secret powers. But they couldn't use them. They were helpless, having been stripped of their ability to transform by the Demons.

A large plank of wood fell inches from Shree. She flinched and looked up at the ceiling. A piece of sheetrock dangled dangerously over her head.

The water was now at Shree's shoulders. She looked to her right, tears streaming from her eyes as she saw her smallest friend fighting to catch her breath, craning her neck to gain one last ounce of oxygen before drowning.

Shree closed her eyes tightly and tried transforming once again. If she could turn into her animal form, she could fly for help.

A loud sound overhead broke her concentration. The boathouse was now on the verge of collapsing. When Shree looked up, she saw the large piece of sheetrock falling down from the ceiling. In a second, it would hit her and likely knock her unconscious.

She braced herself for the blow.

Shivering from the cold water that surrounded her, she repeated the words that helped her turn into a different species.

But it wasn't working. Nothing was working.

Shree was going to die. And she'd be responsible for the death of her friends and the destruction of Harvard University.

Chapter 1

Leaving The Bronx

An hour after her going-away party, Shree woke up with her head on her mother's shoulder and drool leaking from her mouth. The clock on the dashboard of the car read 5:30.

Inside the cramped green station wagon, Shree sat squished between her mother and father. Her family's possessions were scattered all around her. Shree knew that if they were still in the Bronx, they'd be firing up the grill and dancing to the music. She thought about feigning sleep, but she felt her mother move beside her.

"How do you feel, honey?" her mother asked.

"How do you think she feels?" her father responded before Shree had a chance to reply. "She is very happy to be attending her new school, are you not Shree?" Dr. Mandvi looked at her and smiled. "You will have many more opportunities there. And you will prove to them that a girl from the Bronx is just as smart as anyone from Cambridge. Will you not?"

Shree was sure her father was right, but he'd just reminded her that in a couple of days she'd be starting the new school year. Normally self-confident, Shree was having doubts about fitting in at her fancy private school in New England. Kids from all different backgrounds went to her school in the Bronx, the only home she'd ever known. Shree loved it there. She wondered what kind of kids lived in Cambridge. Would they see her as different—or worse?

She looked at her father, whose smile disappeared as he turned from Shree to the road ahead. He fumbled with the portable GPS system he had bought for the trip and continued talking about her new school. Shree tried to act as if she was listening, but she had tuned him out. Around their ancient station wagon a sea of cars could be seen, barely moving. It was Friday rush-hour traffic and they were lucky to be inching along Interstate 95. They hadn't even gotten out of New York City yet, and they'd been on the road for almost an hour.

"Oh, stop lecturing your daughter, Rajandra." Mrs. Mandvi winked at Shree and elbowed her in the ribs, never dropping a stitch. Her mother was an avid knitter and could put together a sweater with her eyes closed. She began to hum an old familiar Punjabi song as she crisscrossed the purple wool around the two metal needles again and again.

"Well, she needs to continue doing well in school, does she not?" Shree's father stopped speaking, looking up for a moment out the window, then back at the GPS device. He dropped it to the floor in frustration. "This device is not constructed as it should be. And look at this traffic. It is slowly going to kill me."

Mrs. Mandvi tied off the ball of yarn she was using and began weaving in the last bit of orange thread. A new ball of yellow yarn lay on the car seat next to her. Shree crinkled her nose at the pattern, and prayed that her mother wasn't making this sweater for her.

Shree looked around the sea of cars again, wondering if they were ever going to make it to Cambridge. She thought about her old home, and sighed. She was going to miss a lot about the Bronx, especially her best friend. Shree could trust Tanya Johnson with anything. And that's why Shree felt comfortable telling Tanya *everything*.

Tanya was the only person who didn't think the weird changes Shree was experiencing were just a result of delayed puberty. Her friend was just as concerned as Shree was about the things that were happening to her. In fact, Shree was certain something was wrong. It was as if her body was fighting a war from within. At times, her eyesight was as sharp as a hawk's. At other times Shree could hear sounds from a mile away, but couldn't see a foot in front of her face. And then there were the bouts of nausea and headaches, the numbness and tingling, and the visions. It all worried her, a lot.

Shree wondered if she'd ever find someone like Tanya at her new school. Probably not, she decided. It was sad to realize that she might never be able to share her secrets.

Shree shook off that last thought and turned on the car radio. She fiddled with the old knob to get to her favorite station, 97.1 FM.

"Oh, no, no, no. We are not going to listen to the hippie-hop. We are going to converse like a normal family." Her mother turned off the radio and placed the knitting needles on her lap. "Look at this traffic, Rajandra. Now it is most certainly your fault, dear, for leaving so late," she admonished. "You and your GPS. See how much that has helped? But no matter, this traffic gives us more time to spend together."

Shree's father did not seem to agree, however. He began honking the horn like a typical New Yorker. "It is not logical. I do not understand these people. You are slowly killing me," he yelled to the cars through the open window.

As if that's going to help, Shree thought. It was difficult to see from where she was sitting, but she was pretty sure that across the top of the dashboard was the exact same sea of cars she'd glimpsed at ten minutes ago. The hoods of all the cars were lined up across the four lanes of the interstate. She gave up. What was the use of looking if all she saw was the same thing?

Shree decided that keeping quiet was the best tactic. Eventually her dad would calm down and things would be back to normal, right?

She realized that she hadn't said a single word since leaving the Bronx, and no one had asked her why. Shree was upset about having to move. She understood that this was a great opportunity for her father, a physicist and biomedical engineer, who had recently landed a job at Harvard University. This gave him the status he finally deserved. It also granted Shree admission to the exclusive

Kennedy Academy, one of the wealthiest and most academically rigorous high schools in the Northeast.

Shree sighed, thinking about how happy her parents were that she'd be going to a prestigious private school in Cambridge, when all she really wanted was to be going back to her old public school in the Bronx. She knew she should be thankful, and she *was* a little curious about what this new place would be like. But she was too bummed out to feel curious or thankful about anything. She was also a bit anxious since she had always been the top student in her class. Shree knew that the kids at her new school were likely to be as smart as her, if not smarter.

Since the car was going nowhere, Dr. Mandvi put it in park and picked up the GPS again. He fiddled with it some more in a last attempt to program the system. He fumbled with the buttons for ten minutes, still unable to make it work. "This darn thing," he mumbled.

Shree looked over at her mother, anticipating what was coming. She knew that her mother could never pass up an opportunity to tease her father, even as she gazed at him adoringly. "One of India's brightest scientists, a Harvard professor yet, and you cannot get that little machine to work?" She laughed long and loud, her shoulders bobbing up and down and jostling Shree about in the small space.

Her laughter had the desired effect, and soon a wide smile made its appearance over Dr. Mandvi's face. He turned to Shree with a wink. "What do you mean one of the brightest? I thought you always said I was the smartest scientist in all of India."

"Oh, do not kid yourself, Rajandra. Your cousin Kaushal is every bit as bright as you, perhaps even a bit brighter.

He has won four awards at University while you have won only three."

"Please remember that my cousin is only a mechanical engineer. If I wanted an easy lifestyle, I would have certainly gone into that field. Biomedical engineering is much more difficult than simple mechanical engineering and—" His voice trailed off as the car in front of him started to move slightly.

He looked in the rearview mirror and then to the right and made a sudden acceleration, almost hitting the car in front of them. At the station wagon's sudden jerk, Shree and her mother were thrown left, then right, into each other. Her father squeezed by the traffic to take the last exit before the turnoff to Connecticut. He missed the exit sign by mere inches, and then they were free and clear.

"I think I know a shortcut," he said, adjusting the rearview mirror.

Shree looked at her mother, and they both rolled their eyes. This was going to be interesting.

Chapter 2

Lost In Salem

Three hours later, Shree and her parents had traveled a great distance, but had gotten nowhere. Trekking along back roads in the dimming light of day, they were now confirmed one hundred percent lost. From the few signs they'd passed, they were probably still in western Massachusetts, although secretly Shree wouldn't be surprised to learn they had reached Canada or Mexico.

Taking one of what proved to be many wrong turns, her father was now directing the station wagon onto a narrow, dark road with little room for oncoming traffic, should there be any. Her father and his shortcuts had added hours to their trip. Shree ached from so much time in the cramped quarters.

She was also tired, but it sounded like her mother was in worse shape. "I told you that we should have stayed on the main highway, Rajandra, but no. You do not listen to what I have to say. And now I have to urinate. Very, very badly. Soon I will have to go by the side of the road."

Shree heard the rare note of annoyance in her mother's voice and was relieved not to have to say anything herself. She looked out the window to see if she could catch any signs of life, but all she could see was the road ahead, and trees, large trees on both sides of the narrow strip of pavement.

Dr. Mandvi, too, had his eyes glued to the road. "Yes, yes, my dear. I am sure there will be a sign to lead us back to the highway soon."

"Hey, what's that up there?" Shree spotted a large sign and pointed to her right. It was one of the old-fashioned kinds with light bulbs that spelled out the letters. So many of the bulbs were out on the big sign, though, that the message was illegible. "–lly's -ine-, —lect–les, and -sed Bo–s," she read.

Her father pulled the car right up under the sign until the headlights lit the sign.

"Oh," Shree said. "Sally's Diner, Collectibles, and Used Books. Cool."

"Let us hope it is open," her mother said. "Rajandra, park over there. Thank goodness we have found some sign of life."

Shree's father slowly drove the car over the gravel into the small lot and parked next to the big clapboard house. Theirs was the only car in the lot.

Shree couldn't be sure in the dusky light, but the diner looked blue and had a faint air of neglect about it. Not very inviting, she thought. Then again, any place with food, books, and "collectibles"—whatever they were—might turn out to be interesting.

Shree and her parents climbed the stairs to the porch that surrounded the house. With every step they took, the stairs complained, sounding loud in the quiet of the early evening.

"This is spooky," Shree whispered.

"Shhh," her mother cautioned. "We do not want to offend anyone."

Finally they reached the front door. A small faded sign hung on the doorknob that read "OPEN" in what had been big red letters that had faded to a pinky-gray. The sign was covered with dust. The screen door hung crookedly from the frame, but the door looked solid enough, made of a beautiful golden wood. Through the windows they could see a long counter and several booths, although the place seemed deserted.

Dr. Mandvi stepped forward and pushed the door. It protested with a loud squeak but opened into the diner. Shree and her mother followed him inside. From there, she could see that it was completely empty. A single dim bulb hung from the middle of the ceiling, casting shadows.

"Hello," her father called. "Is there anybody here?"

For a moment none of them spoke or moved, straining to hear an answer. Then, just as Shree was about to suggest finding the bathroom and taking off again, they heard a faint voice from somewhere in the back.

"I'm coming, I'm coming," the voice said. And sure enough, in another moment a tiny bird of a woman had entered from the kitchen behind the counter, wiping her hands on a light brown towel. She was muttering what sounded like, "Didn't expect them until a little later, did I," but Shree knew that was impossible. She must not have heard the woman correctly.

Shree liked to think that she'd seen it all, especially growing up in New York City, but this woman was one strange-looking being, all wrapped in a long black shawl and an even longer black skirt. Beneath some kind of a bonnet, which she tied under her chin, a cap of snow-white hair stuck out in all directions. The woman's face was a mass of deep lines and wrinkles. She had to be at least a hundred. Two tiny piercingly green eyes peered out from their sockets, lit up with something—anticipation, glee, cunning—Shree wasn't quite sure what. And her narrow pointy ears added yet another dimension of strangeness.

The woman spoke again in a voice that alternately purred and almost screeched. "Don't just stand there dawdling," she said. "The name's Twichett, Sally Twichett. Come in. The restrooms are just over there behind the register."

Shree's father seemed to have lost his capacity for speech. Now he cleared his throat and made an attempt to state his family's business.

"Well, yes, um, we *are* in need of food and the facilities. You see, we took a wrong turn somewhere. We're on our way to Cambridge." Dr. Mandvi's words drifted off. He turned helplessly to his wife.

Shree's mother took over smoothly. "What my husband is trying to say, is that we have been on the road for hours and—"

"Yes, yes, of course," the woman said, dismissively. "I'll just go into the kitchen and get the food ready." Then she looked at Shree. "The bookstore is straight through there, my dear," she said, pointing down a hallway to the left of the kitchen.

"How nice," her mother said. "Our Shree does love books, and I am sure she would love a couple of new ones. Shree, we do not have long, so pick out one or two books while Mrs. Twichett is preparing our meal. Find something you have not read, dear, perhaps by that author you like so much—you know, the one who wrote *Twilight*."

"Yes, deary," Mrs. Twichett chimed in. "Go on now. There are thousands of books to choose from. See what you can find."

Even from a few feet away Shree could see the whiskers on the woman's chin, and a small scar hidden underneath the right side of her lip. Shree nodded, though going down that long dark hallway was not something on her list of must-dos. And yet, Shree couldn't pass up the opportunity to explore the bookstore—and the rest of the house.

Chapter 3

A Path In Motion

The hallway had very little light and the floorboards creaked with every step Shree took, but she had to admit that she was intrigued. Soon her parents' voices had diminished until she heard nothing at all except her own breathing.

The walls were covered with paintings of different sizes. They all looked very old, the canvases shiny and with the occasional crack, the frames large and ornate, many covered in gold leaf. One group of paintings caught her eye. They were the same size, lined up in a row. Their frames were all similar as well, but these were not like the fancier ones; they were plain and made of wood, and Shree was sure she smelled mildew, which seemed appropriate considering the state of the rest of the diner.

She walked slowly past each painting, noting that as a group, they seemed to be telling a story. In the first, a beautiful young woman with pale hair and green eyes was dragged towards a clearing. In the second, that same woman, to Shree's horror, was burned at the stake. It was a gruesome image and Shree felt goose bumps rise on her arms. In the third painting, the woman had risen from the ashes and transformed into the form of a witch. In the last painting, the witch was surrounded by the villagers who had attacked and killed her—but this time they were all dead. The woman had exacted her revenge.

Oh my God, Shree thought. Could they have driven clear past Boston and ended up in Salem, Massachusetts?

Shree took a few steps back, staring at the last painting. It was difficult to make out any detail in the woman's face, but her eyes told it all: hatred, revenge, agony. Shree felt lightheaded.

Suddenly, she caught something moving from the corner of her eye, but when she turned and stared down the hallway there was nobody there.

Shree thought about retracing her steps and heading back. But she was too excited to quit her search. She took a deep breath and kept walking towards the foyer, shooting occasional glances back over her shoulder. Each step she took was accompanied by a high-pitched creak.

The further she got from the dining room, the darker it got until all she could think about was how creepy the house was. Outside Shree could hear the wind, which had picked up speed and was now howling through every one of the old house's cracks.

Finally she saw the room of books up ahead. She cried out in delight and forgot everything but the room filled from top to bottom with thousands of books, just as Mrs. Twichett had said.

As she walked towards the back wall of the library—for it was more of a library than a bookstore—she felt the warmth of the fire, which was crackling in the hearth. She knew it was still hot outside in the summer air, but inside the diner it had been decidedly chilly and she was grateful for the heat.

Shree looked at the titles of the books and noted that they were arranged by subject: mysteries and magic took up a whole wall, and next to these were history books of all kinds. To Shree's right, almost hidden by the dark paneling, was another smaller hallway.

Curious, she followed it as far as it led to another room, much smaller, colder, and even darker than the rest of the house. Again, Shree caught something moving, this time from across the doorway. She stood perfectly still and stared out, but she couldn't see anything. Feeling that she was trespassing but unable to keep her curiosity in check, Shree felt along the wall for a light switch and was pleased when her hand found it by the door. She turned it on and looked around. It was a kind of sitting room apparently, with a couple of small tables, a comfortable-looking armchair, and several small objects scattered on every surface. This must be the "collectibles" mentioned on the sign hanging outside.

This room was also lined with paintings. They revealed the same girl pictured in the prior set of paintings in the hallway, but this time the girl was being harassed by a band of older school children. The paintings showed the girl being shoved from a third-story window, falling to the ground, and finally, lying on the ground after the fall. But the last painting was the most unusual one of all. Because instead of the image of a hurt—or dead—girl crumpled on the ground, there was something else. The girl's fingers had lengthened and her nails had become sharp and pointed. Her back had become curved and her eyes slightly slanted. In fact, the girl was no longer a girl at all. She had become a cat. And the only thing left of the girl of the previous paintings was her face—a human face that, as Shree drew closer for a better look, was now on the head of the cat. It was none other than a younger version of Mrs. Sally Twichett herself.

Shree took several steps back, covering her eyes with her hands. She stopped dead in her tracks as she heard the sound of footsteps coming from the other end of the room. Her heart pounding, she turned and ran out of the room and back down the hall into the library. But after a couple of steps, Shree realized she'd forgotten to shut off the light. She expected Mrs. Twichett to be standing there, shouting in anger. But nobody was there. Again, Shree heard what she thought were footsteps, this time coming from the long hallway leading back to the diner, and she whipped around. "Mrs. Twichett? Is that you?" Shree whispered.

But there was no one there. Nothing.

Shree ran back to the small room and quickly shut off the light.

Back in the library she turned on the single lamp. She was instantly drawn to a hardcover volume with a tan leather case. It rested against the mantelpiece of the room's single fireplace. Shree picked up the book eagerly but handled it cautiously, seeing that its cover was threadbare and its thin pages were nearly falling out. The words, *My Search for John Harvard's Treasure: Gold, Silver, Jewels, and the Secret Key, by Sir Malcolm Winthrop*, were printed in an ornate faded gold script. Shree turned one page over and then the next, careful not to let any of the loose pages drop to the floor, feeling excited. She kept getting the strange sensation that she was being watched, but every time she looked over her shoulder the room was empty.

Shree noticed right away that the book she held was arranged in a very peculiar way. The first half of the book was a collection of journal entries written by the author, while the second half was a series of detailed hand-drawn maps. Shree attempted to read some of the excerpts, but it was difficult to make sense of any of it. Not only was the writing hard to make out in the dim light of the room, but most of it was written in some kind of ancient English. She caught the occasional word or two, but definitely not enough to decipher what the author had written.

The most interesting part of the book was its collection of maps. Each map was beautifully drawn and depicted a different view of Cambridge, Massachusetts. The first was a bird's-eye view of the entire city. Next, there was what looked like a map of Harvard University, labeled "Harvard College, 1638." Several other maps followed. The most interesting one was the last map of the book, which caught Shree completely by surprise. It showed a close up of Harvard Yard with tiny, almost illegible scribbles in the margins. An arrow pointed to an "X," which was marked in thick black ink with a note to the side. Shree didn't have to understand the funky old English to know what the "X" meant: a hidden treasure.

This was it. This was the book she wanted. Shree looked up and was startled when she caught sight of herself in the big window across the room. Just a reflection, she thought. Suddenly, her reflection was joined on the right by that of another—Mrs. Twichett's—and she spun around. But no one was there. Shree didn't know whether to be scared or annoyed.

Then, from behind her a voice spoke. "I see you have found what you were looking for."

Shree jumped a mile, clutching the book to her chest.

Mrs. Twichett stepped forward to stand only inches from her face. "A treasure hunter, eh? Of all the wonderful books in my collection, you choose this rubbish?"

"Well," Shree floundered. Couldn't the woman announce herself like everyone else? "M-my father says that a good book always finds you, and this one looked kind of interesting."

"Don't be fooled, young lady. Treasure of this sort is unlikely to exist—and many who have tried to find it have the scars to prove it. Some have even died in its pursuit." Mrs. Twichett's voice had taken on a decidedly hysterical quality. "A secret key that can unlock unlimited treasures— hogwash! Nothing but myths and ramblings, ramblings and myths." Mrs. Twichett turned to go. She gave Shree a final hard look. When she spoke again her voice had returned to its former calm. "It's time to return to the diner, dear. Your parents are waiting."

Shree didn't know what to think about Mrs. Twichett and what she'd said, and she was torn between returning to the diner to eat and settling in the library for a long look at the treasure book. But she knew her parents would be looking for her. Too much time had already passed.

Shree shook her head. She felt disoriented. She knew one thing, though. Hearing the old woman talk about the treasure the way she did made Shree more interested.

Mrs. Twichett was clearly waiting for Shree at the entrance to the hallway. Shree had to go. But she didn't want to leave the book. Slowly, she went over to Mrs. Twichett, the book still in her hand. When she got about a foot away, the woman reached out her bony arm and grabbed her. Shree's instinct was to pull away, but the woman held her tight and leaned in close.

"Listen to me," she said and gave Shree a long look as if deciding whether or not to say what was on her mind. "It is true that this book is meant for you, my dear. And you must follow what has been set in motion. But do not abuse what it holds within. Go about it alone and you will suffer the consequences of your actions—and fail just like the others before you."

Shree looked down at the book. The faded gold letters now sparkled as she slowly moved the book from one hand to the other. When she looked up, Mrs. Twichett was gone. Instead, Shree saw a black cat crossing the hallway and disappearing into the distance.

Suddenly, she felt herself being pulled to the right by a strong hand. Shree gasped and clutched the book against her chest once again.

"Shree, where have you been?" Her mother looked petrified. "What has taken you so long? We must eat quickly and get back in the car. Have you found a book?"

She looked around at the collection of books that lined every inch of the room. "This place is very, very spooky."

"Hi, Mom. Sorry for taking so long, but I was speaking to Mrs. Twichett. She's letting me have this book, it's really cool mom, it's actually a treasure—"

Her mother cut her off, looking irritated by Shree's comment. "What do you mean you were speaking to Mrs. Twichett? Mrs. Twichett has been in the kitchen making us our dinner. Let us not start any nonsense young lady. Let us go back and eat. I will not have any fibs from you tonight."

"But—" Shree looked hurt and confused. She attempted a feeble protest, but it was no use. Her mother had taken the initiative and was already four or five feet in front of her, walking back quickly towards the kitchen.

With each step she took, Mrs. Mandvi shook her head and muttered, "Very, very spooky indeed."

Twenty minutes later, Shree and her parents pulled out of the diner, attempting once more to find their way to Cambridge. As they drove out of the lot, Shree glanced back to see if Mrs. Twichett was watching. But all she saw was a dark parking lot, a decrepit sign swinging on its hinges, and a big black cat with piercing green eyes resting comfortably by the window sill.

Chapter 4

The Demon Twins

Shree groaned and pulled her pillow over her head. The light was killing her eyes. She didn't want to wake up yet. She had plans with Tanya to go to the park, but maybe she'd just stay in bed a few more minutes.

Suddenly, Shree realized where she was. She was not at home in the Bronx. She and Tanya had no plans that day. Slowly the details of where she was and how she got there came creeping back.

They'd arrived in Cambridge at about 10:30 last night. Shree hadn't been able to see much of her new house because it was so dark, and they were so exhausted that after opening up the house and unloading the air mattresses and a few blankets, they'd all gone straight to bed. The movers weren't arriving until later that morning with the rest of their things. Shree groaned again, thinking about all the unpacking and organizing she'd have to do to get ready for school.

Finally, she lifted the pillow from her face. She smelled something delicious. But how could her mother cook without any pots or pans? Her parents were speaking loudly; she could hear them all the way from downstairs. They always did that whenever they wanted to wake her without actually coming into her room, and she was notorious for sleeping in until they forced her to get up.

Oh well, she might as well check it out. She was hungry.

Shree didn't bother dressing first. She put on her favorite robe over her boxers and t-shirt and tied the sash. It was ratty, she knew, but she'd wait until it fell from her in tatters before she ever let it go. A gift from her grandmother in India, it was one of her most special belongings. On went her slippers and then she was ready to see what smelled so good.

"Shree, is that you?" she heard her mother call.

"Yup. I'm starving. What smells so good?"

"Your father went out to the bakery," Mrs. Mandvi said. "Come, have some hot chocolate and a muffin."

Shree sat down, chose an apple cinnamon muffin from the plate, and looked around her new home. The cabinets of the kitchen were an unusual shade of lavender, but Shree decided she liked them.

Her mother saw her gazing at them and put her hand up to the cabinet by the sink. "What do you think, honey? Are they too much? I think I might like the color, but we could always repaint."

"No," Shree said definitively. "I like them. I think they're different."

Just then Dr. Mandvi came into the room. He was carrying an enormous container of what Shree knew would be English breakfast tea, his favorite kind. He used to drink only chai, but when he'd come out to visit Harvard a couple of months ago, he'd developed a taste for this stuff. Last year Shree's mother had bought him a travel mug which read, "Smile if you love an engineer," and now he was never without either of them. He picked up a chocolate chip muffin and gave a contented sigh. "Aaahhh, these are good, are they not, Indira?"

Just as she was about to answer, the doorbell rang. With a start, her mother started barking orders. "That must be the movers," she said. "Rajandra, please go open the door. Shree, go get dressed. Quick! We have so much to do today."

Shree heard the no-nonsense tone in her mother's voice and headed for the stairs with her hot chocolate. She planned to put on her jeans and go explore the neighborhood until the movers were done unloading the truck. Hadn't her mother mentioned that a girl about her age lived next door?

In ten minutes, Shree had brushed her teeth, thrown on an old shirt, and pulled on her jeans with the holes in the knees. She added the brand new yellow-and-black-striped Adidas sneakers Tanya had given her as a going-away present, and was out the door, her backpack with the treasure book slung over her shoulder. As she left she yelled to her father, who was gesticulating to the movers as they guided the sofa into the living room, to let him know that she'd be out looking around. His lips formed the message, "Do not go too far," and then he turned back to direct the two men in baseball caps and back braces.

The first thing Shree noticed was how open everything was in her new neighborhood. Instead of tall buildings and cement as far as she could see, huge old trees graced every yard, and none of the homes were more than two or three stories. While the Mandvis' house was much smaller than the two on either side, Shree still thought it looked nice. Instead of white with dark green shutters that the other two had, 25 Berkeley Place was pale yellow with wooden shutters and black trim, which seemed to fit perfectly in this old section of Cambridge.

Shree got as far as the sidewalk before remembering the girl in the house next door. Her mother had pointed out their kitchen window to the house on the left, the one with the rusty swing set in the yard. Didn't look like it got much use anymore, that was for sure. Shree automatically scanned the house, looking for signs of life. Was it too early to ring the doorbell? As she answered her own question (yes), she thought she saw the curtain in a window on the second floor move. She stopped for a better look, just glimpsing what she thought was the flick of a ponytail and a pink shirt before the curtain dropped back down again. Hmmm. Well, maybe she wasn't ready to come out yet, Shree thought. Maybe the girl was shy. She'd come back later and try again.

Shree took a left at the end of the corner onto Berkeley Street, another narrow street. In the Bronx, Shree had relied on the fact that all the avenues and cross streets were laid out in a grid-like fashion. Here, the streets were curvy and of different lengths. After a hundred feet she got to the next corner, which curved twice before intersecting with a slightly wider street. The street sign was bent and had been pummeled with something hard, maybe a rock, but was still legible—Craigie Street.

Which way to go now? Shree decided to take a right, making sure to note the turns she was taking so she could get back home. A little way down Craigie Street she passed Craigie Circle. First Berkeley Place and then Berkeley Street, then the two Craigies—couldn't they come up with any new names for these streets?

After walking another block, Shree saw a little park up ahead on her left. Excellent. Shree loved to rollerblade, even if she did spend a lot more time on the ground than on her feet. The streets were full of cracked sidewalks where the trees had broken through the cement; it'd be nearly impossible to skate on them. But Shree could see as she approached the park that the walk surrounding the grassy area was ideal for skating. She also noted that there were several wooden benches lining the south end of the park, shaded by giant maples and oaks. It looked like a great place for writing in her journal and for reading her new book. If only Tanya could be there to hang out with her.

Shree was about to sit on the bench over by the big marble fountain when she felt a light draft. She stepped quickly off the sidewalk, and almost before she knew what was happening, she had narrowly missed getting hit by the figure that came speeding down. It was a lanky African American boy who seemed to be flying, rather than running, down the path at full speed. Shree realized that he was being chased by a second figure, who trailed behind by only a few feet.

As the first boy was making the turn, he looked back and smiled. Shree could've sworn he wiggled his large ears at her, but she was probably seeing things.

The grin on the boy's face, though, quickly disappeared when a third figure appeared from out of nowhere and tackled him, knocking the kid with the big ears to the ground.

A few minutes later, Shree heard laughter coming from behind the trees. Curious, she approached slowly and heard the voice of one of the boys pleading, "Come on, guys, back off. It's not my fault you're stupid. You may be brothers, but that doesn't mean you have to share one brain."

Shree took a few more steps until she was past the big trees. The path opened onto a wide expanse of green lawn. She could still smell the scent of newly-mowed grass. But the scene was ruined by the two boys with Red Sox caps worn backwards on their heads. They each held the shoulders of the third boy, the thin black kid. The boys were taking turns slapping him around. They seemed furious, Shree guessed, about that last comment the kid had made.

Despite being beaten, the boy on the ground was talking non-stop, trying to make the bullies back off by making jokes. Obviously, this technique wasn't working. In fact, it seemed to be making them angrier. Just as Shree was about to yell at them to stop, one of the Red Sox kids saw her standing there. "What the hell are you doing in our park?"

"Who—me?" Shree asked. *Their* park?

"Yeah," the other kid said. "You."

Shree saw that the two boys weren't just brothers, they were identical twins. Their dark hair was the exact same color, almost black, and stuck out from under their hats. They were big guys and looked like they knew their way around a hockey puck or a football. At their feet lay the poor kid. What was their problem anyway?

"Listen, I don't want any trouble," Shree said. "But you need to leave that guy alone."

"Like we care what you think," the first one said, a baseball bat held threateningly in his hand. "Get the hell outta here. This is our park."

The boy on the ground mustered the courage to mimic his tormentors in a high squeaky voice. "Yeah, this is *our* park. We own it. We pay rent. We're big tough guys with little p—" His sentence was cut short by a blow to the stomach.

For someone who was so messed up, he sure wasn't hesitating to give his opinion, Shree thought.

"Hey, shut up, you big-eared freak. Did you hear that, Tim? I guess Dumbo Dave wants another beating."

"I heard him, Tom. I guess he hasn't learned his lesson yet. We'll just have to fix that, won't we?"

Dumbo Dave? Learned his lesson? Who were these idiots anyway? Shree usually didn't hesitate to speak her mind, but now she found herself tongue-tied. Who were these jerks and what had this guy Dave done to them? She could see where he got the name, though. His ears were huge, poor guy. She'd better keep her mouth shut—for the moment—and leave. It went against her nature, but without a better plan—and without backup—she was in no position to argue.

"She's nothing, just ignore her bro," the twin called Tim said. At least she thought it was Tim. It was impossible to tell them apart.

His brother held Dumbo Dave down by the neck. He stopped hitting Dave long enough to chime in, "Yeah, just turn your butt around and go back where you came from."

Shree decided she had to do something—anything— to stop them. But just then Dave spoke again. "Don't worry about me, babe. They'll get tired of kicking the crap out of me sooner or later. Save yourself."

Shree didn't want to leave but couldn't think of anything she could do to stop these demon twins either. And she'd promised her parents she'd stay out of trouble. With a long look at Dave, Shree turned around and headed back to Craigie Street. Around the corner she could still hear them laughing. Poor, poor Dave.

Chapter 5

The Myth Of The Secret Key

The incident with the twins had taken away Shree's initial joy at finding the park. After walking for ten minutes, Shree reached Berkeley Place. She jogged up the path. It would take a while before she'd feel normal about coming up to this house and calling it home, but she already liked the fact that she could hear the wind in the trees and see green, not gray, all around.

The moving truck was in the driveway and almost empty now. A few boxes were still lined on the long metal ramp that sloped from the van to the ground, and the last pieces of furniture sat on the lawn. Shree picked up a lamp that belonged in her father's study and said hi to one of the moving men who was coming out the door.

Then she saw that the girl from next door was standing by the end of the porch where the two yards met. Shree started and almost dropped the lamp. Why was the girl just standing there? Why didn't she come over and say hello?

Shree decided she'd take the initiative. "Hey," she said. "How's it going?"

The girl glanced sharply at Shree but said nothing.

"I'm Shree," she tried again. "You live next door, right?"

"Right."

The girl fairly snarled her answer and again Shree was taken aback. She had perfect blond hair, deep baby blue eyes, and a perfect tanned body, but she wasn't very polite. What was up with that? First the boys in the park and now this. Cambridge wasn't a friendly place if these guys were any indication.

The girl eyed Shree up and down. "So, you're supposed to be the smart girl from the Bronx." She shook her head. "I'm not impressed."

Shree didn't know what to make of that comment, so she ignored it. "What's your name?" Shree asked.

"Katherine." This was said grudgingly, but at least it was a start.

"Well, Katherine, it was nice chatting with you," Shree said. It hadn't been, but Shree was trying to be friendly, even if this girl couldn't manage it. Shree stood on the porch a moment longer, but since Katherine said nothing more, Shree figured their conversation was over. "Well, see you later." She turned, rolled her eyes, and went inside to find her mom, leaving the girl and her cold smirk on the lawn. Whatever. If that was the way she was going to be, Shree would look elsewhere for friends.

"Hey, Mom, where are you? Where does this lamp go?"

"Oh, good, you are back," her mother's voice came from somewhere in the house. "I am upstairs. Come help me move these bookshelves, Shree. They belong on the other wall."

Shree took the stairs two at a time and looked into a couple of rooms before finding her mother in the third one, obviously meant to be her father's office. His desk had already been placed to face the door and boxes of books and papers were stacked chest high. Her mother stepped out from in back of one of the stacks. She was covered with dust and her hair was a mess. Shree couldn't help it. She burst out laughing. To see her mother with even a hair out of place was rare, if not a once-in-a-lifetime occasion. And it was even more unusual to see her wearing anything other than a sari.

Immediately, Mrs. Mandvi looked down at her jeans and then felt her head. "Oh, my, I imagine I look quite the sight. How do books gather such dust while they are stored in boxes?"

Assuming it was a rhetorical question, Shree said nothing, but went over and picked a big dust bunny out of her mother's hair.

"Thank you, dear. Here, I will take that lamp. It belongs on your father's desk. Are you hungry? Is it lunchtime already? Come downstairs, I will make you something to eat. I think the dishes and silverware boxes are on the table—at least I hope they are."

Her mother was not usually so scattered, but then they didn't move every day. Shree knew her mother missed her own friends, especially Tanya's mother, Sherika. The Johnsons lived only two doors down and the two families

31

were very close. On top of that, Shree suspected that her mother was a little concerned about making new friends among the mothers of the kids at the private school and her father's colleagues at Harvard. Shree reached out and gave her mother a hug.

"What was that for?" her mother asked, but Shree saw she was pleased, and was glad she'd done it.

"Nuthin'. Let's go eat," Shree answered.

"Noth-ing," her mother reminded. "Please use correct diction."

"Yes, ma'am." Shree saluted playfully, and then followed Mrs. Mandvi down the carpeted stairs to the kitchen.

After lunch, her father took his tea out to the porch and sat down on the top stair. "Shree, come sit by me for a moment," he called.

"Okay, be there in a minute."

"Rajandra, let the poor girl alone," her mother chastised him. "She has unpacking to do. She must get ready for school."

"Now, now, Indira, I am going to talk with my daughter for a few moments, that is all. Leave us be."

Shree saw her mother smile and shake her head.

"Hey, Dad. What's up?" she asked, preparing for the lecture that was coming.

"Of course I am fine, Shree. Come tell me what you think of your new neighborhood."

"Well, I couldn't picture it at all when we were in the Bronx, but now that we're here, I guess it's kind of cool. I mean, I already miss all the different smells and languages everywhere, but it's really pretty here. I found a park down the street too, where I can read and rollerblade." Shree purposefully neglected to mention what had happened with the demon twins and the boy with the big ears.

"I thought you would like it," her father said. "See the birch trees and pine trees? So many different plants and flowers. Those over there are irises. Did you know that, Shree? And those climbing the fence are lilacs."

Her father could never pass up an opportunity for a teaching moment. But she did love the flowers and the smell was divine.

"And the Charles River is just a short distance that way," Dr. Mandvi pointed. "Next weekend we will all take a long walk and explore the area together. You will need to learn the neighborhood so you can get around on your own. I will drive you to school on your first day, but after that I think you will be able to walk there by yourself. It is not too far."

With the reminder that her first day of school loomed a few hours ahead, Shree got quiet.

"Shree, I know it is hard to start a new school, but you will be fine. You must be on your best behavior and study hard. You understand that, do you not, Shree?"

Oh, Oh. The lecture had begun. "Yeah, I know," Shree said grudgingly.

"Remember, you can accomplish anything you put your mind to, as long as you are clear about your goals."

"I know, I know, Dad." Her father didn't ordinarily go on and on like this, so Shree wondered if he was just as nervous as she was over the fact that she was starting a new school.

"Good. You realize, my daughter, that as human beings we have the power to control our own destinies. It is the choices we make everyday that guide us through this life and lead us to our ultimate path: for example, doing well in school and attending university at an institution like Harvard."

Normally, Shree would daydream whenever her dad got too philosophical, but she saw this talk as a perfect opportunity to bring up John Harvard and the treasure she had read about in her book. She knew her father was trying to steer the conversation in a different direction, but this was too good to pass up. "Um, yeah, I guess you're right. By the way, Dad, have you ever heard anything about John Harvard's treasure, or a secret key?"

Her father was as distracted as Shree hoped he'd be. "Hmm, yes, it seems to me that I do remember something about a treasure and a key of sorts. I heard about them when I had my tour of the campus recently. But I am sure it is only a myth, my daughter. These things tend to be nothing more than legends based on superstition, you know. Secret keys, the power to walk through walls—to fly—although possible, I would have to say these things are highly, highly improbable at best, at least with what we know today."

"Yeah, but what exactly did they say?" Shree asked.

"Let us see—they mentioned John Harvard's book collection and his untimely death—and the building of his statue. The tour guide spoke about how John Harvard had taken his entire fortune of gold, silver, and jewels and hidden it underneath the university campus. Most people think it is somewhere in Harvard Yard, near Widener

Library. But again, I think that it is just nonsense that they speak of."

"Well," Shree paused, trying not to appear too excited. "What about the secret key? Did the tour guide say anything about that?"

Dr. Mandvi rubbed his chin and stared in the distance. "Let me think." He spoke slowly, taking a sip of his tea as he pondered the question.

Shree was now at the edge of the step, waiting eagerly for her father to continue.

"Yes. There *was* mention of a secret key, supposedly also hidden somewhere on the campus. The guide was quite enthralled with the myth of the key. She said that without the key one would not be able to open the chest—I believe she said a wooden chest—that is said to hold John Harvard's treasure. What I found particularly interesting was her statement that this key also had some other kind of power. It would allow its user the ability to fly or to walk through walls or perhaps to enter other dimensions." Her father's voice trailed off as if he himself was entering another dimension.

Shree tried to bring him back down to earth. "What else, Dad?"

"What? Oh, yes, forgive me, dear. Let me see. Oh, yes, the myth of the secret key. Unfortunately, Shree, I do not think the tour guide's information was in any way sound scientifically. In fact, I found it highly suspect, at least in terms of the laws of physics. But I do believe that—" Her father turned his head around and looked towards the kitchen. "Was that your mother calling, Shree? Coming, dear," he called into the house. "We must go help your mother. We can talk about this another time, yes?" He got up and wiped off the seat of his pants.

Shree wanted to say yes, but somehow she knew she wouldn't bring it up again. Somehow she knew it was better to keep her mouth shut.

Chapter 6

Hindu Gods

Shree's first day at her new school had arrived. She had expected a little more fanfare, some sign that something big was happening. But it was quiet. Really quiet. Instead of the constant sounds of traffic and the honking of car horns, she heard only the occasional twitter of a bird, and her mom singing as she always did when she worked in the kitchen.

Shree looked over at the chair by her desk. She had unpacked most of her clothes the night before, but still hadn't decided what to wear. At home (she had to stop saying that) she'd never really cared what she wore, but if she wanted to make a good first impression, she should at least try to look—wait, what was she thinking? She'd never cared before about the impression she made. She wasn't going to start now.

With a burst of energy, she made her way through the sea of clothes and paraphernalia. She had unpacked the day before but hadn't quite gotten to the putting-away part yet. Yes! The tail end of her favorite shirt was peeking out. It was a little wrinkled, but that was okay. And where were her jeans? The ones with the embroidered pockets—they were so comfortable—there they were. Shree shoved at the pile to pull them out and knocked everything off her chair onto the floor. She sighed loudly and began putting all her books back in her backpack. As an afterthought she added the treasure book to the stack.

"Shree? Shree! You must come down here right now. You will be late for your first day of school. Shree, are you ready?"

Shree jumped up. She'd been daydreaming for who knows how long and she hadn't even brushed her teeth or combed her hair. "Coming, Mom. I'll be right down," she called.

She buckled the backpack and set it aside. She pulled her jeans on and slid her feet into her new favorite pair of shoes, the yellow-and-black Adidas that Tanya had given her.

She headed downstairs. Her mother was still clucking to herself, mumbling something that sounded like, "That girl. I must talk to her about using her alarm clock before I simply go mad." Shree sat down and quietly picked up her juice.

Her mother turned from the stove. When she saw Shree she shrieked. "No, no, no," she exclaimed in horror. "Do you not remember? You must wear your new uniform to school. Now you will be late. How could you forget? Hurry, go back upstairs and change. Your uniform is hanging in the closet. Go, now. Your father is taking you to school and he is leaving in two minutes."

Shree looked at the clock. Her mother was right. She had exactly two minutes to get upstairs and change. She raced for the stairs, complaining loudly. "I don't understand why I have to wear a stupid uniform to school anyway."

Sure enough, hanging in her closet were the pale blue shirt and black linen pants of Kennedy Academy. At least it wasn't a plaid skirt like she'd seen on so many of the Catholic schoolgirls in the Bronx. That would be even more of a disaster. Still, the clothes were uncomfortable and binding, not like her jeans and cotton shirt. The pants were a little short, too, for her legs. Ugghh. But there was no time to make adjustments now. She should've tried them on again like her mother had suggested. Shree ran back downstairs, out of breath.

"Mandatory uniforms ensure that there will be less competition among students," her mother said as if their conversation hadn't been interrupted. "There is less pressure to impress people with fancy clothes. It helps students concentrate on their studies. I just wish I had time to iron your shirt again."

"I know, I know," Shree said. The logic did not impress her. "But we didn't have uniforms in the Bronx and no one seemed to care."

Then her mother noticed Shree's shoes. "Shree," she said. "Are you certain you want to wear those sneakers? They are awfully, well, they are quite bright and—"

"No time for ironing or shoes," her father said. "Shree does not want to be late for her first day of school, and

I must not be late for my first day of teaching. It will be very bad if I am late for my first day. Very, very bad. We must make a good first impression on our first day, yes?" Sporting a brand new vest and tie, Dr. Mandvi looked at Shree for confirmation.

Shree nodded absently and took a slice of toast off the plate on the table. "I'm ready, let's go."

"But Shree, you have not eaten anything," her mother protested.

But Shree and her father were already halfway out the door.

"Shree, here is your lunch," Mrs. Mandvi said, running after them. "And Rajandra, do not forget your tea."

"Thank you, my dear. You are always taking very good care of us," he said, and kissed her on the cheek.

Once in the car, Dr. Mandvi fumbled through a collection of scientific journals scattered on the seat between them while they waited at the red light on the corner of Berkeley and Craigie. "I hope I did not forget that article," he said. "I am presenting it today. Shree, can you see it here? Look in this pile. It is entitled, *Antimatter and the Subconscious: Using the Mind to Transform Matter*."

Shree combed through the journals. Her dad was always surrounded by a moat of papers. "Here it is. What's antimatter, Dad?" The articles seemed to be written in another language altogether, the words were so foreign. The few she did recognize, like proton, neutron, and electron, were few and far between other ones with weirder sounding names, like quarks, neutrinos, and alpha particles. She read a few words of one that was on "string theory," thinking that might make sense, but stopped when she realized it had nothing at all to do with real string.

Dr. Mandvi pulled across the intersection. "Antimatter is the opposite of everything you see in the world. The theory that I am working on has to do with the possibility of being able to access this antimatter from the subconscious, especially during moments of stress. It takes concentration and will power, along with a bit of knowledge on the basic principles of quantum mechanics. But, under certain circumstances, human beings can potentially tap into this antimatter, which would mean an infinite amount of power."

They had reached the second and final light before the turn to the school on Garden Street. Shree looked at her father. "Dad," she said, thinking about the treasure book in her backpack. "Can this antimatter stuff help you in real life?"

"Well, yes, I suppose it could. Hypothetically speaking, human beings have the potential for changing into different life forms or objects, or even for taking on new powers, if we can find a way to tap into our subconscious. The possibilities are quite fascinating, really."

"What do you mean?" Shree asked.

"Look at Indian culture. Hinduism is full of gods that have part-human and part-animal qualities. It is precisely why I went into the field of biomedical engineering. You see, antimatter, when appropriately utilized, can allow a person to take on the powers of anyone or anything." Dr. Mandvi paused, taking a sip of his tea. "The god Ganesh, for example. He is part-elephant and part-human. As an elephant, he is the remover of obstacles, and as a human he is known for his wisdom and intelligence."

"Why would anyone want to be an elephant?" Shree asked, confused about that particular god's selection. Shree thought about which animal she'd choose if she were a god: a lion, an eagle, a shark, maybe a bear. But definitely not an elephant.

"It is not that simple, my daughter. Back then, our ancestors consulted the oracles for advice before choosing. Unfortunately, they did not always have this luxury. Sometimes circumstances in their lives prevented them from making their own selection. Sometimes destiny decided for them."

Shree had tuned out her father's last words as they reached the school. She thought about the paintings in Mrs. Twichett's hallway and the book, not understanding how the Hindu gods could have anything to do with helping her find the treasure.

"It is as I have taught you all along, Shree," her father was saying as they pulled into the long driveway of the school. "You can accomplish anything you put your mind to. Anything. You must only focus on what you want and allow your inner spirit to do the rest. Somehow everything else will fall into place."

They pulled up to Kennedy Academy in the green station wagon. Shree was nervous, hesitating to get out of the car. She saw the BMWs and Range Rovers in the lot and knew her father had seen them too. She felt a little embarrassed for him, but saw he was smiling encouragingly at her. He didn't seem to mind the obvious discrepancy in their vehicular status—or lack thereof. She put her hand on the door handle but didn't get out, even though she could see that she was late and other stragglers were rushing to get to the doors before school started.

"Shree," her father said gently. "It will be okay. You are a very smart girl and you will find your way in this new place. Remember, you are a Mandvi." He gave her a big smile and patted her once on the back.

Shree opened the door and stepped out of the car onto the curb. Just as her father pulled away she remembered his new job. "Good luck, Dad," she called, but wasn't sure he heard her.

Shree began the long walk up to the stairs of the school. The brick building was clearly old but well-maintained. Over the massive arch and doorway it read, KENNEDY ACADEMY, *Veritas Supremus Totus*, with a fancy crest underneath the words. The entrance to her school in the Bronx had simply read, "Public School #54." Shree pulled back her shoulders. As she jogged up the stairs, she felt a slight jostle on her right.

"Oops, s-s-sorry," a voice said.

Shree turned to see a plump, red-haired boy with a zillion freckles. "That's okay," she said. But he'd already dropped his gaze and taken off into the building.

Shree followed him through the door and looked around. A sign for the administrative offices hung on the wall just inside, pointing down the hall to the left. She walked through the throng of kids who were high-fiving, throwing fake punches, and generally acting up after not seeing each other all summer. Shree felt the sharp pang of missing her friends as she opened the door to the office.

The cool quiet of the room was a relief. An impressively tall woman stood behind a long counter. Plants were everywhere; ivy leaves paraded up the walls and spider plants hung from the beams in the ceiling. Shree timidly made her way to the counter and stood behind two teachers, who talked to the woman whose hair was stacked high on her head in some kind of a beehive-looking thing. Her clothes were a real contrast—a pattern of bright green and orange. Shree kept her face from reacting but she wanted to cover her eyes from the glare. Finally, the two teachers parted and Shree stepped up.

"Yes," the woman said, not unkindly. "Can I help you?"

"I'm Shree Mandvi," she answered. "I'm new here. I need to get my class schedule, please."

"Oh, yes, Ms. Mandvi. Take a seat. I'm Mrs. Steiner. I'll pull your file and get you a map of the building so you can find your classes. It'll be just a moment."

Shree took a seat on one of the metal chairs against the wall. She hoped Mrs. Steiner would make it quick so she wouldn't be late for her first class. She didn't even know where it was.

The door to the office opened and in walked a girl with long blond hair. "Good morning, Mrs. Steiner. I have to—"

"Just a moment, Ms. Jenkins. I'll be right with you."

The girl rolled her eyes and tapped her foot impatiently. Shree couldn't believe it. It was none other than her friendly neighbor, Katherine. Their eyes met. Shree wasn't going to let this person get the best of her. "Hi, Katherine. Here for the party?"

Katherine looked at Shree like she was crazy. Not too quick, huh, thought Shree. And no humor either. Tanya would definitely have something to say about *that* if she were here.

Just then Mrs. Steiner came out from behind the counter, saving Shree from further pain. "Ms. Mandvi, here is your paperwork. Please give each one of your teachers the correct form to sign. At the end of the day, stop by the office and return the forms to me." Then she addressed Katherine. "Ms. Jenkins, your timing is perfect. This is Shree Mandvi. She has just joined Kennedy, and you are in most of her classes. Please act as her guide today and see that she gets to them without getting lost."

"But—" Katherine protested.

"I know time is a consideration, Ms. Jenkins. But I have a note here in case you are tardy."

Katherine looked miserable, but there was no room for argument in Mrs. Steiner's eyes. Katherine took the note, spun on her heel, and moved for the door.

Shree got up and thanked Mrs. Steiner, who nodded to her briefly before marching back behind the counter. Katherine hadn't waited and was already moving down the hall. Shree hurried to catch up.

Of all the guides in the world, she had to have this one.

Chapter 7

Shree, Shree, The Bumblebee

Two minutes, two flights of stairs, and three corridors later, Shree and Katherine reached room 208. The class was still bustling and the teacher was writing on the board. A spitball flew past Shree's head. Ignoring Shree, Katherine went straight to her seat and started an animated conversation with the boy to her right. His black hair was spiked up in different directions and his eyes glinted. Shree recognized him immediately. It was one of the twins from the park.

Shree walked over to the teacher and presented her with the form for her to sign. This was English class, her favorite—at least it had been her favorite at her old school.

"Hello, Ms. Mandvi, is it? I'm Mrs. Tillman. Welcome to Kennedy. Let me know if there is anything I can do. Take any seat—perhaps there?" Mrs. Tillman's clipped tones told Shree she was likely from England. The teacher pointed to the only unoccupied seat, located all the way in the back. It was a seat in the very last row, and Shree had the sense that it was placed there as an afterthought to accommodate the new kid in class. Mrs. Tillman handed back Shree's signed form and turned to the blackboard.

Shree took her time getting to her seat, walking slowly and scanning the students in the classroom, trying to find a friendly face in the sea of strangers.

Mrs. Tillman turned away from the board to face the class, which immediately went silent. "Good morning class. My name is Mrs. Tillman and I will be your English Literature teacher this year.

"I gather you all had a productive summer," she continued, not pausing for an answer. "Good. School is now in session and your vacation is over, so please pay attention. We have a lot to get through this year. Let us begin."

Shree was shocked at the change in atmosphere inside the classroom. You could hear a pin drop. In the Bronx there was always a whisper or a pen scratching or a giggle. Here the only sound was of textbooks and notebooks opening. Shree snuck a look around and saw the straight backs of each and every kid in the class.

Mrs. Tillman picked up a piece of chalk and began writing a list of authors on the chalkboard. Without being told, the class began to copy the list. Shree followed suit, but after the first two or three names she stopped and smiled to herself. With the exception of one author, Shree was familiar with every name on the list. In fact, she could recite by memory the books she had read by each. Most of them hadn't been assigned in school; she'd read them on her own. It wasn't always fun being an only child, and at times she'd prayed long and hard for a little brother or sister, but it had left her plenty of time to her own devices. It would definitely help her now.

"Since you are sophomores," Mrs. Tillman said, "you will have more responsibility. There will be a greater course load and the lessons will be much more difficult, I assure you, than they were last year. This class in particular will require your utmost diligence." Shree felt the collective groan that went around the room. "We will commence with William Shakespeare, reading his plays and poems. Some of the works may be advanced for your age group, but that is why you are here at Kennedy Academy: to excel above your peers."

At this point Mrs. Tillman paused, looked down at her notebook, turned a page, and began the lesson. "Can anyone tell me when Shakespeare wrote most of his works?"

There was dead silence in the room. Who would be the daring person to answer the first question, on the first day of class, and be labeled the teacher's pet forever? Shree held her tongue even though it was hard. She instinctively knew that wouldn't be the way to start off at Kennedy Academy.

Mrs. Tillman waited a full minute and then looked at the class list. "Colleen O'Connor."

A girl sitting three seats to the right and one row ahead of Shree looked up. Shree saw her hand down by her side, holding her cell phone. Not smart, Shree thought.

"Yes, Mrs. Tillman?"

"I asked you about William Shakespeare, Ms. O'Connor," Mrs. Tillman reiterated. "His life was plagued by controversy. Before we begin our discussion, can you tell me when Shakespeare wrote most of his plays?"

Colleen cleared her throat. It was obvious she didn't know the answer. But when she spoke, Shree was impressed by how confident she sounded.

"I believe William Shakespeare wrote most of his plays in the early 1900s. My favorite play has to be *Romeo and Juliet*. Leonardo DiCaprio played an awesome Romeo."

The class laughed. What!? Shree couldn't believe her ears. Colleen sounded as if she knew exactly what she was talking about, but what she said was ridiculous. Mrs. Tillman, clearly, was not impressed.

"I am glad that you have taken an interest in Shakespeare's plays, Ms. O'Connor, but you are off by a few hundred years. Let's see. Ms. Mandvi?" Mrs. Tillman looked down at the class assignment to confirm her name. "Shree Mandvi. Can you tell us what you know about Shakespeare?"

Shree looked up. She really didn't want the attention, but she *did* know the answer. "Um, well, Shakespeare was born in the mid-1500's and he wrote most of his plays and the majority of his poems at the end of the century. The fact that he wrote so much in such a short period of time, especially since he didn't have a typewriter or a computer, makes people question whether or not he was the author of all the works attributed to him."

Mrs. Tillman was quiet for a moment. "Thank you, Ms. Mandvi. A very well thought-out response. Who else can tell me something about Shakespeare's works?"

Shree stifled a smile. A number of her classmates seemed impressed by her answer, but others were looking at her as if she had insulted them. Katherine and the boy from the park had their heads together, and Colleen O'Connor sent Shree a piercing glare before rearranging herself in her chair.

Okay, thought Shree. I guess I know where I stand with them.

Shree picked up her pen and looked back up at the board. That's when she saw the thumbs-up from the girl in front of her.

The girl wore her hair in tight pigtails that stretched her head. Tall and skinny, with incredibly long arms and legs, Shree found out as the day wore on that her name was Eleanor Martinez, that she was from the Dominican Republic, and that she was in two more of Shree's classes. But the girl always ran out the door before Shree could say anything to her. Shree had been obligated to stick with Katherine, who had ungraciously dragged Shree from class to class saying not a single word. What had Shree ever done to her anyway? And they were neighbors. It would've been so nice if she had a friend like Tanya next door. But Shree had to stop thinking like that. Nobody would ever take Tanya's place. And it was obvious Katherine was not interested in being friends.

Shree made it through her first morning of school, including gym class, never her best, without too much difficulty. All the other teachers had introduced themselves, welcomed her to Kennedy, then signed her paperwork and left her alone. Shree hadn't had time to find her locker so her food was still in her backpack when it was time for lunch.

Katherine unceremoniously left her standing in the doorway to the cafeteria without a backwards glance. Shree needed to put down her heavy pack and get something in her stomach. Kids were everywhere, finding their usual tables and sitting with their friends, but Eleanor was nowhere to be seen. Shree located a small table by the window and headed over, shrugging off her pack onto the back of the chair with relief. She took out her lunch and opened up the containers of Tupperware her mother had packed so carefully. Normally Shree would be grateful not to have to eat the cafeteria food. The stuff they called food at her school in the Bronx had been barely edible. But here the food looked unbelievable-salads and pizza and subs. Shree would have to start bringing money to school. She didn't eat meat as a result of growing up Jain, but maybe if she took the pepperoni off the pizza she could eat it.

"Hey, how about sharing some of that curry crap with us?" a voice at her elbow said. Shree looked up. Looming above her were the two boys from the park whom Shree had dubbed the Demon Twins in her mind, and Katherine. Colleen was standing a little further away, wearing a football jacket.

Shree decided to ignore them. Maybe they'd just go away.

But no such luck.

"I said, how about sharing some of that crap?" Demon Twin #1 said again, his voice hard and menacing, pointing to Shree's tofu-coconut curry. She now knew that their names were Timothy and Thomas Smith after roll call in homeroom, but there was no way to tell them apart.

"Leave me alone," she said. "I haven't done anything to you." Shree could feel the interest of the other kids around her and was dying of embarrassment. She wanted to fade into the chair and disappear.

"Leave me alone," Demon #2 mimicked. "Oh, we'll leave you alone." And with that he reached over and swept Shree's lunch to the floor. "Oops," he said, laughing. "What a mess. Now you'll have to clean it all up."

Suddenly the room went quiet, the clattering of dishes back in the kitchen the only noise Shree could hear. She gazed down for a second. When she dared to look up again, a beefy kid had joined the pack. Shree hadn't seen him in any of her classes, but she figured out that he was a junior and on the football team. He was obviously Colleen's boyfriend and the owner of the jacket she wore. He slung his arm over Colleen's shoulders and laughed with the rest of them.

"Listen," Shree began again. She was already madder than a—well, than a she-didn't-know-what. But she kept hearing her father's words about staying calm. She knew she had to keep her cool. "I don't want any trouble."

But Timothy—or was it Thomas?—cut her off. "You don't want any trouble?" he repeated. "A smarty-pants Indian geek who likes to make other people look bad." He looked over at Colleen, who had obviously felt dissed by Shree's previous display of knowledge.

That is so unfair, thought Shree. She was only answering when she was called on in class. It wasn't like she was showing off. Answering the teacher was what she was supposed to do.

She started out of her seat. She might be new here, but she wasn't going to take that from anyone.

Before Shree could get up, Colleen jumped in front of her and addressed Shree with a thick, fake Indian accent. "Oh, yes, and it is very, very good. And you know my daddy works at a 7-11 and sells hot dogs and Slurpies for a living. Oh, yes, it is very, very good."

Shree felt the blood rushing to her head. Then she started experiencing the weird symptoms that had plagued her in the Bronx. She felt dizzy and nauseous. Her lower back started hurting and she had the sensation of having pins-and-needles all over her body.

The gang of Demons began to laugh and mimic Colleen, bobbing their heads back and forth, giving each other high fives and repeating her version of an Indian accent: "Yes, it is very, *very* good. Very, very, very good."

Colleen walked over to Shree and pointed at her shoes. "Look at those repulsive shoes," she said in a loud voice. "Whatever were you thinking? Bright yellow and black? Ugghh!" She shuddered. "What do you think you are, Shree, a bumblebee?" At this point Colleen looked surprised—and delighted—as if she was stunned that she'd thought of something so unexpectedly brilliant.

Jason, Colleen's boyfriend, chimed in. "She *does* look like a bee, with those big eyes and those yellow shoes." He started to laugh, a loud, unattractive noise.

And then one of the twins added, "Yeah, look at those buggy eyes and skinny arms. Hey, Shree the bumblebee, do you go around stinging people?" His imitation of a heavy Indian accent sounded ridiculous, but no one else seemed to notice.

Shree's head threatened to explode. She saw red. Literally saw red. Everything had turned a shade of crimson.

"You think you're so much better than us," Colleen said.

"Yeah, go back to New York, you stupid bee," Katherine added.

It was too much. Shree stood up. She wouldn't take one more minute of it.

"What's going on here?" The gym teacher, Mrs. Murphy, was suddenly at the end of the table. She looked at the food spilled all over the floor. "Ms. Mandvi, is there a problem?"

Shree heard the words from afar. Slowly she dragged herself back to earth. The red turned to pink and then the color faded all together. She looked down at the food on the floor. "No, Mrs. Murphy. My food, um, it just fell. I'll clean it up."

"Good. Ladies, gentlemen, move along then. Let Shree clean up before she's late for class."

Grinning in triumph, the Demons left the cafeteria. Tears sprang to Shree's eyes. She got a mop from the janitor and cleaned up the mess, still hungry and ashamed, only stopping briefly in the girls' bathroom to mop up her own tears. Naturally, Katherine hadn't bothered to wait, so Shree had to find her own way to her history class. She slid into her seat as the door was closing.

For the rest of the afternoon Shree thought of nothing else but getting revenge. She didn't care that it went against everything her parents had taught her about their Jain beliefs. The Demons deserved it.

Shree didn't know how, but she'd find a way.

Chapter 8

Regarding The Treasure

When Shree got home, her mother peppered her with questions. How was her day? Did she like her teachers? Were the kids nice to her? What did she need from the store? Shree tried her best to be patient and answer her mother's questions, but the truth was that for the first time in her life, school wasn't as enjoyable as it had always been. And for the first time in her life, Shree felt irritated with her mother's well-intentioned interest.

After she peeled off her uniform to add to the pile her mother had by the table for tailoring and washing, she took off upstairs. She jumped straight to bed and started crying, the tears that had accumulated during the day bursting out from the emotional dam she'd built inside. Shree had expected to feel awkward and out of place on her first day of school. But she hadn't been prepared to be humiliated and ganged-up on in front of the entire student body.

She placed her pillow over her face to prevent her mom from hearing her cry. The last thing she wanted to do was explain what had happened at school. She thought about her friends from the Bronx and started to cry even harder. It wasn't fair that she had to start a new life in a strange school after living in one place for so long.

After fifteen minutes had passed and she had balled up a dozen tissues, Shree finally stopped crying. Thinking of her best friend Tanya, and how she'd have reacted to the creeps at school, helped Shree pull herself together. No doubt she and Tanya would come up with a way to get revenge. Shree would just have to do it on her own, that's all.

Shree wiped the final tears from her face and emptied the contents of her backpack on the floor. She grabbed the treasure book and went back to lie on her bed. Her homework could wait until later. She'd much rather think about John Harvard's treasure than homework, or those stupid Demons.

Shree saw that Winthrop's book was actually a lot more detailed than she had originally thought. Now that she looked at the pages more carefully, she noted that some of the original journal entries were in fact brief descriptions of the life of John Harvard and the events that led up to the hiding of the secret key and the treasure.

According to an entry dated June 19, 1639, Sir Malcolm wrote that John Harvard wasn't really the founder of Harvard University at all. In fact, Harvard had led a life of "adventure and crime" in England prior to his arrival in America and before settling down to pursue the life of an academic. Harvard had lived a very short life, from 1607 to 1638. Some people thought that his father had known William Shakespeare in Stratford on Avon where they had both lived.

Shree was intrigued. This guy's life of "adventure and crime" must have something to do with the treasure map in the book. She propped herself up on her pillow and read on, no longer thinking about the Demons.

The introduction described a "secret key" that could open "unlimited treasures," including the treasure chest hidden by John Harvard somewhere in Cambridge. Harvard had brought the treasure and the key when he moved to New England with his wife. It didn't take much math to figure out that since he'd emigrated in 1637 and died in 1638, he'd only been in Cambridge a short time. And, somehow, during this brief time in the Bay Colony, he must've found a way to bury the treasure.

Shree also discovered that Sir Malcolm had sold his home and sailed for New England in 1637, meeting and befriending John Harvard upon his arrival. Winthrop implied that Harvard had confided in him about bringing a large treasure from England to America. But Harvard had died before Winthrop learned where the treasure, supposedly "of gold, silver and dazzling jewels," was hidden.

Shree looked up. Could the maps copied in the back of Sir Malcolm Winthrop's journal lead to the treasure? Had Winthrop written his own book after Harvard's death to keep the treasure maps hidden? It couldn't be. But what if it was? What if she held in her hands the only book that held the location of John Harvard's treasure and the "secret key"?

Shree flipped back to the maps at the end of the book. The date in the corner was 1638. There was no indication of who had drawn the maps. But to Shree it was clear that Harvard's treasure was hidden beneath the campus of the university that bore his name. And who better to find it than someone like her?

Shree could feel her excitement building. She needed to talk to Tanya. Maybe she'd call or email her after dinner. Not that it'd be the same as having her there, but it would have to do.

A quiet knock came while Shree was leafing through the various maps. "Yeah?"

"Shree, may I come in?" her father asked.

"Um, sure, Dad." Shree stuffed the treasure book under her pillow. As her father walked in, she remembered the collection of used tissues still on the floor by her bed. She prayed her dad did not look down.

"Well, my daughter, I wanted to know how your first day of school went." Dr. Mandvi took a step forward after closing the door behind him. He looked at the tissues on the floor. "Is everything all right, Shree?"

"Sure, Dad. I guess so." Shree had decided not to tell her father about the Demons. He'd worry and likely tell her mother—and then everything would be a big deal.

Her father paused. Shree knew that he wasn't buying her response.

"Hmmm. I suppose those were tears of joy, then?" Dr. Mandvi asked.

Shree did not appreciate her father's attempt at humor. "Well, Dad, let's just say it didn't go as well as I had hoped, that's all." Shree wished he would change the topic, but once her father's curiosity was piqued he hung on for dear life.

"Well now, I am sure it is not as bad as it may seem." He sat at the edge of the bed as if he were settling in for a while.

Shree remained silent for a minute, staring down at the floor. She could not help it. Fresh tears started to form in the corners of both eyes and suddenly she was crying again. "Dad, it was awful. I got ganged-up on by a bunch of bullies who made fun of me for being Indian and for having large eyes and for wearing the shoes Tanya got me." She left out the part about the 7-11 and the Slurpies. Somehow Shree knew that would wound her father deeply. "They made fun of my name, Dad, and called me *Shree, Shree, the bumblebee.*"

Her father stared at Shree for a moment, a perplexed look on his face. He repeated her words aloud, almost as if he was speaking to himself. "Shree, Shree, the bumblebee?" Seconds later he was laughing, his shoulders bobbing up and down, both his arms tightly wrapped around his pot belly.

Shree stared at her dad and then started to cry even harder. How insensitive could her own father be?

Dr. Mandvi stopped abruptly. He looked down and started to speak. "My daughter, how could you let these people get to you? You are stronger than that—and smart enough to know that what they say is nonsense. Making fun of your name and what you wear and your appearance—this is ignorance. Certainly you know that. And you cannot let them hurt you."

Shree protested, wiping her tears with the corner of her shirt. "Dad, you weren't there. You have no idea how humiliating it was for me, on my first day of school, in front of everyone."

"But my daughter," her father said, "you cannot take these things to heart. There will always be people who will make fun of you for being different, for not being like them or thinking like them or being from the same background. But you need to understand that our strength lies in our differences."

She nodded apathetically, not quite convinced, and Mr. Mandvi went on. "Shree, it is those people who embrace their differences that end up developing their skills, who realize their full potential, and who achieve greatness in life."

It was turning into another lecture and Shree was too distraught to pay attention. She guessed he was trying to be supportive, but it was just too hard to listen to what her father was saying, much less believe it.

It was time for dinner. Her father assured Shree that he wouldn't tell her mother about her day if Shree promised to cheer up before coming down to join them.

A few minutes after her father left, Shree got up from bed, washed her face, and put the treasure book back in her backpack. She opened the door and headed downstairs to join her parents, even though all she really wanted to do was to climb back in bed and cry.

Chapter 9

Back To School

By the time Thursday arrived, Shree had begun making a long list of possible excuses for getting out of school for the rest of the year. Things had gone from bad to worse in no time. Despite the fact that she had decided to stop wearing the shoes that started the whole "Shree the bee" thing, there had been no let-up. From the moment she got to school until she left to go home, the Demon Twins and their friends were there to make her life miserable. The only thing that prevented her from fighting back was her father's warning about staying out of trouble.

First there was the name-calling. Colleen took advantage of every chance she got to make fun of Shree, lifting her arms up and pretending to buzz around like a bee. Shree couldn't decide which was more unbelievable—Colleen's love of idiocy or the fact that the teachers didn't seem to notice what was going on.

Then there was the other stuff.

Shree had overheard Katherine speaking to the twins about her, telling them that she had heard how well Shree had done at P.S. #54 in the Bronx, how her father was a famous engineer and how Mrs. Stein thought she'd end up being valedictorian. Katherine seemed really bothered by this fact, almost as if she hadn't expected anyone at Kennedy to compete with her for top student. It finally made sense to Shree why Katherine had been so mean to her when she'd moved into her new house. Apparently, Katherine's mom was on the board of governors at Kennedy and had told her daughter about Shree's academic record.

But Shree had no desire to compete with anyone. All she wanted was to do well in school and make new friends, so what was up with Katherine's attitude?

In fact, Shree was purposefully avoiding answering questions in her classes, trying to attract as little attention as possible. But it didn't matter. The Demons were determined to make her life at Kennedy Academy miserable. On her way to gym that morning, Shree tripped and went sprawling, landing face first on the floor. When she looked up she saw the retreating backs (and hair spikes) of the Smith twins. She heard their laughter and felt her cheeks burn all the way down the hall. They weren't as dumb as they looked either. They knew that in between classes their actions would go largely unseen by the hall monitors, who were always stationed in the same places and were easy to avoid.

Then Shree was getting her books from her locker before biology class when she felt a hard shove from behind. It was Jason. The sharp pain stunned her momentarily and she dropped her books and her forehead hit the hard metal of the locker's edge. Tears stung her eyes. She would've fallen if it weren't for the fact that out of nowhere a hand appeared at her elbow and steadied her. It was Eleanor.

"Are you okay?" Eleanor asked quietly.

"Yeah, I guess. Thanks," Shree answered.

But Eleanor was already moving off into the crowd. She might not be a friend, but at least she hadn't joined in the abuse.

Shree felt as if surviving each day at her new school was going to take a lot of effort. Would she make it to her next class unscathed? Would she make it through to lunch? It was becoming a big burden and she felt absolutely possessed by the need to fight back.

Today she decided to take her lunch outside. It was easier to eat alone in the courtyard than in the cafeteria where Colleen or any of her evil friends could harass her.

Shree knew just from the little she'd seen in the halls and outside in the schoolyard that the Demon twins were the ones responsible for bullying the weaker kids in school. She also knew by now that Katherine's crew was considered the most popular at Kennedy, supposedly from the elite families of Cambridge. All beautiful, athletic, and rich, they were the ones who had the parties and knew all the right things to do and say. Of course, Colleen was obviously some kind of exception to *that* rule. Shree allowed herself a moment of smugness as she ate her lunch. Those guys would be considered such losers back in the Bronx. They wouldn't last a day at P.S. #54.

She stayed under the radar and made it back to her history class safely. She liked history, and this whole treasure thing about John Harvard and the university had really captured her interest. Mr. Roberts wasn't boring either. He liked telling stories and acting things out, which made what they were studying—American history—more interesting. Shree sat down and opened her notebook.

But no sooner had Mr. Roberts begun writing on the board than Colleen pretended to buzz like a bee, shaking her body from side to side as she ran around the room. Then the twins took over, bobbing their heads, placing an index finger to their foreheads, apparently thinking they looked Indian. They were absolutely silent, miming everything. But eventually a few giggles escaped from a couple of kids in the back and one of the twins let out a big chortle.

Mr. Roberts turned around. "Mr. Smith, I take it you have something to say to the class?"

"Um, no, Mr. Roberts."

"Then I suggest you sit in your seat, face forward, and provide me with your utmost attention. Am I making myself understood?"

"Yes, Mr. Roberts," Tim answered as he sat down.

Shree was relieved and again picked up her pen to take notes. Mr. Roberts was saying something about how the Iroquois Indians' excellent marksmanship allowed them to conquer vast areas of land and become leaders among the neighboring tribes.

Shree accidentally dropped her pen, which clattered to the floor. Mr. Roberts cleared his throat. "Ms. Mandvi, are you with us?"

"Yes, Mr. Roberts. I'm here," Shree answered.

Mr. Roberts gave her a look and then continued with his lesson. Shree made an effort to sit up straight and listen. It didn't help that she knew that behind her Colleen was probably rolling her eyes.

Keeping her body rigidly facing forward, Shree dropped her arm down and tried finding her pen under her seat. Suddenly, there it was in her hand. How? Looking down she saw someone else's arm retreating. But whose? She looked up and saw Eleanor winking at her.

Shree smiled back. Finally, she thought, a friendly person in Cambridge. Maybe the shy Hispanic girl with the pigtails and the long arms might be interested in being her friend?

Mr. Roberts continued with the lesson despite the interruptions. "Can anyone tell me which other tribe, this one located in the Southeast, competed with the Iroquois for dominance of the United States?"

No one volunteered an answer. The teacher looked around. Shree had only been half-listening, but she knew the answer, and whispered it to herself. Mr. Roberts caught her. Oh-oh. She'd *so* rather he didn't call on her, but she saw that was exactly what he had in mind.

"Ms. Mandvi, would you care to share your response with the rest of the class?"

Shree had spent an afternoon the previous summer with her friend Jerome, who was half Chinese and half Native American, researching various tribes on the Internet. Jerome had been fixated on learning where his ancestors came from. He was pretty sure that he was part-Cherokee. And the Cherokees came from the Southeast.

Shree took her time answering, acting as if she were thinking hard. She could feel the waves of hostility Katherine and the others were sending her way, and although part of her wanted the teacher to know she knew the answer, the other part wanted to stay out of the line of fire. Finally, when she saw Mr. Roberts was running out of patience, she said quietly, "I think it was the Cherokees."

Mr. Roberts let out a long sigh. "Thank you, Ms. Mandvi." He turned around, wrote down "Cherokees" on the blackboard, and began a long discussion about the tribe, jotting down fact after fact that the class would need to memorize for the upcoming quiz.

Behind his back, Colleen took the opportunity to make fun of Shree. She grabbed a blank piece of paper and in large letters wrote, "INDIAN BEE SAYS HOW TO HER PEOPLE." She held it over her head so the entire class could see while Mr. Roberts continued to write. There was some strangled and barely audible laughter and some nudging, but again the kids were careful not to get caught.

Shree looked down, her face burning. It was proof that what her father had told her was true. There were lots of ignorant people and Colleen was one of them. Did she really think that Indians from Asia were the same as Native Americans from North America? Even the dumbest kids at her school in the Bronx knew that Christopher Columbus was wrong when he landed in America and thought he'd reached India, and that was why Native Americans had been mistakenly called "Indians."

The bell rang shrilly. Shree rushed to write down the last notes Mr. Roberts had written on the chalkboard before they got erased. Class had finished and, unless she did something, she'd be finished too.

Chapter 10

A Close Call

Free at last. Shree grabbed her books from her locker and walked-did-not-run until she reached the front exit. Then she skipped down the stairs. One more day until the weekend. She'd almost made it through the week. It was a beautiful early fall day and the sky was cloudless. It was a great day to walk home and maybe stop in the park for a few minutes—if no one else was there. Maybe she'd spend some time reading the treasure book.

She began to hum one of the Punjabi tunes her mother was always singing around the house. She thought about Eleanor and wondered why she never saw her at lunch. Shree hadn't seen her sitting in the cafeteria or outside, not even once. Eleanor was really nice. It'd be great if she turned out to be someone Shree could talk to.

Shree loved her walk home from school. She loved smelling the fall flowers that lined the yards of most of the houses on the way, and she loved being alone with her thoughts. But mostly she loved it because it meant that she had survived another day of torture. She didn't know how long she'd be able to put up with the abuse, but she kept reminding herself of how upset her parents would be if she got in any kind of trouble—whether it was her fault or not.

The bike path was lined with fading daisies and chrysanthemums. Shree was surprised by how strong their scents were, almost as if she were tasting the flowers rather than smelling them. Each flower had its own unique scent, which seemed to stand apart from the others. By the time Shree had walked to the end of Garden Street, she was identifying each type of flower by its smell rather than by what each looked like.

She supposed that part of this fascination was because she'd never had much exposure to nature in the Bronx. Her family had gone picnicking in the Botanical Gardens once or twice a year in summer, and there had been the occasional trip to Lake George in upstate New York, but other than that Shree was a nature dweeb. She could see that it was going to be different in Cambridge. She reached down to pick up a beautiful pink daisy, which had fallen from its stem, and inhaled deeply.

Suddenly, she knew she wasn't alone. Even the air had shifted. She looked around. Sure enough, the Demon Twins were only about fifty feet away and gaining fast. Shree forced herself to look forward and picked up her pace. There was no telling what they'd do to her without any teachers around. Her heart began to race. It was difficult to keep from panicking; her face and hands were covered with sweat already.

Couldn't she have just one day without the Demons? Couldn't one day go by where she didn't feel afraid?

It took all her willpower not to turn around, but she could hear from their footsteps and voices that the twins had seen her. And they knew that she had seen them. It was now or never. She had to get away before they caught up to her.

Shree dropped her heavy book bag and started to run. The footsteps behind her also picked up speed. It would only be a minute before they'd catch her.

Shree had walked home from school the previous couple of days and knew her way pretty well, but now as she raced down Garden Street she saw that she'd overshot her turn. It was too late to go back. She took the next left, breathing heavily, and ran down a short street and then onto Fink Drive. The big "DEAD END" sign by the crosswalk did little to lessen her sense of desperation. They'd be there any second and there was nowhere to hide.

Three houses lined the end of the street, each with a wooden fence and a gate. She tried the gates but they were all locked. Her breath ragged and her stomach cramped from the exertion, Shree chanced a look back at the corner and considered her options. Heading back where she came from meant running right into the twins. Staying where she was meant she'd be dead meat. Frantically, she searched for a potential hiding spot.

Her heart began to race. She felt the weird dizziness and nausea again, her vision clouded, and then the world went dark.

The twins tore onto Fink Drive less than a minute later. It was a dead end—a perfect place for them to trap Shree.

Snickering, they sauntered past the first two houses.

"Shreeeee. Oh Shree, Shree the bumblebeeeee," they taunted. "Come out, come out, wherever you are."

But they couldn't find Shree anywhere.

"Where'd she go, Tim?"

"I don't know, bro. She has to be here somewhere."

The twins approached a blue Cadillac that sat parked on the street by the third house. Tom poked his brother in the ribs and gestured with his head towards the car, smiling.

Tim gave Tom a thumbs-up and then spoke loudly. "Gee, Tom, I don't know. I don't see her anywhere. But where could such a pudgy, buggy-eyed bumblebee be hiding?" Tim walked around the Cadillac to the passenger's side and Tom went over to the driver's side door.

"I mean all we want to do is talk to her."

Winking at each other, the twins leapt forward, expecting to find Shree crouched on the other side by the hood of the car. But the street was empty. They searched under the car. They tried the gates of each house, all locked up tight.

Finally, they stopped. "How could we have lost her?" Tim asked angrily. "She was here a minute ago."

Tom looked at his watch. "I don't know, bro, but we gotta get the hell out of here. We're gonna be late for football practice."

Tim lagged behind, making a final sweep of the street for any sign of life. "Hey, what's that buzzing noise?"

Tom looked around nervously and pointed to a distant tree. "I'm not sure, but there's a beehive right up there. And you know I'm allergic, so let's get the hell out."

A curtain moved in the yellow house on the end and a woman peered out.

"Come on, Tim. It's not worth the trouble. Let's leave before that woman calls the cops."

Shree didn't know how much time had passed before she came back to her senses. She was sitting on a branch high above the ground, surrounded by the crimson leaves of a massive oak. She had no idea how she'd gotten up there. Somehow she had managed to climb the tree and crawl into the branches to avoid detection.

How had she gotten there? Had she blacked out? She'd heard about people with brain tumors who couldn't remember what they did or where they went. Could she have a brain tumor?

It took a long time to get down, partly because Shree was shaking so hard. She was almost more afraid of her apparent blackout than she was of the twins. There was no telling what they'd have done to her if they had found her. She concentrated on retracing her steps. When she got to Garden Street, she could see her backpack lying exactly where she'd dropped it, in the middle of the street. For some reason the twins hadn't taken it. Relieved, she picked it up.

That's when she saw that it had been opened. Holding her breath, Shree fumbled through the contents, gasped, and dropped the bag to the ground.

Her treasure book was gone.

Chapter 11

Target Practice

Shree felt another bout of nausea coming on. The pungent smell in biology class was too strong, making her sick to her stomach. She covered her mouth and closed her eyes tightly. What was happening to her? Dissecting a frog was not the most enjoyable experience, but she had never been the least bit squeamish. Now, all of a sudden, she was Miss Sensitivity.

But it wasn't only the nausea that bothered her. For the past few days, she had a massive headache, too, like the ones their old neighbor in the Bronx, Mrs. Lillienthal, used to complain to Shree's mother about. Migraines or something. And her ears had begun to ring and she was having a hard time focusing. Sometimes the symptoms lasted a few seconds; they came in waves and made Shree want to curl up in a ball and die. They were the same symptoms she had experienced in the Bronx, only more intense.

The one saving grace was that Eleanor had ended up being her lab partner.

"What is wrong, Shree? You do not look so good." Eleanor spoke with a thick Dominican accent, rolling her r's the way Shree's Hispanic friends did in the Bronx. Shree looked up and saw Eleanor holding the scalpel and doing all the work. Shree's eyes were fixed on her textbook as she tried to avoid looking at the frog cadavers, which were in various stages of dissection around the classroom.

"I'm not sure, Eleanor. I'm just not feeling so good." The ringing in her ears began again. Shree took some deep breaths and tried to ignore it.

"Well, a lot of people get grossed out doing this stuff, so do not feel bad. I am getting destroyed in English, math, and history, but this is one class that will definitely boost my overall GPA."

Eleanor's hands moved quickly but delicately as she followed the tracings of the dissections to the letter. Shree's new friend was a natural, handling the blade as if she was a surgeon.

Shree looked around to see how the rest of her classmates were doing. They were at least six or seven steps behind her team. Shree gave a weak smile. "I'm so glad you're my partner. I could've ended up barfing all over Tim or Tom, if I'd been paired up with them. Of course, I don't know if that would've been such a bad thing."

She and Eleanor broke into laughter. Shree started to feel a bit better.

"Hey, Eleanor, can I ask you something?"

"Sure."

"How come you're never in the cafeteria? Don't you eat?"

Eleanor looked embarrassed. "Last year, when I was the new kid, the twins used to bother me a lot. I started spending lunchtime in the library. Mr. Leopold is really nice and lets me eat in the corner. He is not supposed to do that and he could get in trouble if anyone found out. Do not tell anyone, okay, Shree?"

"Definitely not. I won't tell anyone. But maybe you could come and eat with me."

"Okay," Eleanor said. "Today?"

"Absolutely," Shree said.

By the time the bell rang Shree was so relieved to get away from the smells and the little dead froggie bodies that she gave Eleanor only a brief wave, jerked her head as if to say "I'll see you at lunch," and headed to gym class. Shree got there a few minutes before any of the other kids, who typically dawdled as long as possible on their way through the halls. She stuffed her books inside her locker and put on her gym clothes and sneakers. What a mess she'd gotten herself into. Sometimes she felt excited about being in a new place and meeting new friends—well, at least one new friend—and then other times she felt like running back to the Bronx. Sometimes she had tons of energy and other times she thought she'd flop with exhaustion. Basically, she felt totally unlike herself.

Shree slammed her locker closed and spun the dial on her lock. She turned around and bumped smack into a girl who was hurrying past her, completely oblivious. It was no wonder the girl hadn't seen her. Her glasses were thick and odd-looking. Shree recognized her as Nancy somebody-or-other, a friend—or at least an acquaintance—of Eleanor's. She was in the same grade but only in one or two other of Shree's classes.

"Sorry," Shree said, but the girl just gave her a disconcertingly fierce look, mumbled something unintelligible, and kept going. Shree shrugged, noting as she did that she was doing a whole lot of shrugging lately. It kind of summed up her current life.

On her way into the gym, she passed a bunch of girls speaking with Katherine and Colleen. They were all whispering and giggling and, although there was really no reason for Shree to believe they were talking about her, that's the way it seemed. Immediately she felt her face flame up.

Inside the gym she was surprised to see that instead of the volleyball nets normally set up for class, six large stands constructed out of bales of hay and wooden legs had been positioned at one end of the room. A row of bows and quivers of arrows sat leaning on the bleachers. Shree immediately went over and picked up a bow. Archery! She'd always wanted to try the sport and was a real fan of all the Robin Hood stories. In her fantasies she was sometimes Robin Hood and sometimes Maid Marian, but always a great archer. This must be one of the perks of going to a place like Kennedy Academy—they could afford this kind of equipment.

A man came into the gym with a clipboard. He waited, impatiently tapping his foot, until all the girls had arrived, and then made the announcement that Mrs. Murphy had been called away for a few weeks due to a personal emergency and that he, Mr. Marr, would be substituting for that time. "Because one of my areas of expertise is archery, and because the weather still permits, that's what we'll be doing until Mrs. Murphy's return. I would like six girls to each pick up a bow, a quiver of arrows, and a pair of gloves. Go to the back of the room and wait for my further instruction. The rest of you stand over there by the bleachers—behind the girls who will be shooting, out of the way. This is a dangerous sport and precautions must be taken at all times to avoid risk of injury."

The girls all took positions, whispers of excitement hissing through the group. Unfortunately, Shree hadn't moved fast enough and ended up in a group that included both Katherine and Colleen. She'd have to pay a lot more attention than that in the future.

Mr. Marr continued. "Before we begin I must remind everyone again that the bow and arrow is a weapon. It has always been a weapon, and is therefore inherently dangerous. There will be no fooling around in this class. There will be no pointing of this weapon at anything—or anyone—other than a target of hay. Doing so will be cause for immediate suspension—from class and from Kennedy Academy. Do we understand one another?"

Shree looked around the room. Everyone stared at Mr. Marr with a blank look. She turned back, excited to start the lesson.

Mr. Marr clapped his hands together. "All right, so let's get to the fun part. The key to shooting the bow and arrow is to be quick with your aim." He leaned down and picked up a large wooden bow. It looked brand new. The frame was black with a yellow pattern crisscrossing the main frame. "The bow is heavy and the string, for obvious reasons, needs to be under a lot of tension in order to propel the arrow to great distances. Therefore, you need a lot of strength to give it a good pull."

He pulled an arrow with green and white feathers on the end and placed the string from the bow between the two plastic perforated edges at the end of the arrow. "If you pull the arrow and take too long to aim, your arm will tire and you'll miss your mark." He shot the arrow. The arrow grazed the edge of the white part of the target and deflected to the ground, landing several feet behind the target.

Whispers of "I told you so" and "what a loser" made it to Shree's ears. She hoped Mr. Marr didn't hear them.

Mr. Marr then pulled a second arrow from his quiver. It was true that, bald and overweight, he didn't look a lot like Robin Hood, but could he even hit the target at all? He inserted the arrow, pulled back the string on the bow, and let go. The arrow sailed through the air and hit the target with a resounding smack, only an inch away from the bull's eye, as if it had been set with a homing device. Shree and the rest of the class gasped in surprise, and Mr. Marr allowed himself a slight smile of satisfaction.

"That's the proper way to shoot. I'll demonstrate again. Place the bow in front of you. Lift up your arms, draw back on the string as you bring the bow back down and to your right side, keeping your eyes on the target the entire time. You will feel the arrow inches from your ear while you make your final adjustments." Mr. Marr moved gracefully and then stood perfectly still as he stared at the target in front of him. "And then you let go." He let the string loose and again the arrow shot forward.

Shree heard the whizzing sound of the arrow as it crossed the short distance to the target and landed just to the left of the first arrow, but still comfortably inside the yellow circle in the center of the target.

Mr. Marr smiled broadly this time and turned to the girls. "Now, don't expect to do that your first time. It can take years of practice to hit a bull's eye."

Katherine edged to the front of the line with the bow and quiver and put on a pair of gloves. No one complained, thought Shree, just like usual. Shree was glad they were so far apart.

"You will each empty the quiver of arrows, and then hand over your equipment to the next girl," Mr. Marr instructed.

Katherine and the other five girls in the first row took their positions.

"Ready. Place your arrows, bring them back, adjust your aim, and shoot," Mr. Marr said.

Shree saw six arrows whizzing through the air, most landing on the floor somewhere in front of the targets—all but one. Katherine's had hit the target almost directly in the middle.

"Who shot this one?" Mr. Marr asked.

Katherine raised her arm, a big grin on her face. "I did, Mr. Marr."

"That's great shooting, Ms.—"

"Jenkins," Katherine answered.

"Ms. Jenkins. Congratulations. Have you shot before?" Mr. Marr asked.

"Yes, sir. For three summers I've taken archery at my camp in New Hampshire. I've come in first place in every competition. The counselor told me I should think about taking private lessons and training for the Olympics."

The class was listening to every word. Shree couldn't believe how vain Katherine sounded, but no one else seemed to notice.

"Well, Ms. Jenkins. Practice does indeed make perfect," Mr. Marr said. He then spoke to the rest of the group. "First row, hand over your equipment to the next row please."

Things went on this way until finally it was Shree's turn. Unfortunately, by the time she got to the front of the line, Katherine and Colleen were directly in back of her. Her plan to stay away from them had backfired. She took a deep breath and steadied the bow. It felt so comfortable in her arms, like it was meant to be there. Then she pulled an arrow from the quiver as Mr. Marr had demonstrated. She lined up the arrow, pulled it back, adjusted her aim, and prepared to shoot.

Just as she was about to let go, Shree heard giggles behind her. "The stupid little Indian thinks she can shoot," Shree heard Katherine say.

"Yeah, make your people proud, Indian Bee, chief of the insects," Colleen said.

Shree turned around, irritated by the girls' comments, and blurted out, "Indians and Native Americans are two different races, you ignorant b—"

"Is everything all right over there? Yes, you with the yellow-and-black set. Take your shots, it's getting late," Mr. Marr said, glancing at his watch.

Saved from herself—and from causing what could've been an ugly scene—Shree turned away from the other girls and began to set up her shot again. But she rushed through it, the whispers behind her interrupting her concentration. Her first shot went only a few feet and crashed onto the floor. Colleen, who was standing as closely as she could get to Shree without incurring the notice of the teacher, giggled loudly.

Sighing, Shree took another arrow from the quiver. She took a breath and stared straight ahead. She was still angry but told herself to relax. She attempted to focus. She took another breath, ignoring the continued chatter of the girls behind her. Finally she felt ready to pull back her arrow. She stretched it taut. And then—*zing*. She let it fly.

Thwack! The entire class had been waiting for Shree to finish, standing in small groups and watching. Shree heard the smack of the arrow as it sailed into the target in front of her at dead center. The whole class began clapping. Shree was shocked.

"Is this your first time, Ms.—?" Mr. Marr asked.

"Mandvi, sir, Shree Mandvi. And yes, it is," Shree answered.

"Well, Ms. Mandvi. You're a natural. Now finish up the arrows in your quiver. It's time to get changed."

"Yes, sir. Thank you."

Shree heard a muttered "beginner's luck" from behind her, but ignored it.

She did as Mr. Marr said, trying to focus on the target, not on the stares and comments directed at her by her classmates. She took another arrow, placed it carefully on her bow and released it. The arrow again struck its target dead center, landing within an inch of the previous arrow.

Shree turned around and saw Katherine staring at her in anger. She turned back to her target. She still had two arrows left.

Shree wasn't sure what possessed her to do it, but she grabbed the two remaining arrows and quickly placed both of them next to each other along her bow. Before Mr. Marr could object, she raised the bow, pulled the string back, used her left index finger to split the arrows slightly apart, and then released the string.

The growing chatter ceased. Mr. Marr stood flabbergasted, one hand resting carefully on top of his large belly, the other scratching the few hairs remaining on his bald head.

"I'll be damned. I've never seen that before. Ah, now you're just showing off, Ms. Mandvi." But he was smiling.

The entire gym class had just seen Shree's arrows travel in opposite directions, one hitting the target at the far right of the row and the other hitting the target at the far left. A double bull's eye.

Shree turned around and winked at Katherine and Colleen, just to spite them. She collected her arrows and then added her quiver and bow to the pile and headed back to the locker room. Katherine and Colleen stood stone still, apparently unable to process what had just occurred. Several of the other girls gave Shree a high five and one even said, "That was amazing, girl," sounding just like Tanya.

Shree changed her clothes and felt the experience of shooting the arrow again and again. It was almost as if she herself were the arrow, fearlessly hurtling through the air towards a specific target, and then landing with perfect dexterity and balance. Still buzzing with adrenaline, Shree promised herself that she was going to get very, very good at hitting her target.

Chapter 12

The Best Laid Plan

Shree's high lasted the rest of the day. She replayed that last shot over and over in her head, the smile on her face becoming a permanent fixture. It was odd that a girl with no technical skills or athletic ability could've done so well at archery, but she was not going to waste her time analyzing what had happened.

Finally, it was time for lunch. Shree was already sitting down and opening her Tupperware when Eleanor got there.

"Hey, Eleanor," Shree said.

"Hi, Shree. Did that really happen in archery?" Eleanor asked, sitting down across from Shree.

"How did you hear about that?" Shree took a bite of her curry.

"My friend Nancy told me. She heard that you kicked Katherine's butt in archery. I did not know you did archery." Eleanor took out her sandwich from her backpack.

"I didn't either, El. It was great. I've never felt so incredibly focused before. It all just happened. I can't even explain it, but it was like I was meant to do it." Shree was too excited to keep eating.

"Well, it is about time someone showed Katherine that she is not the only one with talent. I just hope it will not come back to haunt you," Eleanor said.

"Yeah, I know what you mean. She wasn't happy about it." Shree was pensive for a second.

"Well, *I* am, Shree."

"Thanks, Eleanor."

They took a few bites of their lunch in silence.

Shree looked around. "Hey, El."

"Yes?"

"I was wondering. About this Nancy person," Shree said.

"What about her?" Eleanor asked.

"I've been seeing her around—what's up with her?" Shree had been curious about Eleanor's relationship with Nancy and finally felt comfortable asking Eleanor about it.

"What do you mean?" Eleanor took another bite of her sandwich.

"Well, how well do you know her?" Shree asked, trying to figure out if she was overstepping her friendship.

"She was in a few of my classes last year and now we are doing an art project together. She is really smart. She gets mostly A's and that is why she is taking a couple of classes with the juniors. She can seem a little cold—until you get to know her. And she has this way of listening to what you are talking about that is, well—you will see."

Eleanor took the remaining bite from her sandwich. "Why, what's up?"

"I'm not sure. I mean, we're in English class together. Sometimes I get the feeling she's looking at me funny. Like she's trying to figure something out—just weird is all. You're in our English class. Haven't you noticed it or is it just me?"

Eleanor grinned. "Well, it is kind of hard to figure out her facial expressions. I mean, her glasses take up half her face."

Shree laughed. "Yeah, I guess you're right. I'm just being paranoid. At this point I think everyone in this school hates me—except for you."

"Hey, you can meet her now." Eleanor looked beyond Shree and waved. "She is coming over here."

Nancy brought her lunch over to the table.

"Mind if I sit with you guys?" she asked.

"Of course not," Eleanor said.

"I heard about what you did today in archery, Shree. Congratulations," Nancy said.

Every word was precisely enunciated. Maybe that's what made Shree feel so strange about this girl, the oddly formal way she spoke.

Shree nodded her thanks. Nancy Yoon was as tiny as a mouse. Her straight glossy black hair hung to her chin and swung in a wall of motion whenever she moved. Everything about her was neat and put together, tucked in where it should be and tied where it needed to be. Her glasses were as Shree remembered them—like Coke bottles—big black rims with thick plates of glass through which Nancy's slightly almond-shaped eyes peered like fish through the depths of a murky pond.

"How did you hear about that?" Shree asked.

"Oh, you know. Around," Nancy said.

Hmmm. Not too helpful, thought Shree. But Eleanor didn't seem to notice. She was babbling happily to Nancy about how Shree had finally stood up to one of the Demons.

"Who are the Demons?" Nancy asked. Shree noticed that although Nancy spoke quietly, something about her voice conveyed a sense of command.

"The Demons are all of Katherine's groupies—you know, besides Katherine there is Colleen and her boyfriend Jason, and then the creepy Smith twins. They have been giving Shree some real trouble. Shree here named them." Eleanor looked over at Shree.

Nancy gave Shree a penetrating look. "Good name," was all she said.

"Thanks," Shree said.

There was silence while the girls finished eating. Every time Shree looked up she felt Nancy's eyes on her—or maybe not on her exactly, but on her backpack. Shree didn't know what to make of that. The only thing she had of any interest in there had been the treasure book, and now that it was stolen it held nothing more than her textbooks and pens.

That reminded her: she needed to ask Eleanor if she wanted to go to Harvard Square with her over the weekend. Shree was hoping her father would get her a Harvard ID so she could do some research on the secret key and the treasure at Widener Library. If they went together it'd give her a chance to tell Eleanor about the treasure and the book—and all the rest.

"Listen, Eleanor, I was thinking about going to Harvard Square this weekend. I have to do some research at the library. Want to come?"

Nancy looked over, and Shree realized that she'd made a mistake by asking Eleanor to join her in front of Nancy. Now she'd have to invite her too. "Nancy, do you want to come along, too?"

Without revealing any emotion, Nancy replied instantly, "Yeah, I'm interested," and then went back to eating her lunch.

Shree could've sworn she caught the trace of a smile on Nancy's lips before she took her next bite.

"Okay, great. We'll make plans tomorrow then, okay?" Shree asked.

Eleanor and Nancy nodded goodbye and Shree took her plastic fork and napkin to the trash bin. As soon as she got home she'd ask her father if he could get her an ID. With all the volumes in Widener Library at her disposal, the origin of the secret key was sure to be hers. It was only a matter of time.

Chapter 13

Changes

It was the loud crash in the kitchen that woke up Mrs. Mandvi. Next to her in bed, Dr. Mandvi continued to snore loudly. She looked at the clock. 5:11 AM. She stared out the window. It was still pitch black, with not a trace of sunlight. The streetlights were as bright as they had been at midnight when they had gone to sleep. Had she dreamed the sound?

She heard the noise again, like the crash of a pot. She was certain it came from the kitchen. She elbowed her sleeping husband.

"Rajandra," she whispered. "I believe there is someone in the house."

Dr. Mandvi mumbled incoherently and turned over. His snoring grew louder.

Mrs. Mandvi elbowed her husband again, this time harder. "Rajandra, there is an intruder in our kitchen!"

His eyes opened slightly and he mumbled something like, "Well, go down and make him your tofu *tikka masala*. It is very, very good and he will like it." He turned over again, pulled the blanket to his chest, and went back to snoring.

"Sometimes you are of no use at all, Rajandra. There is an intruder in this house and you are sleeping. What a husband I have." Mrs. Mandvi glared at him. She would just have to take it upon herself to find out what was going on. She looked around. The only thing she could possibly use as a weapon was a small lamp, which sat on the dresser next to her. She held it in front of her chest and slowly crept down the stairs.

The noise got louder as she approached the kitchen. The overhead light was on. If this was a burglar, he was not only noisy but also stupid. Mrs. Mandvi peered around the corner, the lamp raised above her head. She could not believe what she saw.

It was Shree, right there in the middle of the kitchen, flour coating her face and batter on her hands—and the counter and the floor. Mrs. Mandvi's relief at finding her daughter instead of a burglar was rapidly replaced by a sense of shock.

"Shree, whatever are you doing?"

"Oh, hi, Mom. I thought I'd make breakfast. I'm sorry if I woke you. I was trying to be quiet."

"But it is only five in the morning—and you do not even like to cook." Mrs. Mandvi looked around. She would have a lot of cleaning up to do later.

Shree turned her attention to the frying pan where two hearty globs of batter sat. "I was really hungry and I got to thinking about how much I love pancakes. I've seen you cook them plenty of times." Shree smiled and used a spatula to flip the ungainly masses over.

Mrs. Mandvi didn't know what to say. What was happening to her daughter? First the weird cravings. Then the mood swings. The night before she had caught Shree sleeping under a pile of blankets, saying she was a "little cold" when it was at least eighty degrees in the house. And now this. Mrs. Mandvi was glad that her friend Sherika Johnson was coming to Cambridge so she could finally see first-hand the nature of these changes.

She looked at the pan again. There was no way in heaven that the blob heating up inside it resembled a pancake.

She shifted her attention to her daughter again. "But how did you know how—?"

"I just followed the directions on the side of the package. Making pancakes is a lot easier than I thought."

Mrs. Mandvi decided to keep her thoughts to herself about the status of the pancakes. She did see that Shree was showing great dexterity and hand-eye coordination. Her daughter scooped up a pancake and flipped it with short, quick movements. Amazingly, the pancake turned in mid-air and then landed perfectly on the spatula again. With a flourish Shree completed this maneuver several times, each pancake landing squarely on the pan. Perhaps her daughter had the talent for cooking after all.

"Are you hungry, Mom? Sit down. You can have the first one. See how they taste."

Forgetting that it was still pre-dawn, Shree's mother sat down as instructed. Shree put a plate with two large lumpy pancakes in front of her. Adding a bit of syrup, she cut off a piece. It did not look appetizing but she did not want to disappoint her daughter. She forced herself to bring the bite to her mouth. Shree was smiling in encouragement. Mrs. Mandvi could stall no longer. She put the piece in her mouth and chewed. Ugghh. What had she put in them?

"So, how is it?" Shree asked.

"Um, it is, well, I am impressed by your attempt, dear." It was so bad that it took all of Mrs. Mandvi's strength to swallow.

"But what do you think?" Shree looked at her mother, her eyes round and eager for approval.

"They are certainly different from the ones I am used to eating. And they are a bit—" Mrs. Mandvi paused, trying to think of the right word to describe the taste without offending her daughter, "—sweet, don't you think?"

"I put some honey in the batter," Shree answered.

Shree's mother looked over at the counter. Next to the kitchen utensils was a large container of honey. It was empty. Shree had used an *entire* jar of honey.

"I'm going to have a few myself," Shree said, and proceeded to heap pancakes onto a plate. She then went into the pantry and pulled out another jar of honey. She opened the lid and poured a generous portion over the stack. "Perfect," she said.

Mrs. Mandvi was so shocked she said nothing. She sat and watched her daughter, the one who had always disliked sweets, polish off a large stack of pancakes loaded with honey. When she was done she picked up the dishes from the table and washed them in the sink.

They were still cleaning up when her father came downstairs. "Good morning, Dad," Shree sang. "There are plenty of pancakes if you're hungry."

Her father looked confused. Mrs. Mandvi just shook her head "later" and turned her attention back to the dishes.

"I found the library card on the table. Thanks for getting it for me, Dad. Mom said I can go to Harvard Yard with Eleanor and Nancy tomorrow. We're going to study together and get books for our, um, project."

"Remember that it is an identification card. You must keep it with you at all times. Do not lose it." Dr. Mandvi stared at the pancakes as he said this.

Shree kissed her father's cheek. "Gotcha. Well, I'm off to school." Shree grabbed her backpack and started for the door.

Mrs. Mandvi went to the window and watched as her daughter made her way down the walk to the street. Dr. Mandvi put three large pancakes on a plate.

"Stop," Mrs. Mandvi warned. "Trust me my dear, you do *not* want to eat those."

Chapter 14

The Transformation

It felt good to have the yellow-and-black Adidas back on her feet. Shree skipped down Berkeley Place, her bookbag thumping on her back. She'd been up for hours and still had enough energy to run a marathon. She felt excited again, as if all her problems had magically floated away and the world was right again. The distressing symptoms she'd been experiencing had left too. No more blurry vision, no more headaches or nausea. Even the ringing in her ears was gone. Shree felt great physically, and this made her see Kennedy Academy in a whole new light; it was now a wonderful school filled with unlimited opportunities.

The Demons weren't going anywhere, she knew that. But somehow she'd find a way to steer clear of their path. Who cared if they called her names or made fun of her? She wasn't going to let them get the best of her. Whether it was all that honey she'd put on her pancakes, or the fact that she and Eleanor had become close friends, Shree felt lighter this morning than she had since she got to Cambridge.

All day Shree held onto her emotional high. She volunteered to answer questions in all her classes without a care in the world for the reactions of the Demons.

Mr. Blayne: What percentage makes up two standard deviations from the mean?
Shree: Ninety-five percent.

Mrs. Tillman: Which of Shakespeare's sonnets describes love as an "ever-fixed mark?"
Shree: The sonnet entitled "Let me not to the marriage of true minds."

Mr. Roberts: Which African American abolitionist worked closely with Abraham Lincoln to help slaves gain their freedom?
Shree: Frederick Douglass.

Mr. Stanley: Which chamber of the heart pumps blood to the lungs?
Shree: The right ventricle.

At least in her current frame of mind it seemed as though the majority of Shree's classmates were okay with her display of brilliance. With the exception of the Demons, the rest of her class nodded and smiled at her after she answered questions.

In gym Shree could do no wrong, either. The bow and arrow settled into her arms like a baby, and she shot two arrows simultaneously again as Mr. Marr asked her to do. The sound of the double bull's-eyes was more satisfying than anything she'd ever experienced.

Shree replayed her performance from the day on her way home from school. She had answered questions correctly. She had impressed her teachers and classmates. She had even made a couple of potential new friends. The fear that had gripped her since the first day at Kennedy Academy was fading fast and being replaced by a sense that she could actually succeed at her new school the same way she had at P.S. #54.

Slowly, though, with every step she took, Shree could feel her feelings of uncertainty begin to return. She was so caught up in her performance in school that she'd forgotten to keep an eye out for the Demons. She was lucky to have avoided them all day, but now for some unknown reason she was frightened. Soon Shree was looking over her shoulder and hurrying her pace. Were those footsteps she heard?

Now she was really going crazy. The first good day she'd had in a long time, and she was ruining it with her paranoia. She made herself slow down and take deep breaths. "There's no one there," she said aloud. "Get a grip, Shree."

But she couldn't help it. She had to look again. As she rounded the corner towards the park, she stopped to make sure that the sidewalk behind her was empty. "See? Nobody. Don't be such a wimp." Shree again forced herself to walk more slowly and wiped her sweaty hands on her jacket. Relieved that she was alone on the street, she turned the next corner.

Blocking her way stood the whole gang of Demons. Katherine stood in front, the twins on each side of her like bodyguards. They held thick tree branches in their hands. The sneers on their faces made clear their intent as they all looked to Katherine and waited for her to speak.

But it was Colleen, not Katherine, who spoke first.

"Well, look who we have here, guys. It's Shree, Shree, the bumblebee. How's it going, bee? You really think you can get away with making me look bad without paying for it?" Colleen laughed.

Shree couldn't speak.

"What's the matter, Bumbles? Scared?" Katherine asked.

Shree's gaze was fixed on the branches in the twins' hands. Slap went the wood against their palms, over and over, making Shree jump with each impact.

One of them picked up Katherine's threat. "What do you think, Tom? What should her punishment be?"

"Hmm, I might be able to think of a couple of things that'd teach her not to mess with our friend." He smiled at Shree.

"Not yet, guys," Katherine said. "First, the girls are going to have a little fun." She turned to Shree. "You think you can embarrass me in gym class like that?" She spat the question at Shree. "You think you can show us up in class? Who do you think you are?" Katherine took a step forward and stopped. "I'll tell you. You're a nobody. A freak. You don't belong here."

Suddenly, Colleen and Katherine were moving forward. Shree stepped back automatically and stumbled over a rock. She was on the ground before she knew what happened and in another second the girls were looming over her. "I told you to go back to New York." This statement was punctuated by a kick of Katherine's boot.

"Yeah," Colleen said, "And what's up with those stupid shoes? I thought I told you they were ugly." The kicks to her side from Colleen's pointy shoe made Shree sick to her stomach. The pain was unbearable and she had a hard time catching her breath.

Katherine dragged Shree up by the hair and pushed her towards Colleen, who slapped Shree's face and sent her with a push back to Katherine. Colleen then reached down and picked up a handful of dirt. "Hold her still, Katherine," she said and then threw the dirt in Shree's eyes.

Shree couldn't see. She was blinded by the dirt and the pain. Panicking, she knew she had to get out of there before they hurt her even worse. But she couldn't open her eyes—and that scared her more than anything else. She had to get out. But how?

Shree heard laughter from Jason and the twins. They were just watching, enjoying the show. She rubbed her eyes but that only made them sting more.

Suddenly, time stood still. The voices of the Demons receded and she heard her father's voice floating around her head. It was the first day of school. What had he said? Something about how when we embrace our differences we gain power. And something about unlimited potential. Yeah, that was it. That was exactly what he'd said.

Well, Shree was being pushed. And she needed help.

A deep calm pervaded Shree's whole body. There was no more pain and no more fear. She allowed her body to stay relaxed, kept her eyes closed, and ignored her surroundings. She sensed the Demons advancing on her. The air around her crackled.

Colleen moved in to grab her hair, but Shree stepped easily to the side and Colleen was left with nothing more than a fistful of air. Katherine threw a punch at Shree, but again, Shree managed to move aside and the punch went right past her. It landed square in Colleen's face, instead. Shocked, Katherine reached for Colleen, who was holding her jaw and trying to stay upright.

Shree waited. She heard the girls' panting and cursing. In another couple of seconds the blows were sure to start again. And they did. They came at her again and again. She dodged one and then another and then another. She cleared each one, feeling like some kind of Kung Fu master.

The girls sputtered and swore in frustration. The boys were no longer laughing. Now they stood gawking, rooted to the spot.

Colleen yelled to Jason and the twins. "Will you guys *do* something. What's wrong with you? Don't just stand there watching. Get her!"

Shree felt the twins coming at her: how, she didn't know. Then she felt the strong grip on her arm. She knew they wouldn't hesitate to rough her up just to appease the girls.

Shree said nothing, but her mind was busy. The weird feelings she had experienced in the Bronx started back up. She couldn't let the Demons get the best of her. She couldn't let them win. She was Shree, and Shree Mandvi never gave up.

And that's when Shree disappeared.

"What just happened?" Katherine said.

"I don't know," Jason said, holding onto Colleen's shoulders. "One minute she was here, and then she was gone."

There was a faint buzzing noise overhead, like the sound of a distant lawn mower. The noise got louder. For a minute no one spoke, listening. "Hey, what's that?" Tim asked.

"Dude," Tom exclaimed. "It's a bee. And it's coming right for us."

They all looked up. Sure enough a big fat bumblebee was dive-bombing from the sky.

At the last minute it steered a path for the twin with the biggest stick.

Tom screamed.

"Run, Tom, run," Tim called out.

But it was too late. Tom used his stick to beat at the air but the bee easily avoided the contact. He threw down his stick. "Get away from me, you stupid bee, get away," he whined. But the bee kept coming, circling above his head over and over again.

Then, suddenly, Tom let out a long wail. "It stung me! It stung me!"

"Tom, are you okay? Your face is all red." Tim ran over to his side.

"No, I'm not okay, you idiot. I just got stung—and I don't have my Epipen."

Tom's breath was coming in uneven waves. He had his hands on his neck. Drops of sweat began to drip down his forehead. Already his face was swelling, puffing up like a sponge soaked in water. He ripped open his shirt. "I can't get enough air. Tim, I—I—can't breathe. My lungs—Tim—call for help."

Tim saw his brother's face start to turn blue. He was going into anaphylactic shock. "He's allergic to bee stings," he yelled to his friends. "Hurry, call the ambulance or he'll die."

As Jason pulled out his cell phone and made the call, the bee spun off and settled on a hydrangea bush about twenty feet away to watch. Tim was begging his brother to hold on until the ambulance got there and Katherine, Colleen, and Jason were standing in a useless little huddle.

Finally, Shree heard the sirens. She hurt all over, aching from her little toe to the top of her head. She looked down and saw that her legs were back to their human form and that, instead of wings, she had arms again. She was breathing heavily as if she'd run the race of her life. Could what she thought happened really have happened?

It didn't seem possible, but she couldn't explain it any other way. Slowly, she picked herself up off the ground, brushing off the dried hydrangea petals from her shoulders. With a final look back at the EMTs, who were radioing their instructions back to the hospital, Shree took off running.

Chapter 15

All About Bees

Shree made it home in minutes. She ran up to the porch. She was about to open the door when she realized what a sight she must be to the outside world; her shirt was torn, her hair was a mess, and she could feel blood crusted on her face. She couldn't go into the house looking like that. What would her mother say?

Shree crept over to the garage and looked in the window. She almost wept in relief. The station wagon was gone. Her mother must still be out. She went around the side of the house and let herself into the kitchen door. She ran upstairs and tore off her clothes. She'd shower and get changed, and if her mother asked about the cut on her face, she'd say that she had tripped over something in gym class.

Ten minutes later Shree was toweling off. Her body still ached from every pore and she felt as if she could sleep forever. She looked in the mirror. The cut across her face was sore looking but it had stopped bleeding and didn't look as bad as she thought it would. She combed her hair and tried to ignore the renewed pounding in her head and the pain in her side where she'd been kicked.

Suddenly, Shree felt woozy and her stomach began to hurt. She sat on her bed for a minute to regroup. The reality of what had just happened—what she, Shree, had done—hit her like a ton of bricks. She had changed into a bee and had almost killed someone with her stinger.

She gave herself up to the memory. She needed to remember everything. She recalled feeling powerless—completely and utterly helpless. So helpless that she felt she'd die with the sense of despair. But then things shifted. Even though she still hadn't been able to see, she knew that the Demons couldn't hurt her, and that she had some kind of power they didn't have. First she'd heard her father's words, and then everything kind of switched. She saw a bright light and then suddenly felt like she was outside her body. She started getting smaller and smaller. She felt things growing from her sides and back. At some point everything had gone black and when she came to she was flying. She could still feel the euphoria. She'd never felt so fast, so fearless, so free.

Then the next thing Shree remembered was the feeling of release as she gave into her urge for revenge.

Oh. My. GOD! Had she really done it? Had she stung Tom Smith?

Shree's eyes welled up with tears. She was a monster. She remembered vividly that once she had realized the twins couldn't hurt her, all she thought about was getting revenge. She recalled feeling hatred and anger and loathing. It went against her Jain upbringing and everything her parents had taught her, but all she could think about after transforming into a bee was hurting those who had hurt *her*.

Shree shuttered. What the hell was happening?

Over the past few weeks she had developed a craving for sweets and honey, her sense of smell had increased, her moods and physical health had been madly up and down. She had become a brilliant archer—and now she had turned into a bee.

She took a deep breath. There *had* to be a logical explanation for this. Shree looked around the room trying to find clues that might help explain what was going on with her. After scanning for a moment, her gaze finally settled on her computer. That was it. She needed to do some research. Maybe the Internet could answer some of her questions.

Unfortunately, when she Googled "bees," she found 26,654,980 hits. Shree sighed. Where to begin? She scrolled down on the page and saw Wikipedia about halfway down. She clicked on the link and waited. In seconds the screen came up with pictures, text and link. She read the first paragraph.

Bees are flying insects closely related to wasps and ants. Bees are a monophyletic lineage within the superfamily *Apoidea*, presently classified by the unranked taxon name *Anthophila*.

O-kay. Whatever. Moving right along.

There are nearly 20,000 known species of bees in nine recognized families, though many are undescribed and the actual number is probably higher.

There were links sprinkled throughout the text. Again, not very helpful. Shree moved on. The next link took her to "bee disambiguation," whatever that was. Shree groaned. At this rate it would take her all day to learn anything useful.

Shree clicked to go back to the original page on bees. Maybe another section further down might be more helpful.

Bumblebee queens sometimes seek winter safety in honeybee hives, where they are sometimes found dead in the spring by beekeepers. It is unknown whether any survive winter in such an environment.

Hmmm. That didn't sound good. Did that mean that she wouldn't survive the New England winter? What if she transformed into a bee again and ended up stuck? Would her parents find her dead inside a beehive?

Shree tried to shrug off those fears. She forced herself to keep reading.

There was one more section that stood out. It was on bee stings. Shree quickly scrolled down so she could read the paragraph. According to the article, when a bee stings something—or someone—its stinger stays behind in the victim when the bee flies off. And then the bee dies.

Shree felt nauseous. *She* was a bumblebee. *She* had stung once already. But why hadn't she died?

She remembered, though, that she still had her stinger when she flew away after stinging Tom. Maybe she hadn't done it properly?

But if there was a next time—and there was bound to be—would she end up dead?

She was deep in thought when she heard the front door slam shut.

"Shree? Are you home?"

It was her mother. Damn. Shree had hoped for a little more time to get herself together.

"Shree? Where are you? Mrs. Johnson is here for a visit. Come say hello."

Shoot. Shree had totally forgotten that Tanya's mother was coming. She really wanted to see her, but why today of all days?

"Hi, Mom. Hi, Mrs. Johnson," she called down. "I'll be right there."

Shree wiped her eyes with the back of her hands and tried to compose herself. She had to go downstairs and act as if everything was normal. She didn't know how, but she had to be convincing.

There was a soft buzzing at her window. Shree raised the shade. A bee with bright yellow stripes and a big black stinger sat on her windowsill. Shree stared at the bee and two big round black eyes stared back at her, as if to say, "You're one of us now." Shree shook her head to dislodge the crazy idea. Just then the bee took off into the room. Shree watched as it swept its way across the ceiling, buzzing loudly, and then down along the windowpane and back to the sill. After a minute it made the journey again. Shree watched it circle around several times. How were bees getting in her room? What were they trying to tell her? She thought bees were supposed to hate the cold, but maybe that's why they were coming in. Maybe they were trying to get away from the colder air outside. But still, it didn't account for the fact that they were coming into *her* room instead of settling down for the winter where they belonged—in their hives with all their honey.

Shree had to face the truth. The Demons had been calling her a bumblebee from the first day of school. Could it really be that she was actually becoming one? A real live bee? But how? And, more importantly, did it mean that one day she'd turn into a bee and never come back?

Shree walked back over to her mirror. Looking at herself—really looking at herself for the first time in a long time—she could see the comparison. Her eyes were large and black. Her waist was round and the fact that she was a bit short and had very thin arms and legs gave her body a sort of insect-like quality. The yellow-and-black sneakers at her feet were just additional pieces of the giant puzzle that was her new existence. But to transform? Into a real bee? How could this be happening? It was crazy, impossible, ludicrous. And yet?

Shree went back to her window. She opened it, making it possible for the bee to leave. But the bee continued to sit on her windowsill, not moving. "What are you waiting for?" Shree asked. "Shoo!"

But the bee was unshaken, resting on its wings and staring out at Shree.

The mid-October breeze filled the bedroom. From a distance, a thousand different shades of red, orange, and brown leaves blended perfectly with the purple-blue sky of the setting sun. Shree stood closer to the window and took a deep breath. The dusky smell of the sole dandelion that grew on the side of Mrs. Rando's house next door filled her nose.

She pivoted and looked further down the street towards Mr. Goldman's garden of petunias. She could smell each and every one of them. They called to her, their overripe pollen begging to be stolen away before the first frost.

"Shree! Where are you? We are waiting for you."

Shree jumped a mile. The sound of her mother's voice on the stairs woke her from her trance. Another inch and she would've fallen out the window. She'd have to be a lot more careful. Her clothes were still on the floor. She didn't want her mother coming into the room. "I'll be right there, Mom," she yelled. "I was just doing my homework." She stuffed her clothes in the back of her closet to deal with later, jammed on some jeans and a t-shirt, and opened the door. She'd have to put on a good act.

Mrs. Johnson gave a big hug. "Shree. How are you, girl? Let me look at you, sweetheart. Why, you look—" She paused and cried out, "Hey, what's that on your face? Are you okay?"

Her mother came running. "Oh my goodness, Shree. What has happened? Are you all right?"

"I'm fine, Mom." She turned to Mrs. Johnson. "I'm fine, really, I just tripped in gym class. I took a shower and cleaned it off. I'm fine, really."

Her mother held Shree's face in her hands. Her penetrating stare was hard to deflect. Finally, Shree looked away.

She turned brightly to Mrs. Johnson, "How's Tanya? I wish she could've come with you. I miss her."

It worked. The change of subject had shifted the conversation.

"Tanya misses you too, honey. She had a basketball game this weekend, otherwise she would've come with me. I told her that we'd try to come together another time. Maybe over the holidays."

"That'd be great. Harvard Square's supposed to be really cool. I really want to take her and show her around," Shree said.

"We just got back, your mother and I. You're right, girl, it's wild. I never thought somewhere outside New York City could be so diverse."

"Yeah," Shree said. "Diverse is definitely the word."

Chapter 16

Not Alone

Seven AM came all too soon. The previous night's dinner could've been a disaster, but with Mrs. Johnson there, most of the attention had been shifted from Shree and onto the adults, who talked for hours while Shree did the dishes. When she said she had to go upstairs and do her homework, no one took much notice. As she left the grownups in the living room with their coffee and tea, Shree overheard Mrs. Johnson saying, "Shree looks good, Indy. That cut? She's always been a bit klutzy, right? I wouldn't worry. It sounds like she's adjusting to Kennedy just fine."

Adjusting? Huh. That wasn't the word that came to mind. Shree knew something big was happening and it was not at all in her control. She'd have to work on that. Maybe practice her flying and learn more about bees. She needed to learn everything she could about what was going on with her.

Right now the last thing Shree wanted to do was to go back to school. At least it was Friday. If she could survive the day without any problems, then she'd have the whole weekend to figure out what was happening.

From downstairs she heard her mother calling. "Come on, Shree. You are going to be late for school. Breakfast is ready."

She was still sore all over, even worse than yesterday. It took every ounce of energy to get herself up from bed. As she walked down the stairs, she held onto the railing tightly, making sure her legs didn't give out.

Shree gave Mrs. Johnson, who was sitting at the table with a huge mug of coffee, a big hug, grimacing at the discomfort. Then she gave her mother a kiss on the cheek.

"Hey, girl. How are you feeling this morning? Your face looks better at least. You didn't eat much at dinner. You must be starving. Here, we got some things at the bakery." Mrs. Johnson spoke a mile-a-minute and pushed a platter of fruit and pastries towards her.

Shree looked at the nectarines and apples and muffins, thinking that there was no way she could eat. But suddenly her mouth was watering. She reached for an apple and for a muffin with chocolate chips and sugar sprinkled on top.

Her mother looked on disapprovingly. "Where are your manners, Shree? Is that how you eat in front of our guest? Please sit down and take a plate."

Mrs. Johnson chuckled and winked at Shree. "Honey, I've seen a lot worse, what with four boys and all."

Shree drank down a quick glass of juice and grabbed two doughnuts she spied on the counter to add to her lunch bag. She said a quick goodbye to her parents and

Mrs. Johnson and then ran out the door. She didn't want to go to school, but if she had to go, she didn't want to be late.

The first person Shree bumped into before English class was Eleanor. Shree was feeling much better after the brisk walk and another doughnut.

"Hi, El. Are we still on for tomorrow?" Shree asked.

"Yes, definitely. My mother is going to drop me off in front of the gate at ten. So we will have all day. You still have to tell me why we are going."

It was a good question. How much did she want to tell Eleanor? She owed her friend an explanation about the treasure, but all this bee stuff? Eleanor might like her, but even a friend would think someone who said she turned into a bee was a total lunatic.

Eleanor gave Shree a closer look. "Hey, what happened to your face?"

"The Demons," Shree said. "Yesterday, after school."

"Did you tell anyone?" Eleanor looked worried.

"How can I?" Shree asked. "There's nothing they can do, and besides I ended up—"

"Ended up what?" Eleanor asked.

"Oh, never mind. Listen. I don't want to tell anyone, El. I need to handle this myself."

"Well, okay, if that is what you want," Eleanor said, sounding unconvinced. "But I think—"

Before Eleanor could finish Nancy walked over.

"Oh, hi, Nancy," Eleanor said. "Can you still come this weekend?"

Nancy glanced at Shree's wound, and then turned to Eleanor. "Yeah, no problem," she said. "I'll meet you at Harvard Yard at ten."

Nancy stared at the wound again, making Shree feel uncomfortable, almost as if Nancy were seeing right into her soul.

The bell rang and the girls rushed in to take their seats.

The class was ringing with talk about Tom's visit to the emergency room after he'd been stung by a bee. Somehow the word got around that Katherine had called 911 and saved Tom's life. Shree couldn't believe her ears. Katherine had done no such thing. She'd been screaming and hysterical when Shree had flown away (it still felt weird to say that) and now she was a hero? Shree was disgusted. The girl just didn't know when to quit.

As she approached Katherine's desk, Shree felt the Demons staring at her. Did they know she had turned into a bee? Because if they knew, and she knew that they knew, and they knew that she knew that they knew, then it'd be a very difficult situation! Shree just prayed that they kept the specifics about what had happened the day before as quiet as she did. Shree tried to act naturally but as she walked by she felt her lower back give a little *zing*, as if her stinger wanted to reassert itself.

Calm, she told herself, stay calm. You don't want anything to happen in school.

She got to her seat and sat down. Tom was nowhere to be seen and she heard Tim saying he'd be out until the following week. Shree tried but couldn't feel bad about what she'd done. The twins were jerks and they deserved it.

Mrs. Tillman started talking about Samuel Taylor Coleridge, an English poet and literary critic, and his most famous poem, "The Rime of the Ancient Mariner." Shree half-listened to what the teacher was saying. She was busy making a list of the supplies she needed to bring with her to Harvard Yard. She was also trying to figure out what she'd tell Eleanor and Nancy. The thing was that Eleanor seemed to trust Nancy. Shree could honestly say she trusted Eleanor, so she knew that if she wanted to confide in Eleanor she'd have to let Nancy in on everything, too.

Shree gave a mental shrug. Even though Nancy seemed kind of strange, she'd just have to assume that Eleanor was a good judge of character.

Shree recalled Mrs. Twichett's speech at the diner, remembering specifically the old woman's warning about the importance of being inclusive in her search for the treasure. Is this what Mrs. Twichett had meant: that Shree should let people in on her secret?

At that exact moment, Shree saw something moving in front of her. She looked up from her book and noticed that Eleanor's pen had fallen on the floor. The pen was closer to Shree than it was to Eleanor, so Shree put down the treasure book and went to pick it up.

But she stopped half-way and gasped.

Right in front of her, Shree saw Eleanor's hand and fingers extending out along the floor as if they were made of expandable rubber. In fact, Eleanor's hand was three times its normal size. It moved slowly underneath her chair, expanding as it glided along until it found the pen.

And then suddenly her hand shrank back to its original size.

Shree was stunned. What had just happened?

A few minutes later, the bell rang. Shree stayed frozen to her seat while Eleanor packed her bag in front of her.

"Are you coming, Shree?" Eleanor asked.

Shree just sat there, staring at Eleanor's hand.

It took Eleanor a couple of seconds, but Shree could see when her friend finally realized why Shree was acting so strangely. The next thing Shree knew, Eleanor was rushing out the door and down the hall.

Shree jumped up, grabbed her book bag, and ran after her.

"Wait, Eleanor. We need to talk." Shree had a hard time keeping up with her. Eleanor picked up her pace as she rounded the corner.

After about a minute's chase, Shree made a last ditch attempt to gain Eleanor's attention.

"I know what you did with your hands," Shree yelled out, her voice echoing in the empty corridor.

Eleanor stopped running and turned, walking briskly back towards Shree. "Listen, I want you to forget what you saw. It did not happen. You did not see anything, okay?"

Shree was taken aback. She had never seen her friend angry before. "But Eleanor, I saw what you did and—"

"Look, I do not want to talk about this here. Let us meet after school." Eleanor sighed. "I will tell you everything then."

With that, Eleanor rushed off to her next class, leaving Shree wondering if she wasn't the only one keeping secrets.

Chapter 17

Ellie Espagueti

Eleanor was waiting for Shree by the double doors when the last school bell rang. Usually, Eleanor was gone before Shree had time to gather her stuff from her locker. But today things were different.

"I thought we could walk home together and talk," Eleanor said, giving Shree a weak smile.

"Okay, El. I need to tell you something too."

An uncomfortable silence fell. They both started to walk down the path leading to Brattle Street.

Eleanor opened her mouth to speak, but hesitated and grew quiet. It seemed like she was trying to choose the right words before beginning her story.

The girls continued to walk in silence. The only sound Shree noted came from her shoes as they crushed the many dead leaves scattered on the sidewalk. The sound was intensified by the quiet air of fall, as Shree waited for Eleanor to start speaking.

"In the beginning it only happened when I got really upset about something." Eleanor began in a halting voice. "The first time was when I was in the second grade. I was living in the Dominican Republic then with my parents and four brothers."

Shree smiled, thinking of Tanya and all her brothers. It was getting chilly, so she zipped up her jacket and hid her hands inside her sleeves.

"When I was seven I started to grow. I mean really grow. Over the course of a couple of months I grew nearly a foot. That meant that I was now taller than everyone else in my class—every single kid. And then I was taller than every kid in the whole school. I was skinny too and they started calling me 'Ellie Espagueti.' Well, that was the nicest name they used. The other ones were pretty mean. Finally, I stayed by myself. Even my friends did not want to hang out with me because they would have to put up with the other kids if they did. And I think they started to get uncomfortable around me, too."

Shree looked at Eleanor's hands. Her fingers were unnaturally long and slender. She felt sorry for Eleanor. It must've been tough growing up like that.

"Anyway, my parents tried to reassure me by telling me that I was going through early puberty, but it did not make me feel better. One day, my friend Melissa gave in and she came over to my house to play soccer with me. She was really good. She was scoring goal after goal, and I was getting more and more frustrated. I had long legs, but I was always so clumsy. We played for a while and then she gave the ball a hard kick towards my goal. I saw it coming and I do not know what happened—all I remember is that I was upset about everything—and suddenly it was as if

I had become someone else. I watched as first my arms, then my hands and fingers stretched out, almost as if they were made out of rubber."

Eleanor stopped speaking for a moment and sighed. "They reached a few feet away for the ball as I dove to block it, snatching it in mid-air and preventing Melissa from scoring on me. Melissa saw the whole thing and just stood there staring, and I got the horrible feeling that I had done something awful. She ran off screaming, and after that day, things were never the same, even though I do not think anyone really believed Melissa's story about what she saw."

Shree remembered stinging Tom in the park. She shuddered, thinking of how anxious and upset she had felt afterwards.

"Eventually," Eleanor continued, "my parents decided to move to America. My mother has a cousin who works at Massachusetts General Hospital, so they brought me here to figure out what was wrong with me."

"Did they?" Shree asked.

They were passing the Longy School of Music, halfway between Kennedy and her house. Shree could hear a string quartet playing Bach.

"Sort of. I had a million blood tests and x-rays. I felt like a human pin cushion by the time they were done. They decided that even though my case did not fit all the criteria, I had something called Marfan's Syndrome. It is a rare genetic disorder that makes some of your tissues grow out of proportion. Of course, this did not explain my new abilities in the least. But I was still keeping those to myself. I was enough of a freak already."

Shree knew just how she felt. "So what happened after that?"

"Well, they wrote up my case in a bunch of medical journals. I have been interviewed by a thousand doctors. I got tired of the whole thing, and so did my parents. But the medical people wanted to keep me around—you know, to watch me grow. To them I was special because they noticed that my fingers were different lengths from week to week. They had never seen that before; they had no idea that I could stretch out any part of my body."

Eleanor smiled. "They told my parents that they would pay for me to go to school here. My parents could not afford Kennedy Academy on their own, but when they heard I would get free tuition, they signed me up. I guess they hoped that I would not stand out so much here."

"Wow. That's totally amazing, El. I love it. But can you do that thing with your hands whenever you want to?"

Eleanor smiled again. She stopped walking and stood in the middle of the street. With no one in sight, she dropped her hands and started shaking them at the wrist. For long seconds nothing happened and Shree was about to say something, when all of a sudden Eleanor's fingers began to twitch. Shree watched as two long arms and ten long fingers began to grow. In the blink of an eye, they'd stretched clear across and over to the nearest fence by the side of the street, snaked over it, and made their way to a branch on the big maple tree in the yard. Eleanor then picked off a big leaf and brought it back to give to Shree. When Eleanor's arms returned to her body, they regained their normal size and hung by her side as if nothing had happened. Shree was speechless. Who'd have thought she'd ever see something like that?

"That was awesome, Eleanor. How did you do that?"

"Do not ask me, Shree, I am still trying to make sense of it," Eleanor said. "The only other person that knows about this is Nancy, so please do not tell anyone."

They continued walking, not saying much until they reached the park where Eleanor turned to go home. Shree was glad that Eleanor had shared her secret with her, but she wondered why she had also confided in Nancy. This was a huge secret. What was it about Nancy that made Eleanor trust her so much?

"So, Shree, were you going to tell me something?"

Shree paused. Arms and legs that stretched were nothing compared to becoming a bee. But Eleanor had just shared her big secret. Didn't she deserve honesty in return?

"I'll tell you, Eleanor, but you have to promise never to tell another soul."

Eleanor nodded.

Here went nothing, thought Shree. And she poured it all out to Eleanor. How she craved sweets and loved flowers and got sick and then had tons of energy and, finally, how she had become a bee and had stung Tom. She even told her about John Harvard's treasure, about how she'd found the treasure book at the diner in Salem and how it'd been stolen by the twins during the first week of school.

Eleanor's eyes got bigger and bigger.

"I guess we are more alike than I thought. That is unbelievable, Shree. But what are you going to do?"

"I don't know, but I do know that I have to learn more about bees to figure out what I can and can't do. And then I plan on getting my treasure book back."

Shree looked over at Eleanor. "Up for some treasure hunting, El?"

"I would not miss it for the world, Shree."

Chapter 18

A Field Trip To Harvard Yard

Just as her father was dropping Shree off at the gate to Harvard Yard the next day, Eleanor was arriving with her mom. Dr. Mandvi and Mrs. Martinez waved to each other, then pulled away into the flow of traffic. Shree had promised to be home by three. She and Eleanor were a few minutes early and Nancy wasn't there yet, so they walked inside the yard to wait for her.

"Hey, isn't that Dave?" Eleanor asked.

"Dave who? Where?" Shree looked around.

"Over there. By the tree. The tall, skinny guy with the big ears." Eleanor pointed to a figure in the distance.

Shree looked. She was pretty sure it was the same guy that the twins had been beating up at the park, on her very first day in Cambridge. Dave was now standing under the big oak tree like he was waiting for someone.

Eleanor waved. "You know it is really too bad," she said. "Dave is a pretty nice guy, even though his mouth is too big for his own good. People make fun of him all the time because of his big ears. They call him Dumbo Dave. His real name is David Jackson."

"I saw the twins beating him up when I first got here," Shree said. "They were in the park. I felt really bad for him, but there was nothing I could do."

Shree paused, recalling the incident. "But even when they were hurting him, he just kept on making jokes. Which really wasn't a good idea since it just pissed the twins off more."

"Sounds like Dave for sure. He never knows when to keep his mouth shut. He is a great mimic, too, but like I said, he never knows when to stop."

"That's probably what got the Demons started," Shree said. "Not that they need a reason."

They reached Dave at the tree and stopped to speak to him.

"What up, girls?" he asked.

"Hi, Dave," Eleanor said. "Do you know Shree?"

"Well, we've never formally met. But I do remember a particular incident in the park."

"Yeah," Shree said, feeling herself blush. "That totally sucked. Sorry I left."

Dave shrugged as if he hadn't expected otherwise. "Where you guys going?" he asked.

"We need to do some research at Widener." Shree jumped in before Eleanor could answer him. She didn't want Eleanor saying anything about their mission.

"That's funny," Dave said. "I'm going there, too. I gotta work on my, um, English paper."

They walked towards the middle of Harvard Yard, away from the South Gate and Harvard Square. Immediately the sounds of traffic and frenzy were diminished, as if hitting university property meant automatic quiet out of a respect for learning.

Shree really wasn't sure she was comfortable with Dave coming with them, but Eleanor didn't seem to mind, and there was really no choice. Eleanor and Shree parked themselves by the fountain in front of Widener Library.

"Why are we stopping here?" Dave asked.

"We are waiting for Nancy," Eleanor said. "We are meeting her here."

"Who? Nancy Four-Eyes? Great. I've known Nancy forever."

"You know, I do not think she would like to hear you call her that," Eleanor said. "She is pretty sensitive about her eyes."

"Aw, she's fine with it," Dave said. "I always tease her. She doesn't mind." Dave hummed for a minute. "This campus is pretty cool, especially that statue over there." He pointed to the John Harvard Statue at the other side of the yard.

Shree didn't agree with Dave. She was sure Nancy didn't like being teased about her glasses. And his comment about the statue bothered her, too. Why did he want to talk about the statue?

"I guess," Shree said. "Why?"

"Oh, I don't know. I've heard some cool things about that old dude Harvard, like how he might've hidden—" he paused and pointed to the far corner of Harvard Yard. "Hey, there she is. Nancy! Over here."

Nancy looked up and stopped in her tracks. Shree waved, at the same time wondering why Nancy had such an angry look on her face.

"Come on, Nancy," Eleanor called. "It is kind of cold out here."

Since they had arrived the sun had indeed disappeared and a brisk wind had picked up.

Nancy seemed to square her shoulders before coming towards them. "What are *you* doing here, Dave?" she asked coldly.

Shree looked over at Eleanor. Clearly Dave and Nancy were not on the best of terms.

But Dave looked unperturbed. "Hey, Nance," he said. "I haven't seen you around. What's going on?"

"Nothing is going on, Dave. I have nothing to say to you."

"Aw, come on, Nancy. That was in second grade."

Shree's head went back and forth from Nancy to Dave. It was like following the ball in a tennis match.

"I don't care. You've never stopped calling me Four Eyes," Nancy said.

"Well, sometimes it just slips out. And you gotta admit that it did jump-start my comedy career, for which I give you total credit, by the way. Just think of it as a term of endearment," Dave added.

"Yeah, right. How about if I call you Dumbo Dave? Would that be a term of endearment, too?" Nancy demanded.

Dave smiled. "Actually, funny you should mention it since that's how—"

Nancy cut him off before he could continue. "I'm through speaking to you. Let's just walk over to the library."

As the three girls followed the concrete path to Widener Library, Dave trailed behind. Shree could see that Nancy didn't look happy about it. When they got to Widener Library, they all stopped in front of the building. There was an uncomfortable silence as Shree looked at Eleanor and Nancy, wondering what to do about Dave.

"All right, I'm off to get my English books." Dave gave a nervous smile to the girls and walked up the long set of marble steps towards the entrance.

Because Nancy and Eleanor wouldn't be allowed inside the book stacks without a proper ID, Shree still needed to figure out a way to sneak them in. Once they were all inside, she'd search for the books and tell Nancy about the treasure.

Shree had made a decision to let Nancy in on everything. She would take Mrs. Twichett's advice about not going after the treasure by herself. Who knew? Maybe Nancy would turn out to be a big help.

Once Shree reached the entrance, the security guard showed her where to slide her ID through the slot in the metal post. She gave a push and the spokes of the gates *cha-chinked* as she walked through. Nancy and Eleanor were issued temporary passes, but Shree still needed to figure out a way to sneak them inside the book stacks.

As the girls entered the main reading room, Shree saw the sign for the reference desk and headed over to ask for help. She could just see the last of Dave's backpack bouncing up with each step as he climbed the staircase on the left of the reading room. What could he be up to, anyway?

"Yes, may I help you?"

The woman behind the desk looked just the way a librarian should, thought Shree. Her name tag read Mrs. Finney. She was skinny and stern, her hair pulled into a bun at the nape of her neck. She was wearing a gray sweater and pearls around her neck. What is it about librarians, Shree wondered. Was this the way she'd end up if she kept up with so much reading? That would be *so* not cool.

"I said, may I help you?" Mrs. Finney repeated, a slightly annoyed expression on her face that said, "I do not have time for this, young lady."

Shree jumped into the present. "Um, yes, please. I'm doing research for my English project and I need to find some information about John Harvard. I have the names of a couple of books."

"Follow me over here to our computerized database. I will set you up with an account so you can browse our catalogue. Here is a map of the library."

Mrs. Finney's mahogany desk faced the entrance into the six-storied section of books, but she had to leave her post to show Shree how to use the computer system. Which was just what Shree was counting on. Eleanor and Nancy stood nearby, pretending to browse through a collection of old encyclopedias on the opposite wall. But as soon as the librarian wasn't looking, Shree made sure to signal the girls so they could sneak in. Shree was certain that Mrs. Finney wouldn't tolerate trespassers into her book stacks, so this was the only solution.

Mrs. Finney asked Shree for her ID card and copied the numbers on the back into the login screen. She asked Shree to type in a password and turned away as Shree typed in "treasure" in the box. Once Shree was logged on, Mrs. Finney gave her a couple of pointers on accessing the database and then got up. "There are pencils and paper by the computer terminals, and the bathrooms are over there." Mrs. Finney pointed down a long hallway. "Do you have any questions?"

Shree shook her head no. She waited until Mrs. Finney had spun around and clicked back on her small-heeled shoes to the reference desk, then made herself at home at the computer terminal.

Fifteen minutes passed in the blink of an eye. On the paper before her, Shree had call numbers for the two books she'd come to get and for three others that seemed promising. She knew she had to get to the stacks before Eleanor and Nancy started to get fidgety. She picked up her backpack and slung it over one shoulder. The map said that the historical references she wanted were up on the third floor in the southwest corner of the library. Call numbers in hand, Shree waved at Mrs. Finney as she entered the book stacks.

Once inside, Shree felt that now familiar twinge in her back as she walked down the long and dark corridor. Every time she thought about how the twins had stolen her book, her lower back started acting up. She really had to start practicing the whole bee transformation thing before she got caught off guard again.

Once inside the stacks, Shree met Eleanor and Nancy.

"Wow, that was a lot easier than I thought," Eleanor said, high-fiving Shree.

"Yeah, let's just not get caught. I have a feeling that Mrs. Finney doesn't deal kindly with trespassers," Shree said.

"What are we doing here, anyway?" Nancy asked.

Shree looked at Eleanor. "Care to give a summary?"

Eleanor smiled. "It is a long story, Nancy, but Shree thinks that there is a treasure hidden underneath Harvard University. It is going to make us rich. She had the book with a map telling us where it is hidden, but the twins stole it. Now we need to do some research and try to figure out how to find the treasure."

Nancy showed no reaction. In fact, she seemed completely indifferent to the news that there might be treasure beneath her feet somewhere. Was she not excited about it, or was there something else that Shree was missing?

She shrugged it off, thinking that it was nearly impossible to read Nancy's expression from behind those thick glasses.

Shree continued walking down the hallway with Eleanor and Nancy following right behind her. Each room they passed was full of books, thousands of them, all colors, all sizes, all ages. Every once in a while Shree heard the shifting of papers or a cough, or the clicking of keys on a laptop. She couldn't see anyone, but she assumed the sounds emanated from students behind the high sides of the stall-like study units by the far wall. Shree decided at that moment that she might never leave. She was in permanent book heaven. When she reached the right room she set her pack down on a carrel by a back window so she'd have her hands free.

Shree tiptoed by rows and rows of books, comparing the numbers on her list to the signs at the end of each row. The stacks were musty, but of course it'd be impossible to dust all the books in a place as big as this. Eventually they all came to the 680s, the section on the history of Harvard University. The first two books on her list were right where they should be.

It was great having Nancy and Eleanor along for the book hunt. Nancy seemed to know exactly where the books were located, while Eleanor helped by extending her arms and pulling the books off the hard-to-reach shelves.

The girls spent the next few minutes searching for the remaining books on Shree's list, but it seemed that the next three had already been taken out. Well, at least they had found two. Shree turned back to load up the books in her backpack, when she noticed that the library had gotten really quiet. The air was hushed and the light had taken on a kind of fragmented quality, as if even the dust was settling down for a rest.

That's when Shree heard the whispers. Or thought she did. Her back started to ache. It was as if she could feel the air bursting with new scents. Deep down she was certain something big was about to happen, but she didn't know what.

Shree stopped so she could hear better, and the whispers stopped. She started walking again and could've sworn the sounds started up again, too. She kept walking and then stopping, over and over. Shree told herself she was being paranoid. Eleanor and Nancy looked at her as if she was going crazy. And they were right. Shree was in the library, for heaven's sake. Everyone whispered in the library.

Seconds later, though, the whispering sound turned into a soft humming noise. Now Eleanor and Nancy stopped walking as well. They must have heard the whispers too, but Shree was sure that only she could feel that the air quality had suddenly changed. She felt goosebumps and another growling sensation in her back, as if her stinger wanted to jump out again. The noise kept getting louder and louder. Then all at once there was a rush of wind, as if a tornado had suddenly swept inside the library stacks. Hundreds of books were thrown off the shelves in all different directions. The girls huddled together and braced themselves as the torrent of wind passed right by them, showering them with volumes of paperbacks and forcing Shree, Eleanor, and Nancy to crouch on the ground and hold onto each other tightly. When it was over, there were books all over the hallway.

"What the hell was that?" Shree asked.

"I do not know, but that was crazy," Eleanor said.

"Well, whoever it was," Nancy said, "must've been in a big hurry." She held onto her glasses tightly.

"What do you mean *whoever*?" Shree asked.

"I mean that someone was responsible for what just happened. I couldn't catch who it was, but it was definitely a person." Nancy stared down the hallway, keeping her hand firmly attached to the side of her glasses.

Shree must have been seeing things, but it looked like Nancy's glasses reflected a thousand images at once, as if Shree was watching a DVD on fast-forward.

"Look, Shree, we will tell you everything later. Right now we have to get out of here before we get in trouble with the librarian," Eleanor said.

Shree wasn't sure what to make of the whole business. What had just happened? And what nonsense was Nancy talking about, that some person was somehow responsible for that bizarre indoor windstorm?

One thing was for certain. Eleanor was right. If Mrs. Finney found the girls in the book stacks, they'd all get in major trouble.

Dave came out of the library just as the girls were reaching the bottom of the stairs. How had he managed to show up at the exact time they were leaving, Shree wondered.

"Hey, you all finished at the library?" Dave asked.

Shree nodded.

"Where are you guys going now?" Dave looked from one girl to the other.

The guy really *didn't* know when to quit. Shree glanced over at Eleanor and Nancy, who were staring at the ground. Big help they were.

"Okay, okay, I get it," Dave said, looking hurt. "I know when I'm not wanted. I'll see you guys around." And he took off across Harvard Yard.

"Gee, now I feel bad," Shree said. "Maybe we should've let him hang out with us."

"No way," Nancy said. "Dave's a jerk *and* a liar. Didn't you guys notice? He said he was taking books out for his English paper, but he was holding a bunch of history books." Nancy paused, and pushed her glasses closer to her face. "And anyway, we have too much to do. We need to keep going. John Harvard's statue next?"

Chapter 19

Inside The Statue

Once they reached the statue, Shree forgot all about Dave. She stood at the base with Eleanor and Nancy by her side, admiring it. Up close, the John Harvard statue was a lot bigger than it seemed from afar—and solid as a rock. It looked impenetrable. Shree circled the granite base a couple of times. From her vantage point she could see Harvard's feet and legs, but that was about it. There was nothing particularly odd about the statue, just a rectangular slab of stone with a big bronze man on top, sitting in a chair with his arm resting on a large book.

"Eleanor," Shree said. "You're the tallest one of us. Can you check out what's up there?"

Eleanor looked around. When she was sure no one was watching, she extended her legs several inches to get a better view of the top half of the statue. "Well, I can see the guy's shoes. They have buckles on them. I can see the bottom of his robe and the chair. That is about all. Oh, and there are a couple of other books lying on the floor next to the chair."

"Have you heard about how people rub Harvard's feet for luck?" Nancy asked.

"Why would they do that?" Shree asked.

"I don't really know. Except they probably can't reach anything else," Nancy said.

"I see what you mean," Eleanor said. "The shoe that sticks out here is shiny. It must be from all the people who rub it, but I do not see how that is going to help us. What now?"

"Good question," Shree said. She let out a big sigh. "If I had my treasure book back, I'm sure I could figure it out."

Shree was beginning to second-guess herself. There was nothing even remotely connecting this statue with a treasure—except the map, of course, with the big "X" on it.

Shree walked around again, taking note of the Harvard insignias on either side of the base of the statue. The emblem consisted of three books with the syllables VE-RI-TAS on them, carved carefully into the stone.

Nancy came around to look at the insignia, too.

"Do you see anything, Nancy?" Eleanor asked.

"Well, actually, I think I do. Inside the statue," Nancy said.

"What do you mean by inside?" Shree asked.

"I haven't told you yet, Shree, but I can—" Nancy began.

"She has x-ray vision," Eleanor jumped in.

"Eleanor," Nancy moaned.

"I am sorry, Nancy, but I could not wait any longer. Go ahead, tell Shree," Eleanor urged. "Nancy has powers, too, just like us."

"Is that true, Nancy?" Shree asked. "You really have x-ray vision?"

Nancy flushed. She looked at Shree through her thick glasses and nodded. "Yes, it's true. I can see through most stuff."

"She can also see things from far away," Eleanor said.

"No way," Shree said. "That's amazing. Can you really see inside this statue?"

"It's pretty dense and dark, but I can definitely see a couple of grooves over there," she pointed to the upper left corner of the insignia, "and there, like door handles."

"Wow, Nancy. You know what that means?" Shree could hardly contain herself. "That means that somewhere inside this statue is some kind of a lever. If we find the lever, we find the way into the statue."

"But then what?" Eleanor asked. "Do you think the treasure is inside the statue?"

"So far it's all we've got," Shree said. "But first, what do you say we go have lunch? I want to hear all about your powers, Nancy, and then we'll figure out what to do."

On the way to Pinocchio's Pizza Parlor, Shree bombarded Nancy with questions about her powers until Nancy said she'd start at the beginning.

"I was only six when my parents discovered I had trouble seeing. I pretended for a long time that I was seeing what everyone else was seeing, but eventually they figured it out. Until I got glasses I didn't know that trees had leaves—I thought they were just big clumps of green.

"Then the doctor told my parents I needed glasses. But I didn't want them. Other kids who wore glasses got made fun of all the time. I was already the butt of jokes in school because I was Korean, and so tiny."

Shree nodded, remembering back to her first day at Kennedy and how lousy it felt to be labeled as different.

"I didn't want to wear anything that'd make me stand out. But I needed these humongous lenses," Nancy pointed to her glasses. "I still do. And like I predicted, everyone started making fun of me when I started wearing them. The kids called me Nancy Four-Eyes and told me to buy windshield wipers to clean my lenses."

Shree could see why people made fun of Nancy. Her eyes were magnified by the size of the lenses, and the frames made her head look smaller than it was to begin with. It occurred to Shree that she was pretty lucky. This was the first time Shree had to put up with kids making fun of her. Nancy and Eleanor had been dealing with that problem for a lot longer.

"What did you do?" Shree asked.

"There was nothing I could do," Nancy said. "I decided that it was better to see than to walk into walls. Then one day last year something really bizarre happened. My science teacher decided to give us a pop quiz. Everyone freaked out. He was a really harsh grader."

"You mean Mr. Carrozza, do you not?" Eleanor asked.

"Yeah, he's the worst," Nancy said. "Nobody knew the answers. We were all turning the pages of the quiz and nobody knew what to do. If we failed the test some of us would end up in summer school—like me. If I went to summer school I'd miss out on my trip to China. I was supposed to be going there to see my grandparents.

"I got so upset sitting there and thinking about failing the test that I couldn't even concentrate on it. It was like I was paralyzed. And I was so mad at Mr. Carrozza. There he was, all calm, sitting at his desk. He didn't care one bit about how we felt. His briefcase was on the desk next to him."

Shree remembered the pop quizzes given by her teachers in the Bronx. Most of her friends at P.S. #54 expected to go to summer school anyway, so there was never any stress when they failed. Thankfully, Shree never had that problem.

"After looking over the quiz," Nancy continued, "I started to panic. I glanced around the room, frantic about the thought of failing. And that's when I noticed that there was something funny about Mr. Carrozza's briefcase. It was like it had a window in it—I could see what was inside. I took off my glasses and cleaned them, but when I put them back on, the same thing happened. Without them everything was blurry, but with them I could see straight through solid objects. It was like looking through a telescope. I saw the answers to the test on a piece of paper in his briefcase."

Shree thought about the first time she'd transformed into a bee. Just like Nancy and Eleanor, the powers were triggered by some extreme emotion. In her case, it was fear. Was this the driving force behind their powers? Did it have anything to do with the antimatter and subconscious stuff her dad had spoken to her about?

Nancy looked down. "I felt guilty about the whole thing, but I couldn't help myself. I couldn't fail that test. So I read all the answers and copied them on my paper. I got to go to China because I aced the test."

Shree was quiet.

"I've never done it again, I promise. Just that one time. But I've developed my skills. I can see through things, and I can focus my eyes so that I can use them like either a telescope or a microscope, with a little adjustment of my glasses. Lately, I've gotten good at seeing behind me, too."

"Behind you?" Shree squeaked. "How's that possible?"

"Honestly, I have no idea," Nancy answered. "All I know is that it has to do with these glasses. In moments of stress, I can use them to help me out. Without them, I'm useless."

"Yes, but do not try to put them on, Shree, because it only works for Nancy. I tried wearing them last year and all I got was a huge headache afterwards," Eleanor laughed.

"There's got to be a reason why you can use your glasses to give you all these great powers and others can't. I mean, there are millions of people out there who wear glasses," Shree said.

"All I know is that when kids made fun of me, the jokes were always directed at my glasses. And my powers didn't start until after I stopped caring about what other people thought of me," Nancy explained.

"Do you think if we get inside the statue you'll be able to see what's in there?" Shree asked.

"I don't know," Nancy said. "But it's worth a try."

Chapter 20

Pinocchio's Lair

Pinocchio's Pizza Parlor was on Winthrop Street, a few blocks from Harvard Yard. Shree had read on an Internet guide to Cambridge that it was a regular hangout place for students and a perfect place to sit and talk. No one would notice them—or listen to what they had to say.

The restaurant was packed. As Shree and the girls walked inside, a group of three guys got up to leave. Eleanor grabbed the table and claimed it. They decided what they wanted and Shree went up to order at the counter. It seemed everyone wanted a hot pizza on a chilly weekend afternoon. They ordered a large pie, with half mushrooms and half peppers, along with sodas. Waiting for the pizzas to bake, they sat back down at their table.

Nancy and Eleanor started to talk at the same time. Eleanor got in first. "Do you think the books you got will tell us more about what we are looking for?"

"I hope so. I'll bet there'll be something in them about the treasure. And the secret key," Shree added.

"Secret key?" Eleanor asked. "You did not tell me about that."

"I didn't?" Shree asked. "Well, yeah, in the treasure book it said something about needing the secret key to get the treasure. I don't know if it's literal, that there really is a secret key, or whether it's like a door or something—or a clue. From what I remember reading, if there is a real secret key, then it's hidden somewhere underneath the John Harvard Statue. I just wish I had the treasure book back. Without it, it's impossible to know for sure."

"I might be able to help with that," Nancy said.

"What do you mean?" Shree asked.

Just as Nancy was about to speak, Shree's name was called. "Hold that thought," she said and went up to the counter and got their pizza.

"Now, how can you help me get my book back?" Shree asked.

"I saw your book inside your backpack the first week of school," Nancy said.

"You did? How?" But after a few seconds, Shree realized the answer to her own question. "Oh, yeah, your powers."

Nancy continued. "It's not something I mean to do all the time, but I'm naturally curious. I saw you had this interesting book in your pack. And then, a few days later, I saw the same book in the twins' stuff. Then I saw it in Katherine's bag. And then when you said they'd stolen your book, I put two and two together."

"So who has the book now?" Shree asked. Her back started to ache in anger, as if her stinger would pop out any minute. "We have to get it back."

"I don't know for sure," Nancy said. "After we had lunch the other day I looked for it, but it wasn't in Katherine's bag anymore. Maybe she has it at home."

"Damn," Shree exclaimed. "But then again, she does live next door. I'm going to have to find a way to get in there and look for it."

"Good luck," Eleanor said. "We all know what a good neighbor she is."

"Yeah, but there's got to be some way. And then once we have the book we can go back to the statue when no one's around and work on getting inside."

Shree was deep in thought for a moment. "Hey, I know. Next Saturday night's Halloween, right? I heard my parents talking about going to some kind of faculty party. You guys could come over and we could all sneak out and go back to Harvard Yard and no one would know about it."

Nancy and Eleanor looked uncomfortable.

"You don't like that idea?" Shree asked.

"Well, it is just that I do not like lying to my parents," Eleanor said.

Nancy nodded. "Me neither."

"It's not really lying," Shree said. "It's just a little omission. Just tell them you're spending the night at my house. I'll take care of the rest."

The girls took a couple of bites in silence.

"Oh, I forgot napkins." Shree got up to go back to the counter, but Eleanor stopped her.

"Do not worry about that Shree. I will get them," Eleanor said.

Shree sat back down. She saw Eleanor looking around the room to make sure no one was watching. Eleanor then shook her right hand at the wrist and stretched out her forearm along the floor and up towards the counter. She grabbed a fistful of napkins and then recoiled her hand quickly. Seconds later, Eleanor had brought back enough napkins for the entire table.

"El, that was amazing. How come you're so good at your powers? I mean, there's no way I can turn into a bee whenever I want. I've tried ever since that day at the park, but I can't figure out how to do it. It's so frustrating." Shree grabbed a napkin and wiped some extra tomato sauce from her face.

"It takes time," Nancy said. "You'll get it, Shree. You just have to keep practicing."

"Yeah, but you guys make it seem so easy. I've only been able to transform once, and that's because I had to," Shree said. "I also feel like I haven't been myself lately."

"What do you mean?" Eleanor asked.

"Well, recently I've been really sensitive to certain smells." Shree paused, gathering her thoughts before continuing to speak. "I don't know how to explain it, but it's like smelling the wrong thing can start me on an all-night vomiting spree."

"My father says that every person is dominated by one of the five senses, and this is why some people are great at music, others at art, and others," Nancy said, turning to look at Eleanor, "are highly tactile. Some people are great chefs and food tasters and some, like you, Shree, are dominated by their sense of smell."

Shree stared at Nancy, puzzling over what she had just said. "So you're saying that my powers have something to do with my sense of smell?"

"I'm not sure. But maybe in our case it makes sense." Nancy shrugged and took another bite of her pizza.

"You know," Shree said. "I did a little research after the incident in the park."

Nancy interrupted. "You mean when you turned into a bee?"

"How did you know about that?" Shree asked.

Nancy pointed to her glasses and said matter-of-factly, "Remember, I see *everything*. So, you were saying?"

Shree stared at Nancy for a few seconds, still trying to figure out how this girl's powers worked. Nancy was nowhere in sight during the incident at the park. Did that mean that Nancy could see things from miles away?

Shree continued where she had left off. "Yeah, so, I was doing research online and it seems like there've been other people throughout history who've had the same kinds of experiences we're having."

Eleanor looked unconvinced.

"No, I mean it. Take Dracula, for example, or Frankenstein or even the Werewolf," Shree continued.

"Dracula?" Eleanor laughed, jabbing her in the ribs. "Now I know you are crazy, Shree."

"No, I'm serious," Shree insisted. "Did you know that the story of Dracula is based on an actual human being— some Romanian kid in the 1300s who was terrorized by his friends because his teeth were pointed like a dog's?

This kid was really pale too, like a ghost, because he had insomnia and slept during the day and was up at night. He didn't get any exposure to sunlight. Soon everyone was calling him a freak. He even loved tomato juice, supposedly."

Here Nancy and Eleanor both groaned.

"Well, we don't know if that part is true," Shree added, "but eventually he was rejected by society and people started calling him a vampire and saying that he sucked blood for food."

"But how is that like us?" Nancy asked.

"I'm just saying, these are people who were shunned for being different and who felt they had to fight back. Some of them took the path of evil to get revenge. That's probably where all the movies and books come from. But even if they're not totally true, most myths and rituals are based, at least partly, on some kind of truth. They have at least some basis in reality. Look at us—no one would believe it if we told them about our powers either, would they?"

"Wait, back to this evil thing. Are you saying you think that could happen to us?" Eleanor asked.

"I hope not, but maybe. Think about it. The one thing monsters have in common is fear. It's how they become evil in the first place. It's either fear or a sense of insecurity that drives most people to harm others." Shree looked around the room and lowered her voice. "I guess what I'm trying to say is that we need to be careful. We have to stick together and not allow our powers to get out of control."

Shree remembered that it was a sense of fear that had led her to transform into a bee at the park. But it was a desire to seek revenge that had driven her to sting Tom Smith. She'd discovered in her research that, even though it can be used in a positive way, many times a sense of fear can lead people to act in malicious ways. It was a fine line that divided the two, and she was very concerned about that.

Eleanor jumped in with a question. "Do you guys think we are the only ones with powers?"

Shree thought about that for a moment before she answered. "Well, it doesn't make sense if we were. I mean, there's got to be others like us, right?"

The girls grew pensive for a minute, as they finished the last bites of their pizza. The conversation then shifted to talk about school and, after a half-hour of gossiping, the girls cleaned up their plates and wiped their faces. Shree had to admit that was some of the best pizza she'd ever eaten, even by New York City standards. They put on their jackets and headed out the door.

"Look," Nancy said. "There's Dave again."

She was right. There he was, about ten feet from Pinocchio's, waving. "Hey, girls. How's it going?"

There was something about this guy, thought Shree. Suddenly he was around *all* the time. It made her suspicious.

"What are you doing here, Dave?" Nancy demanded.

"Just came for a little lunch myself," Dave said. He pulled open the door to the pizza parlor. "See you later," he said, giving another jaunty wave, and then the door closed behind him.

"Well, that was strange," Eleanor said.

"Tell me about it," Nancy said. "That guy really gets on my nerves."

Shree had to agree that things with Dave didn't seem quite right, but maybe he was just another weird guy. "Come on," she said. "Let's get going. I promised my parents I'd be home on time."

Chapter 21

First Flight

Shree got home on the dot of three. Eleanor and Nancy had gone to Eleanor's house, while Shree had continued on to Berkeley Street. Shree was excited by the turn things had taken. Who would've ever thought that there'd be three of them with such unusual powers? Just like her father said, sometimes power comes when you really need it. Shree still hadn't figured out the subconscious thing yet, but she knew that eventually it would all make sense.

The girls had decided that on Saturday night they'd go back to Harvard Yard to search for more clues on how to get into the statue. It'd be Halloween, too, a perfect night to be out and about without creating too much suspicion. Now, if only Shree could get the treasure book back.

She saw her mother waiting at the door when she turned onto their walk.

"Hi, Mom."

"It is a good thing you are back, Shree, I was getting worried. Did you get what you needed at the library?"

"Pretty much," Shree said. "We had lunch at Pinocchio's, too. They have great pizza."

"Well, I am glad you had a good time," her mother said. "It is nice that you have friends here."

Shree saw her chance. "Do you think a few of them could come over next Saturday night and hang out?"

"Next Saturday night? Is that not Halloween? I believe your father and I have been invited to a faculty party that night. We will discuss it and see."

"Okay, thanks, Mom. I'm going upstairs to read for a while."

"No snack?" Mrs. Mandvi inquired.

"No, not right now. I'm kind of beat." Ignoring another one of her mother's sidelong looks, Shree climbed the stairs to her room.

She was tired, but she felt good. Talking about being a bee and having her friends' acceptance made her feel less like a freak and more like a normal person with a special talent. Shree decided to take a short nap. But first she went over to her window to see if her fuzzy little friend was there. Nope. Not today. Maybe it was finally too cold. Shree took off her shoes and socks and flopped on the bed. Soon she was fast asleep.

When Shree woke up, only a streak of light was left in the sky. Her back was still sensitive in some places, but other than that she seemed no worse for wear. She thought about what Nancy and Eleanor had told her, that she needed to practice if she wanted to use her skills more effectively. Somehow during the last few hours she seemed to have accepted the idea that she, Shree, was really, at least sometimes, a bee.

A car door slammed and Shree went to the window. Surprised, she saw it was Katherine and a man, probably her father. He was tall with graying blond hair, and carried a big briefcase. Katherine didn't look very happy. Not that she ever did, except when she was making fun of other people.

Shree watched Katherine and her father get into the car. Then she looked at the Jenkins' house. She got an idea. Could she? No, definitely not. But why not? It was the perfect opportunity. And she needed to practice, didn't she? That's what Eleanor and Nancy said. She heard a voice from deep down inside calling out to her, "Practice being a bee and find out where Katherine is keeping your book."

She looked at the door to her room, as if expecting her parents to have heard her thoughts. The house was quiet. Her door stayed shut.

She would *not* try to transform into a bee and sneak over to Katherine's house. She would *not* see if she could see into the window of Katherine's room. And she would definitely *NOT* try to get into the house and look for the treasure book. Positively not.

Could a bee be arrested for breaking and entering?

Two minutes later Shree was sitting on the floor, trying to concentrate her way into becoming a bee. The only thing happening was that she was getting a sore tailbone from the hard floor.

Frustrated, she got up and stretched. She moved into her beanbag chair by the window. Hey, there it was. The bee was back. It was moving slowly, gracefully, buzzing around the frame of the window, then settling on the ledge, then buzzing around some more. Shree watched, hypnotized by its methodical movements. Her breathing slowed and she allowed herself to relax. She thought about her father's words.

And then Shree was on the windowsill, too.

She'd done it! And it had been easy. She was a bee again. Elated, Shree felt the excitement of being a tiny creature full of energy and freedom. The other bee on the window ledge was looking at her oddly, but since Shree didn't yet know how to speak bee, she just buzzed companionably and looked for a spot to squeeze out the window.

There, over in the corner. It was a tiny opening. But for a bee? Easy. That must be how the other bees were getting in. Shree made a couple of passes around her room, resting in between each one. She flew diagonally across the room, then back and forth a few times. She couldn't afford to tire herself out, but she couldn't afford to go out without practicing first, either.

Finally, she felt ready. She checked the clock by her bed. Katherine and her father had left about twenty minutes before. She gave herself ten minutes max to get over to Katherine's, see what she could find, and then get out. That should give her plenty of time. After a last mini-rest on the window ledge, she headed for the crack in the corner. And she was out.

The air was chilly, but not too bad. She felt herself sort of kick off very naturally and suddenly she was high in the air, nothing but sky and grass above and beneath her. In seconds she was at the house, on the ledge of the window she believed to be Katherine's bedroom. She peered inside, more than slightly relieved to have made it without a hitch. The desk light on Katherine's desk was on, schoolbooks opened on top, as if she'd been studying and her father had called her to go out. Shree saw that the screen at the top of the window did not quite meet the frame. There might be just enough room to crawl inside.

Success. Once in the room, Shree looked around. It was a girly room with lots of pink and frills, the kind of room that made Shree feel all itchy. Katherine had tons of clothes, too. Her closet was filled with sweaters, skirts, dresses, and coats. It looked like a department store. Surprisingly, she also had as many books. In fact, Shree was amazed at the variety of books she found in her library. Not just romances, but Katherine had a bunch of Shree's favorite classic novels, too.

She was wasting time. That's not what she'd come for. Shree needed to get going and look for the treasure book. She buzzed over to Katherine's desk. Spanish, English, history—it was all there. No treasure book. It must be in her backpack. Nancy said she hadn't seen it in there for a while, but Shree should check it anyway. But how would she get to it—and get it out of there if she found it? She was a bee for heaven's sake.

Shree thought for less than a second. All she had to do was change back into her human self, find the book, grab it, and leave. Easy.

Unfortunately, Shree did not hit the landing the way she had anticipated. As her body whizzed down from the window onto the desk, a gust of wind behind her made her miss the plush pillow that rested on Katherine's chair, forcing Shree to drop at full speed, crash-landing on the floor.

Shree laid stunned on the carpet. Thankfully, she was still in one piece. She had to transform back to her human self.

"Turn back," she said over and over, "turn back to Shree."

It took a full minute, but finally she was human again. After shaking her head to clear the bit of residual fog, Shree reached for Katherine's knapsack and pulled it open. Nothing. Shoot. Where else could it be?

She scanned the room. The bedside table. She sprinted over. The treasure book made great nighttime reading. She pulled open the drawer and searched frantically. There was nothing but magazines.

Just as she was closing the drawer, she heard voices. She jumped back—and bumped into Katherine's coat rack. She kept it from falling to the floor in the nick of time, but it knocked a cup of pens and pencils off the desk onto the floor. She froze.

"Who's there?"

Shree heard a man's voice: probably Katherine's dad.

"Katherine, there's someone upstairs. Hand me that baseball bat. And call the police."

OMIGOD. Baseball bat? The police? What was she going to do?

Shree heard footsteps coming up the stairs. She had to get out of there. She leapt the few feet to the window and tried prying it open. But how was she going to change into a bee when she was so terrified? She needed to be relaxed. Relaxed? She had to be kidding.

There was no time. A hand was on the door handle and was turning it. The door was opening. Come on, Shree, come on, she screamed at herself. DO IT!

Suddenly, she was on the floor again, looking up at the window from the perspective of a very small insect. Shocked, Shree gathered her wits and took aim. She landed on the windowsill.

Thwap! Something slammed right next to her, so close it almost knocked her off the ledge. Shree took off again and felt a whoosh in the air behind her and another loud crack. Katherine's father was trying to kill her with a magazine.

Shree was so shaken up that she barely made it out the window. Thank goodness for that tiny bee-sized crack.

The last thing she heard was Mr. Jenkins saying, "Damn. Whoever it was must have gotten away. Nothing but a big old bee."

And Katherine's voice at the window. "A bee, huh? Well, how do you like that?"

Chapter 22

Girls Just Want To Have Fun

"So you see, you must attempt to place the 'X' on one side of the equation by first multiplying it by eight, which then allows you to solve for 'X' by dividing the other side by eight, thus leading to the solution: 'X' is equal to 'Y' plus twelve divided by eight."

Like most days in Mr. Blayne's class, Shree struggled to stay focused. That was one thing that hadn't changed when she had transferred to Kennedy; she still hated math. When Mr. Blayne decided to give the class some study time during the last fifteen minutes of the hour (likely due to the blank faces he got after solving the last equation), Shree didn't waste a minute. She immediately slid one of the books she had taken out from Widener Library behind her math book and dug in.

Assuming they found a way into John Harvard's statue on Saturday night—and that was one assumption Shree was going to make—they needed to have some idea about what they might find inside. There had to be some clue in the book about what was down there.

Shree turned to the last page, surprised that it revealed a map that closely resembled the one found in the original treasure book. This map, though, was a little different. It was a drawing of an intricate maze. Shree thought it was simply an interesting puzzle at first, but after studying it closely for a few minutes, she realized it was an actual map of tunnels that ran underneath the John Harvard Statue and Harvard Yard.

If there were tunnels underground, she had to figure out which route to take. The problem with the map of the maze was that there wasn't a scale, so she couldn't tell how far the tunnels went.

Shree also noticed that there were a bunch of notes sprinkled on the margins of the map, but she couldn't make any sense of them. They seemed to relate to landmarks, but the map was from hundreds of years ago, so who knew if the landmarks—if they *were* landmarks— still existed? Plus, many of the passageways lead to dead ends; one false step might lead them down the wrong path and they'd be lost forever.

Shree picked up her pencil. She'd always been good at puzzle books and mazes. This one shouldn't be so hard. She placed the pencil on the start of the passageway nearest the statue, and began to make her way. After six tries she had hit a dead end each time and had to start all over again.

She was still penciling and erasing when she heard a gasp. It was Katherine in what sounded like outrage. The class looked up.

Mr. Blayne looked up, too. "Ms. Jenkins, do you need something?"

Teachers always said that when they wanted you to know you'd done something wrong.

"Uh, no, Mr. Blayne. I just thought I felt something— never mind."

Mr. Blayne went back to his paperwork and the class went back to their studying.

Two minutes later there was another gasp and Katherine said distinctly, "That's enough." She was talking to Robert, a friend of Jason's from football. "Stop it."

Robert's expression was pure shock. "What did I do? I'm just sitting here doing my work."

"Ms. Jenkins, Mr. Kadinsky, that's quite enough," Mr. Blayne said.

"But I haven't touched her, I swear," Robert protested.

"I said that's enough, Mr. Kadinsky. You can't afford to miss any extra study time in this class. You either, Ms. Jenkins. Settle down."

"But—" Katherine started.

"Either go back to your studying or I'll see you in detention," Mr. Blayne commanded.

It seemed like Katherine was shocked that anyone, even a teacher, would speak to her that way. Her eyes narrowed and she took a breath. The class waited for the showdown. But then she said, "Yes, Mr. Blayne," and cast her eyes sullenly down at her book.

That girl is a master manipulator, thought Shree, shaking her head.

That's when she saw Nancy and Eleanor in the back, laughing silently behind their hands. Nancy winked at

Shree—at least she thought she saw a wink behind all that glass. What were they up to?

Craning her neck to get a better view, Shree saw Eleanor's left index finger curled several times over. Slowly, it began to uncoil. Eleanor sent her finger down to the floor and along the baseboards, then inward to the last seat in the third row where Colleen sat, totally unaware, filing her nails behind her math book.

When Nancy gave a thumbs-up, Eleanor crept up past Colleen's red backpack and jabbed her in the arm, just enough to give her a jolt and send her math book flying to the floor.

"Hey!" Colleen blushed furiously. Her nail file was plainly visible without the book as cover.

"Ms. O'Hara? Can I help you with something?" Mr. Blayne asked pointedly.

By then Eleanor's finger was back at her desk. Shree was impressed by how fast Eleanor could make her hands move.

"No, Mr. Blayne," Colleen said, following Katherine's lead. "I'm sorry for the interruption."

Katherine and Colleen shared a long glance and then looked around. But by then it was too late to catch Eleanor.

Shree had a hard time keeping her laughter to herself. She hid her face in her hands. She knew she shouldn't give anything away.

Once more the room was quiet. Shree saw Eleanor shaking her wrists and extending her hands, this time in Tim's direction. What was she doing now? In a minute Eleanor had untied Tim's sneakers and retied them to each other. Shree was delighted. And then, as a grand finale,

Eleanor pushed Tom's textbook with a strong jolt. The book went flying in mid-air and landed on the floor with a loud crash, just as the bell rang.

As Tim jumped up from his seat to leave, he fell on the floor, hitting his face hard and letting loose a curse. He looked furious, searching around wildly for the person responsible for making him appear clumsy. Tom, too, tried to figure out who had pushed his book off his desk.

Mr. Blayne went to say something but the bell had interrupted him. He stared at the twins, a look of irritation on his face. "I suggest you boys learn to keep your hands to yourselves in the future or you'll find yourselves sitting in detention for a very long time."

Everyone looked on and laughed as Tim attempted to untie his shoes and get up from the floor at the same time. Shree had the feeling most kids weren't terribly unhappy seeing the twins being the butt of a joke. She giggled and joined Eleanor and Nancy at the door. The last thing Shree saw was Tim's face, mortified with embarrassment.

Chapter 23

The Other Freak

"That was brilliant," Shree exclaimed. "I can't believe you did that, and right under Mr. Blayne's nose."

"I cannot believe it, either," Eleanor said. "But I am tired of those guys. They needed someone to give them a dose of their own medicine."

"I couldn't agree more," Nancy said. "Let's go get lunch."

The girls were still laughing and comparing notes on what they had just done to the Demons when they got to the cafeteria.

"I forgot my lunch today," Shree said. "I'll meet up with you guys in a couple of minutes. Do you want anything?"

"Yes, could you get me a chocolate milk?" Eleanor asked.

"Sure. Nancy?"

"No, I'm fine."

Shree went to the end of the line and looked at the day's menu. There were the usual pizza, fries, burgers, but there was also macaroni and cheese. That would work. The line moved slowly. The boy ahead of her was heaping food onto his tray. Wasn't he the guy in her biology class, the one who had bumped into her the first day of school? Poor kid was so shy; she'd barely heard him speak in all that time. Ralph, that was his name.

Shree studied him from behind. He was very overweight and had red hair, with more freckles than Shree had ever seen, not just on his face but on his neck and what she could see of his arms as well. Shree felt bad for him and was about to say hello when she felt a foot on her toes.

"Ouch!"

"Oh, s-s-sorry, gee, I'm so-sorry, I didn't see you. Um, are you okay?"

To top it all off, he stuttered, too? The poor kid was doomed to constant teasing, Shree thought.

Ralph had stepped on her foot, leaving a dirty mark on her sneaker. Shree was about to say something she might regret when she saw the look on his face. She couldn't do it. "That's okay, no problem," she said. "I'll survive."

Ralph's face was beet red with embarrassment.

"Hey, aren't you in my biology class?" Shree asked, trying to make conversation.

"Y-y-yeah."

"Well, I'm Shree."

"Ralph."

Shree was trying but it was like pulling teeth to get anything out of this guy.

"You want pizza or a burger?" the lunch lady asked Ralph.

"Oh, both, please. And an extra s-s-serving of fries, please," Ralph said, turning back around with obvious relief.

Shree got her macaroni, a dish of soft-serve yogurt, and a chocolate milk, and then headed back to the table to eat, leaving Ralph waiting for his order.

She sat down and looked at Eleanor and Nancy. It was time to make a decision. Eleanor was her friend and Eleanor seemed to trust Nancy. If she didn't she never would've let Nancy join them on their trip to Harvard Yard. And Nancy seemed to trust Shree with her own secret. Shree needed help finding the treasure. When you added it up, it meant that they were willing to share their secrets with her; it was time she shared hers with them.

"Listen, I just figured out what's down there. You see," Shree paused and pulled the book out of her bag. She opened it to the last page and turned the book around to face Eleanor and Nancy. "Once we get inside the statue, we're going to encounter a series of tunnels that will take us underneath Harvard Yard. They're all part of one big maze. The secret key to the treasure is located here," she pointed to the end of the maze. "To get there, we need to find the right path. But so far I've had no luck figuring out which one that is." She grabbed her pencil and began tracing the maze once again, showing the girls her failed attempts at finding the solution to the maze.

For several minutes, Nancy and Eleanor gave the maze a try. Nancy stared at the map while Eleanor used her extended pinky finger to trace her own path. Each attempt ended in failure.

"Check it out," Nancy said.

"What is it?" Shree asked.

Nancy pointed to the microscopic scribble written on the margin of the map of the maze.

"It's really, really tiny. I don't know how anyone could've written so small, but you won't believe what it says."

"What?" Eleanor asked.

"It says that once we have the key, we need to head to the river to retrieve our first treasure."

"Are you sure, Nancy? The river? Our first treasure? Here, give me that." Shree pulled the book from her and put it down where they could all see it. "Wait a second, that must be it. See where the maze ends down there?"

Nancy and Eleanor nodded.

"See that squiggly line there?"

They nodded again.

"I think that must be the river. Yeah, that's got to be it—the Charles River. We did it. We figured it out."

They hugged and gave each other high-fives.

"But I still don't know what the key thing is all about. What is so secret about it? Unless it's because it's hidden underneath the statue somewhere," Shree added.

"And what is this thing about the first treasure?" Eleanor asked. "Does that mean that there is more than one treasure?"

"I don't know," Shree said. "But we're going to find out."

Their celebration was cut short when they heard a crash from across the lunchroom. When Shree looked up from the map, she saw Jason standing in front of Ralph's table. It was obvious Jason was up to no good.

"What've you got there, fat boy?" Jason's voice carried clearly over to where Shree and her friends were sitting.

"Poor Ralph," Eleanor said. "He gets picked on so much."

Shree agreed and shook her head. Poor, poor Ralph.

Just then they heard Jason laughing loudly.

"What's his problem?" Nancy whispered. "Can't that creep see that Ralph just wants to be left alone?"

Shree nodded, wishing they could use their powers to help Ralph. "It's sad that the Demons deal with their sense of insecurity by picking on others."

Shree saw Jason and the twins standing over Ralph. Sadly, Ralph sat alone, as usual, with a tray full of food in front of him.

Jason repeated his original question, this time a little louder. "I asked you, fat boy, what've you got there?"

"M-m-my lunch," Ralph stuttered.

"M-m-my lunch," Jason mimicked.

Colleen followed Jason over and now was draped over his arm, laughing. Then Katherine sat down beside Ralph. She was wearing her cheerleading outfit and made sure to sit really close. "Hi, Ralphie," she sang, getting him to blush a deep pink.

"That lunch sure looks good, Ralphie boy," Jason went on. "But it's got to be too much for one person—even if that person's a big, fat, blubber-filled whale. I'll just relieve you of some of that food. You *do* want to share it, don't you?"

Ralph looked down and nodded, the picture of misery.

Shree was disgusted.

Colleen laughed when Jason picked up Ralph's burger and held it over Ralph's head.

"Hey, give that back." Ralph made a grab for it.

"I'll give it back all right. But next time I want the usual—turkey club on sourdough, hold the mayo. This is nothing but cafeteria garbage. I expect something gourmet, do you hear me?"

Ralph sat stone still.

"I said, do you hear me?" Jason demanded. And then he dumped the burger on Ralph's head.

For a minute there was silence. But Jason wasn't done. He poked Ralph hard in the chest. "No club sandwich? No sweets? I'm very disappointed with you, Ralphie."

"I'm s-s-sorry," Ralph started.

Shree couldn't believe what was happening. Where were the teachers when you needed them?

"You're sorry?" Jason asked. "Just to show you the kind of guy I am, I'll give you another day to make it up to me. Today I'll just take it out on your fat." And he reached over and ripped open Ralph's shirt from top to bottom.

Ralph gasped and sputtered.

"All that whale blubber must have felt pretty confined under there," Jason added.

The twins laughed.

"I'll tell you what, Ralphie. One last chance. Give me your money and I'll let it slide today." Jason stopped and took hold of Ralph's collar and pulled.

"But I d-d-don't have any money," Ralph cried out.

"What, no money? Hmmm. What's this?" Jason's hand closed around something that hung from Ralph's neck.

"Not bad, whale blubber, not bad at all. I tell you what. Today, just for today, I'll let you go. But only if you give me that gold chain around your neck."

From across the cafeteria Shree felt her blood start to boil, and that little place in her back start to ache. Shouldn't she do something? Poor Ralph was at the mercy of these thugs.

"No, you c-c-can't have that." Ralph tried to dislodge Jason's hands, but he was no match for Jason's strength. "That belonged to my father. It's all I have left."

But Jason was already taking the chain in his fist to rip it from Ralph's neck. "What do you mean, I can't? Of course I can. Can't I, Katherine?"

"Absolutely, Jason."

"Can't I, Colleen?"

"Of course you can, honey."

"Tim, Tom, come over here. Pick up this fat boy for me."

The twins stepped in and yanked Ralph, who was shaking in what Shree assumed was fear, up from his seat. The only word that came out was, "No, no, no."

They picked him up from his chair and dragged him inside the janitor closet. It was difficult to see from where the girls were seated because Jason blocked their view, but it was obvious that the twins were doing a good job holding onto Ralph while Jason attempted to rip the gold chain from his neck.

Shree gave a quick look around. Still no teachers. She saw that Jason was having a hard time getting the chain off Ralph's neck and was now making a fist and pulling his arm back. Oh, no. He was going to hit Ralph.

Ralph's body seemed to pull into itself, anticipating the punch that was coming. Jason gave a final wrench and off came the chain from Ralph's neck. Ralph let out a wounded cry.

Finally, Shree couldn't take it any more. She needed to help him before he got hurt. She got up from her chair.

"Shree," Eleanor whispered loudly. "Where are you going? What are you doing?"

But Shree barely heard her. She took two steps forward.

And then Jason flew by her. Then Tim. And Tom. Their bodies lingered in mid-air and then gave a loud thump as they hit the floor.

Coming to her senses, Shree looked for Ralph, but he was nowhere to be seen. A crowd had formed around Jason's inert body.

Shree looked at Eleanor, not understanding what had just happened. Eleanor shrugged, a bewildered look on her face.

Shree quickly made her way across the room, trying to squeeze through the large crowd. It seemed like everyone was interested in checking out the twins, whose bodies had been contorted into funny shapes during the landing and now were twisted in a spectacular pose. Shree had to literally push people aside to get to the utility closet, but when she got there, Ralph was gone. She looked around but he was nowhere in sight.

Shree walked back to her table.

"What the hell just happened? One minute Ralph's getting beat up and the next the twins are flying across the room." Shree looked over at Eleanor, who appeared just as shocked as she was.

Nancy, on the other hand, didn't seem surprised at all. She looked over at Shree and smiled, "I have a feeling Ralph may be one of us."

Chapter 24

Discovering Ralph

Nancy spotted Ralph a mile away and signaled to Shree, who hid behind a tree waiting for him after school. When he finally made the turn, Shree jumped out from her hiding spot.

"Hey, Ralph. How are you?" Shree smiled and started walking beside him.

Ralph looked flustered. "H-h-hello."

Eleanor was next to appear. "*Hola,* Ralph. How is it going?"

Then Nancy right after her. "Hello, Ralph."

Ralph appeared more frightened than confused. "Hi g-g-girls." He started walking faster.

"So, what just happened at lunch?" Shree asked as she picked up her pace to match Ralph's.

"I d-d-don't know what you're talking about." Ralph made the turn on Brattle Street. Shree and the girls were right beside him.

"Why were you so upset about that chain?" Shree asked, trying to make small talk.

"It's the only thing I have from my dad. He d-d-drowned when I was two years old. I'm not allowed near the water because he died." He stopped speaking suddenly.

Nancy looked confused. "But I always see you by the pool at school. And you're at every swim meet, aren't you?"

"Yeah, but my m-m-mom doesn't let me go near the water. She's afraid that I'll d-d-drown. She doesn't know about the swim meets."

Ralph crossed the street. Shree could tell he wasn't happy about having three girls following him home.

"So, Ralph," Shree lengthened her stride to match Ralph's. "Are you going to tell us what happened today at lunch?"

"W-w-what do you mean?"

"Come on, Ralph," Eleanor said. "We all saw what you did to Jason and the twins."

Ralph was silent. He started sweating, and Shree wondered if it was because of the physical exertion of walking briskly or because he was getting nervous over his informal inquisition.

"I'm not sure what you're talking about. I d-d-didn't do anything."

"Listen, Ralph," Shree said. "I understand that you're worried about talking to us, but we're like you—in more ways than you think. Tell us what happened and maybe we can help."

A brief smile made an appearance on Ralph's face and for a second Shree saw what he'd really be like when he was happy. But it was gone in a flash.

He looked down at the ground and continued to walk without saying a word. Shree thought they were out of luck. Ralph might just be a true loner—or too afraid to say anything to them.

"You know Ralph, I saw when you did that thing with your tail," Nancy added.

"Tail? I don't know what you g-g-girls are talking about," Ralph said. He was now sweating profusely.

Shree overtook the group, got in front of Ralph, and started walking backwards while she spoke. "It's okay, Ralph. We know that you have powers. We all do."

Ralph was forced to stop. He stared warily at Shree, then looked at Eleanor and Nancy, but didn't say a word.

"I'm going to tell you something you won't believe," Shree said. "But it's true. Eleanor here has a talent. You could call it more of a skill. And she's not the only one. Nancy does too."

Nancy nodded and smiled, pushing her glasses closer to her face.

"And so do I. All of us do, Ralph. So believe me when I tell you that you're not alone," Shree said.

Ralph stared at Eleanor. "What kind of t-t-talent?"

They had all stopped walking, and Shree realized that they were in front of Ralph's house. They stood on his front porch without saying anything.

Shree turned to Eleanor and nodded. Eleanor looked around and made sure nobody was looking. She stared at the house next door and saw a golden retriever lying by the gate. Slowly, Eleanor's right arm began to stretch, longer and longer, hugging the fence and continuing on until she grabbed one of the dog's many toys. The golden retriever stared in awe at Eleanor's hand, shaking his head from right to left as it followed it out the yard. Seconds later, Shree saw the dog running to the opposite end of the yard and hiding his head behind a tree. And immediately afterwards, Eleanor's arm returned to its original size.

Ralph's eyes grew. Shree looked at him, waiting eagerly for him to say something.

When he spoke, he stared right at Shree. "What about you? What kind of p-p-powers do you have?"

"Eleanor has had her powers a long time. Mine are brand new—and I can't show you here so you'll have to take my word for it. But—" and here Shree lowered her voice, "I can turn into a bee."

"No way," Ralph exclaimed. "I never thought anyone else could—" He stopped abruptly in mid-sentence.

Shree laughed. "Oh my God! I can't believe you're one of us," Shree looked at Nancy. "You were right. Ralph can turn into a whale whenever he wants to. That's incredible." She turned back to Ralph. "That's a lot cooler than any of our powers. I bet you can swim underwater without using oxygen."

Ralph looked around nervously. "Shhh, if my m-m-mom ever hears about this, she'll kill me. I d-d-didn't mean for my tail to come out like that. It just k-k-kind of happened. It never did that before. Please k-k-keep it down." Ralph started walking towards his front door. "My mom will be here any m-m-minute, and if she finds out about what happened at school, I'm g-g-going to get in trouble." He turned around and took out his house key.

Eleanor put her slender fingers inside her book bag. When she pulled out her hand, it held something shiny.

"Hey, Ralph. I bet you will be happy to have this back." She grabbed Ralph's necklace and dangled it in front of him. The sunlight shone brightly against the charm.

Ralph ran towards Eleanor. "How d-d-did you find it? I thought I'd never see it again."

Eleanor let Ralph grab the necklace from her hand.

"Listen, Ralph," Shree said. "We all have secrets and special powers, just like you do. All we want is for you to join us next Saturday night. We're going in search of a treasure that's buried somewhere in Harvard Yard, and we may need your help."

It was obvious that Ralph was interested. "You mean there's a t-t-treasure hidden in the yard? My mom works at Harvard." He paused, his look of happiness disappearing instantly. "But I'm sure she would d-d-definitely not let me go."

"Just tell your mom that you're going trick-or-treating with us. It's Halloween. She has to let you go," Shree said.

"I'm not sure. Treasure hunting sounds kind of d-d-dangerous and—"

Shree saw a Toyota Corolla pulling up the driveway. Ralph turned and shot a pleading look at her. Shree ignored him and ran towards the car to greet Ralph's mother.

"Hi Mrs. Snodgrass, how are you doing?" Shree was the first to reach her. Nancy and Eleanor followed closely and stood behind Shree, smiling.

"Well, hello young ladies. You must be in Ralphie's class." She turned to Ralph, squeezing his cheeks. "Just like your father. My little ladies' man."

Shree could see that Ralph was mortified. He stood at the same spot smiling and attempting to hide his nervousness.

Nancy joined in. "Mrs. Snodgrass, we just invited Ralph to come trick-or-treating with us on Saturday. He really wants to come, but he wanted to run it by you first."

Mrs. Snodgrass watched as Eleanor and the girls picked up the groceries from the trunk and helped her carry them to the front door.

"Well, thank you young ladies," Mrs. Snodgrass looked at her son. "I suppose it would be okay, Ralphie. It's nice that you are finally making friends. And how much trouble can you get into with these three lovely girls?" She smiled and walked into the house, grabbing the bags from Eleanor at the entrance and waving at the girls warmly.

"Okay, Ralphie. We'll see you on Saturday night, then. And don't be late," Nancy said, laughing as she joined Eleanor and Shree.

The girls left the driveway and walked back down Garden Street to Eleanor's house, arm-in-arm, laughing loudly.

Shree thought about what Mrs. Snodgrass had said and smiled. How much danger could three girls and one overweight boy get into?

Chapter 25

Halloween Night

On Friday, the day before Halloween, there was a distinct air of pre-holiday energy circulating about Kennedy Academy.

Mrs. Tillman had to remind everyone twice to be quiet during homeroom. Then the twins took it upon themselves to release a quart of earthworms during biology. Between the shrieks of the girls and the teacher giving orders for their capture, there was total chaos.

Her father had dropped Shree off that morning in the green station wagon because she'd been running late. Shree was up early, but hadn't been able to get going. The air was cold and the bed was so warm. Her body had hummed with pleasure and before she knew it she'd fallen back to sleep, and her mother had to call her twice for breakfast.

In the cafeteria, Shree opened her Tupperware container of basmati rice and vegetables. It was a meal she generally enjoyed, but lately her lunches seemed so boring. She might need a frozen yogurt for dessert—only to keep her energy up, she told herself. She took a bite of her rice and looked around for Nancy and Eleanor, but they had told her they'd be late because of some kind of meeting with the art teacher about an exhibit over Thanksgiving.

Shree looked around as she ate. There was Dave again, hanging about, not really talking to anyone. Now that she'd actually met Dave, she was seeing him everywhere. It was funny how he constantly had his head cocked to one side, as if it was too heavy or something. She tried to study him without being too obvious. He really wasn't a bad-looking guy, just skinny. But those giant ears—well, let's just say he had his challenges in that department. Shree felt instantly guilty. Thank goodness he couldn't hear her thoughts.

The plan for Halloween night was coming together. Eleanor and Nancy had agreed to meet at Shree's house, then they'd all walk over to Harvard Yard and meet Ralph. The Mandvis had plans to go to a faculty costume party. Shree's mother hadn't been too keen on going at first—she didn't feel comfortable dressing up in strange costumes—but Dr. Mandvi had convinced her she didn't have to wear a costume, and that it'd be a good time to meet some of his colleagues and their wives. Eventually, she had given in and, in a moment of weakness, agreed that Shree could stay home with her friends and hand out the bite-sized candies she'd bought for the anticipated trick-or-treaters.

Eleanor and Nancy entered the cafeteria and rushed over to Shree. "Sorry we are so late," Eleanor said. "The exhibit is going to be a lot of work, though, and they are going to hand out awards."

Not for the first time, Shree wished she had a little talent in one of the arts. Eleanor had a real knack for painting and Nancy played the violin like a pro. "That's okay, you guys eat. I'll tell you the plan, see what you think." The girls nodded and unwrapped their sandwiches.

"Okay, we'll meet at my house at six. I'll order pizza so we can have dinner before we head out to Harvard Yard. My parents are leaving at seven so that should be perfect. Once they leave, we'll wait a bit and then head out ourselves. We need to be back before they come home. What do we need to bring, besides the map and a couple of flashlights?"

"We definitely need a Swiss army knife," Nancy said, fiddling with her glasses.

"And how about some rope?" Eleanor added.

"Rope? What for?" Shree asked.

"Well, you never know," Eleanor said.

"I guess you're right, it couldn't hurt." Shree jotted that down on her list and they finished their lunch just in time to get to their next class. On the way, the girls discussed what they'd do with their share of the treasure. Eleanor thought about buying her family a bigger house with her portion. Nancy wanted to start saving for college. Shree, on the other hand, had something completely different in mind. She'd head back to the Bronx, gather her best friends, and go on a trip to Europe; they'd have croissants in Paris, waffles in Brussels, and pizza in Rome.

Thankfully, everything went according to plan the next day. At the Mandvi house, the doorbell rang and Shree jumped up to answer it. The trick-or-treaters had been arriving steadily since five, Eleanor and Nancy had arrived promptly at six, and the Mandvis were tidying up to leave for their party at seven. They'd already emptied one bowl of candy and Shree had opened two more bags. She loved Halloween, seeing all the little kids dressed as bunnies and witches and pumpkins. Ever since she was little she'd wanted to explore the "trick" part of the equation, but so far she'd kept herself in check.

She opened the door expecting to hear, "Trick or treat!" but instead the pizza delivery guy was on the porch. "Oh," Shree said. "Wait a minute, I'll get the money." She put the bowl of candy down on the hall table and ran into the living room to get the twenty-dollar bill her parents had left on the coffee table. "The pizza's here," she said to Nancy. "Put out the plates, okay? Eleanor, can you get the sodas? They're in the fridge."

Two minutes later they were chowing down on pizza from Pinocchio's. Nancy and Eleanor had gotten permission to spend the night at Shree's, and Ralph was prepared to meet them at Harvard Yard. He was kind of a nervous type and Shree hoped he wouldn't cause too much trouble, but so far they were in luck. Ralph's overprotective mother told Ralph she was going to a faculty Halloween party, too. Shree didn't think it was the same party her parents were attending, but it didn't matter. Either way it put him in the clear.

Shree and the girls took turns answering the door. Shree had no idea there were so many kids in her neighborhood. Their parents escorted them to the end of the walk with flashlights, then stayed back while the kids came up to the door to get their candy. The doorbell rang again. Shree had a dripping piece of pizza in her hand.

"I will get it," Eleanor said.

Eleanor had told Shree that she loved Halloween. It was the one time of year she could really let go and people wouldn't question things too much.

Shree saw Eleanor stand back from the door and send out her arms to do the work for her. Slowly she let her hands open the door. Three children who looked about five or six stood on the stoop with hopeful expressions. "Trick or treat," they sang, and then looked at the candy bowl. Only Eleanor's hands were holding the bowl— no one was there. Shree smiled as the kids followed the hands that held the bowl into the house, mouths wide open, until they spotted Eleanor in a white gown with slits for her eyes. The three little pigs, for that's how they were dressed, screamed.

Eleanor announced, "Happy Halloween, kids. Choose a candy," and held out the bowl a little farther.

There was a scramble of piggy bodies while the three kids fought over who would get down the porch steps first. The last one recovered enough to grab a few of the candies from Eleanor's hands before charging after his friends and into his father's arms. Eleanor waved to the dad, who waved back. Eleanor laughed and laughed.

"Eleanor, you scared those poor little kids to death," Shree said.

"I am just adding a little trick to the treating," Eleanor said, grinning. "Now where is the rest of that pizza?"

Shree shook her head. Never mind, she thought. At 7:30 they would shut off most of the lights to discourage any more stragglers, and it was almost that time. Eleanor couldn't spook too many more kids before then.

The girls finished eating and cleaned up their dishes. Shree didn't want to leave a mess, or give her parents any reason to be suspicious. Shree gathered the supplies and made sure they were ready when the time came to depart.

Chapter 26

An Uninvited Guest

It was a moonless night and would be a dark walk around Cambridge, but luck was with them in the weather. A warm front had come through, causing one of those rare fall nights in New England when it felt more like spring than late fall. They wore their coats, and stuffed hats and gloves into their pockets anyway; it was bound to get colder as the night wore on. Shree tried ignoring the nagging fear she'd been experiencing over the coming winter and how the cold might affect her powers. She'd find out sooner or later.

Before they left, Shree made sure to leave a light on in the foyer and one on outside the door, then added a few mini Snickers, Musketeer Bars, and Reese's Peanut Butter Cups to her pack—sustenance for the adventure. Before closing the door and locking it behind her, Shree looked over at Katherine's house; it had become a habit she couldn't kick, and she did it every time she went in or out her front door. Most of the time there was nothing to see, but sometimes, like tonight, she got the chills, like she was being watched. But the whole house was dark, except for the little desk light in Katherine's room. Shree noticed Katherine left it on almost all the time—whether on purpose or by mistake, she didn't know.

"We've been lucky that the Demons have left us alone lately," she commented. "I think Ralph made them think twice about messing with us."

"Yes, that was awesome," Eleanor said. "Jason and the twins probably still have no clue what hit them. Where is Ralph meeting us, anyway?"

"At the statue," Nancy said. "At eight."

They walked on in silence, the dead leaves on the ground crunching beneath their feet. The darkness enveloped them immediately. Even though Cambridge was a big town, when night came the little side streets stayed relatively quiet and dark. They could see the flashlights of trick-or-treaters shining on the sidewalks, but it was getting too late for the little kids, and the steady stream was turning into a trickle.

By the time they'd reached Garden Street, their brisk pace was making Shree feel the unusual warmth of the night. She was delighting in the higher-than-average temperatures, however. Lately what everyone else felt was comfortable had Shree feeling like she was at the North Pole. Bundled up in her jacket with her yellow-and-black sneakers on her feet, she felt a decided strong connection to the bee within.

They didn't talk as they continued walking. None of them had done anything like this before and they were all aware that if they got caught they'd be in serious trouble. But they all agreed that the payoff was too great to resist; treasure won hands down.

At the light on the corner, Shree pressed the button to cross through Harvard Square and into the yard. They were almost there. The bright lights and traffic of Harvard Square were startling after the quiet and Shree watched as goblins, Barack Obamas, Hagrids, ghosts, and devils paraded through the streets.

Harvard Yard itself was almost silent in comparison, a few students crossing quickly with books under their arms. The solid buildings of brick and stone kept the worst of the traffic noise at bay. The leaves of the big old trees rustled in the breeze as Shree and the girls took the cement path towards the John Harvard Statue.

Suddenly, a stereo began blaring music in one of the dorms and Shree jumped. Two guys in togas then crashed out of the doors and ran past her, stumbling and holding bottles of beer. Obviously, a party in the dorm behind them had begun. Shree, Eleanor, and Nancy giggled nervously and made a beeline for the statue.

Ralph was waiting for them. He looked terrified.

"Hi, Ralph," Shree said. "What's the matter?"

"N-n-nothing."

Shree looked at Nancy and Eleanor. If Ralph didn't get it together, he might ruin everything. He had some great powers, but none of the self-confidence that should go with them. Shree could only hope that if something happened where they needed him, he'd rise to the challenge the way he had with Jason and the twins.

"It is okay, Ralph," Eleanor said. "We have everything we need. Here, take this flashlight and help us with our search."

Ralph took the flashlight and turned it on, which seemed to put him a little more at ease. "Thanks, Eleanor. I don't know, guys, t-t-treasure hunting seems pretty dangerous."

"Nah," Shree said. "It's just that it's dark, that's all."

"Listen, Ralph," Nancy said. "It's going to be okay. I'll be able to see things in advance. We'll be fine. Now, come on. We're wasting time."

Shree was relieved at Nancy's no-nonsense approach. She was definitely ready to start their search.

When the gorilla showed up, however, it put a crimp in their plan.

"What now?" Eleanor whispered, sounding panicked.

"We need to wait for him to leave, I guess," Shree said.

A guy in a hairy gorilla suit had come bounding across Harvard Yard from one of the dorms, followed by a pale-faced guy in khakis and a bowtie. Gorilla Boy whooped and hollered until he reached the statue.

Shree, Ralph, Eleanor and Nancy dashed around the back of the statue and leaned against it in the dark shadows. Shree heard some scrambling and a curse or two and peered around the corner to see what was happening.

Pale Face linked his fingers to provide a boost for Gorilla Boy to get on top of the statue, but Gorilla Boy was so drunk he couldn't get his balance. Finally, after a lot of swearing, Gorilla Boy made it up and over the edge.

He threw down his gorilla head and let out a Tarzan yell, thumping his chest.

"Come on, dude," the pale-faced kid said. "Hurry up. The guard could be back any minute."

"Yeah, yeah, I'm hurrying. Give me a minute."

The next thing Shree knew, there was a sound of a zipper going down. She froze. A few seconds later she could hear the steady stream of urine splashing over John Harvard's feet down to the ground.

"Eeew," Eleanor whispered.

"Gross," Nancy agreed.

Ralph looked mortified.

Shree didn't know whether to laugh or run. Her father had told her about this ancient male ritual at the university, the act of peeing on the John Harvard statue. But she never would've believed it if she hadn't seen it with her own eyes.

Gorilla Boy must have drunk an awful lot of beers, because he had enough liquid in him to make a couple of "X's" and several circles in mid-air before finishing up with a flourish.

"You were a freaking artist up there, dude. Come on, let's go." Pale Face put up his hands and Gorilla Boy backed down the statue, losing his grip and crashing to the ground on top of his friend. Finally the two of them managed to get up and they stumbled off, singing what sounded like the Harvard Fight Song, back to their dorm.

When they were fifty feet away, Shree motioned everyone out from behind the statue. You could still smell the pungent odor of urine in the air.

"That was disgusting," Nancy said.

"Yeah, but now we have to hurry. Those guys are right," Shree said. "The guard's probably going to be making his rounds soon. We don't have much time. Nancy, take a look inside where the insignia is and tell us if you see anything. Eleanor, try to find a crack where you can slide your hand through and see if you can find a latch or a lever. Ralph, you stand over there, in front, and be our lookout. If anyone comes this way, give us a warning."

"A w-w-warning? Like what?"

"I don't know, just a warning. Clear your throat or say something—anything—but don't use our names," Shree added.

"Okay, b-b-but hurry."

Shree walked around the side to join Eleanor and Nancy. Eleanor had her enlarged hands exploring every inch of the stonework around the insignia, as if she were a blind person reading Braille. Nancy held her hands by the frames of her glasses and stood at the base of the statue staring. Shree kept quiet, not wanting to disturb her concentration.

Finally, she couldn't stand it anymore. "See anything, Nancy?" Shree asked.

"Nothing yet, it's really too dark in there."

"Eleanor, how about you?"

"Nope."

Shree kept her flashlight pointed at the stone. Suddenly, Nancy exclaimed, "Shree, over here. I think there's a crevice of some kind. Eleanor, see if you can fit your fingers through this crack."

Shree pointed the light at the insignia's upper left corner where the letters "VE" were carved onto the image of a book.

"See," Nancy said, "there's an opening over here."

Eleanor's hand reached the spot and groped around. "Yes," she said, "I feel it. I will just flatten my fingers to get inside."

"Be careful," Shree said urgently. "We don't know what's in there."

Eleanor was already probing around. "Nancy is right. The stone goes for a few inches, but then it is empty space. I think we found it."

Eleanor gave a squeal and, with her other hand still outside the statue, slapped Nancy a high-five.

Shree knew they didn't have time to waste. "Listen, Eleanor, feel around. There's got to be a lever."

"Okay, feeling, feeling, fee—yes. I got it. There is something here, but it will not move and there is something on my—oh, yuck. There is something on my hand."

Shree pulled at Eleanor's arm from behind. "Eleanor, are you all right? What is it?"

Eleanor snapped her fingers back and shook them violently. "Eeew. That was so disgusting, something slimy was on me. I do not know what it was."

"Did you feel anything, though?" Nancy asked.

"Yes, there was something. It was definitely like a lever." Eleanor wiped her hands on her jacket.

"Do you think you could go back in and see?" Shree didn't want to be pushy, but they were so close.

"Yes, just give me a second. That was awful." Eleanor took a couple of deep breaths and stuck her flattened fingers back into the crack.

In the meantime, Shree referred back to the map. There was something that was ringing a bell, but she couldn't remember what it was. She stared at the legend of the map. She tried deciphering the last line when suddenly she recalled the missing clue.

"Nancy, I need your help. Look at this. It's the legend for the map. Doesn't it say something about feet showing the way?"

Nancy focused her gaze on the map where Shree was pointing. "Shree, you're right. It says, 'With luck, the feet will lead the way.' That's it. It must be John Harvard's—"

Suddenly, Eleanor yanked back her hand. "I did it. I pulled down the lever. But nothing is happening."

Disappointed, Shree thought about what to do next. Then suddenly the base of the statue began to slide inward. There was a screech of stone on stone and the sound of ancient gears cranking. "Oh my God," Shree said in a whisper. "We did it. It's opening."

The base of the statue shifted about a foot before stopping. There was no way of knowing if this was the extent of the opening, or whether time had rusted the hinges and this was as wide an entry as the ancient portal could manage.

All three girls pointed their flashlight into the hole. It was pitch black.

"What now?" Eleanor asked.

"There has to be another lever. There's no way any of us can fit through that opening," Shree said.

"Well, I suppose we could—" Nancy stopped in mid-sentence, and turned abruptly away from Shree and Eleanor. Shree followed Nancy's gaze. She didn't need special glasses to identify the dark figure that loomed from the shadows of the statue.

Chapter 27

The League Is Formed

"What are *you* doing here?" Nancy demanded.

Dave ignored her question, turning to Shree, who stood next to the portal's opening. "Well, are you gonna stand there or are you gonna go after the treasure?"

"Dave, how did you get here?" Shree asked, jumping a mile. "Where's Ralph?"

"I'm right here." Ralph stepped out from behind Dave. "Um, he k-k-kind of caught me by surprise."

"Caught *you* by surprise?" Shree asked. "My heart's still racing. Great guard you are." She turned back to Dave. "Seriously, what are you doing here?"

"I'll tell you everything," Dave said. "But right now, don't you think we should get inside the statue before someone sees us?"

Shree couldn't argue with that. But inside? With Dave? They'd have to tell him about the treasure. Shree looked at Eleanor and Nancy, who shifted their gaze from her to Dave and back again. She sensed they were waiting for her to make a decision.

She turned and stared back at the opening. Looking inside the portal with her flashlight, Shree could see that it revealed a narrow paved walkway that led underground in a downward slope. It was difficult to see farther than a few feet from where they were standing. Shree turned to Dave. "We're not going inside until you tell us what you're doing here."

"Yeah," Nancy said, her voice heavy with suspicion. "Have you been following us?"

"Calm down, all of you," Dave said. "I haven't been following you—exactly."

"Exactly? What does that mean?" Nancy asked.

"Let him talk," Shree said. "I really want to hear this one."

"Thank you," Dave said. "It's really quite interesting how I came to be here tonight."

"Cut the crap," Eleanor blurted out. "Tell us what we want to know."

"All right, all right. You women are so impatient," Dave said. "The reason why I know what you've been up to is that I, well, I've been listening."

"You mean you've been spying. Why does that not surprise me?" Nancy exclaimed.

"Listen for a minute," Dave said. "I have this, um, this thing I can do."

This was sounding awfully familiar, Shree thought.

"Come on, Dave, what are you talking about?" Eleanor demanded again.

"Just admit it, you've been spying on us. Bumping into us at Widener Library a couple of weeks ago, and then at Pinocchio's—and now here. You're unbelievable," Nancy said.

"Just give me a minute to explain. It's not what you think. You're so tough, Four-Eyes," Dave said.

Nancy glared at him in anger.

"Oops, sorry. Well, anyway, to get to the point, I've always had these big ears, right?" Dave asked.

Shree rolled her eyes.

"Yeah, I know, but at some point I discovered my hearing was better than it should be."

Shree and the others just stared at him, so Dave continued. "It's like this. Basically, I can hear a pin drop in New Jersey."

"New Jersey?" Shree said, sounding unconvinced. "Really?"

"Well, maybe not New Jersey, but pretty damn close. I know how it sounds, but it's true. I can hear things miles away. And I know that the twins and the others— these Demons as you call them—are up to something, something big, and they know all about the treasure, too."

"But how do you know about the treasure?" Eleanor asked.

"Yeah, and how do you know we called them the Demons?" Nancy asked.

Dave looked furious. "Have you guys not been listening to anything I've been saying?"

"So you have been spying on us?" Shree cried. "That's unbelievable. How could you do such a thing?"

"It's not like I meant to," Dave said. "It just happens. I've been listening to things since I was six. Once when I was about ten I heard a bank robbery going on a mile away and called the cops anonymously. Of course I got no credit for it, but at least they caught the guy."

"Come on, Dave, stick to the point," Eleanor said.

"Well, that *is* the point. I hear things, I always have. And it helps me to know what's going on all around me. Sometimes it's confusing because I hear so many different conversations, but for the most part I can weed out the most boring stuff. As a matter of fact, that's how I knew you guys were gonna be here tonight—it's how I knew about the treasure. And it's how I know that the twins have been trying to find it before you guys do. That's why I came here tonight, to see if you were still gonna look for it—and to warn you."

Shree was still not convinced.

"Look, the Demons have been making your lives miserable," Dave continued. "Well, they've been making all of our lives miserable. But I'm telling you that they want to find that treasure just as bad as you do. I'm not here to spy. I'm here to help."

"Help us how?" Shree asked.

"I can help in lots of ways," Dave answered. "I'm like a secret weapon. Think about it. I can keep you updated about what they're planning and make sure they don't get in our way."

Shree was torn. If he'd been listening like he said, then he knew all about Nancy's powers, and probably Eleanor's and her own, too. If he'd been listening all this time, he probably knew everything. If they didn't invite him in on the treasure hunt, he could easily change sides and help the Demons. They had no choice. They'd have to let Dave in.

"What do you really want, Dave?" Shree asked.

"Come on, Shree. Don't look at me like that. I don't want anything—well, not much, anyway. Maybe my fair share of the treasure. I've always wanted a Ferrari. Plus, I just want in on the action. I want to join your little treasure hunt. And, like I said, I can be helpful, really. I can make sure no one is following us by using my keen sense of hearing." He cupped his hands around his ears and gave a big smile.

None of the girls spoke. Ralph stared in apparent awe at Dave's ears.

"And besides," Dave put his hands down. "I can keep a secret. In fact, I'd never tell anyone about any of you."

"What do you mean?" Nancy asked.

"You know what I mean. I'm not the only one with superhuman powers, am I?"

Nancy's face flushed, but she didn't say a word.

Shree put her flashlight up to Dave's face. "How much do you know, exactly?"

Dave's face was shiny in the darkness. "Well, I know about Nancy here. Um, and about Ellie Espagueti, too."

Eleanor looked like she was ready to take on Dave with her bare hands.

"Oops, sorry, Ellie—Eleanor. And, um, I guess I know about you too, Shree."

"You know about me?" Shree asked. "About me being a—?"

"Yup. A bee," Dave said.

No one spoke for a full minute. Finally, Shree broke the silence. "Well, that does it. We're all in this together," she said, looking at Nancy, "whether we like it or not. We all have something in common and we need to keep it to ourselves. Does everyone agree?"

"No problem here, Shree. We freaks gotta stick together," Dave said.

Shree hated to admit it, but she liked the idea: a league of freaks, using secret powers to search for a long-hidden treasure. It made Shree feel like she was a part of something bigger than herself. She looked at Eleanor and Nancy for confirmation, and then at Ralph. "Are you guys okay with that?"

Ralph nodded. Eleanor smiled, while Nancy shrugged her shoulders.

"Good. Then it's final. We have a bond of silence. Not one word about the treasure or about our powers to anyone—right?" Shree asked.

They all nodded solemnly. Shree put her hand out. Eleanor put her hand on top and one by one Nancy, Ralph, and Dave added theirs. "We swear to stick together and keep our abilities and our treasure hunting a secret," Shree said. "Now everybody swear."

In unison they all said, "I swear."

There was silence.

"Good. Now that we got that over with, we don't have time to stand around here whining. We have to get down this passageway and see where it leads." Shree turned to Dave. "I don't know if you heard this part," she said, "but we think there's a key down there that'll open the treasure, once we find it. We also think that the maze in my book is the way to get to the key. I've mapped out the only way I could find that takes us from here to there—wherever *there* is. So everybody follow me. Except Ralph and Dave, that is. You guys need to stay here and guard the entrance."G-g-guard? Again?" Ralph asked. "But I was the guard before, and I didn't like it. What if s-s-something happens?"

"We need you up here, Ralph," Eleanor said. "You are potentially the strongest one of us. We need to know that you will protect us while we are down there. Please?"

Ralph immediately seemed to grow in stature. "Oh, well, okay then. I'll stay here—but m-m-make it fast, all right?"

"There's no way I'm staying," Dave said as he grabbed onto the statue's foot for support and tried climbing up the top of the marble base to get a better look at the opening. "I'm going down with you."

Shree sighed. Dave was already being a royal pain. "Okay, we'll let you come with us, but you're not the leader. I have the map, and it's the map we're going to follow. Take it or leave it."

Dave didn't look pleased, but nodded in agreement. As he climbed back down from the base, he grabbed onto the opposite foot of the statue. All at once, the opening at the base began to expand another two feet.

"What the—? Oh my God, Dave, you did it. That was the second lever," Shree said, running back to the base of the statue.

Eleanor, Nancy and Ralph joined Shree. They all stood closely together and stared down the dark hole.

"I guess you were right about the foot, Nancy," Dave said and smiled. With a bend of the waist and a sweeping bow, Dave sent Shree and the girls on ahead.

Chapter 28

The Secret Key

The tunnel was dank and cold. Shree's nose began to run almost immediately, and the hairs on the back of her neck stood straight up. She kept her light on the map. She'd spent a lot of time trying to figure out the actual distances involved in the maze. If she counted how many feet it was to the first turning point, she should be able to figure out how far the other corridors were. She'd marked the route to the exit in a green highlighter and now took the first stretch, counting each foot she took. After ten steps, she saw an opening on her right. That was easy because there was no place else to turn. Right it was.

"Down here, everyone, follow me," she whispered.

Shree knew it wasn't possible, but it seemed even darker after they made the turn, as if they'd left all life behind and were burrowing into the center of the earth. She shivered. They walked ten or so feet and she noted that the tunnel came to a "T." Shree quickly referred to her map. "I think we need to go left here," she said.

After several more lefts and rights, Shree was afraid to admit it, but she felt a little turned around. It was one thing to look down at a map and follow a highlighter, but quite another to physically walk the maze. She also sensed that the others were getting tired and frustrated. Despite having walked a long distance, the group seemed to be getting nowhere.

At the next intersection, Shree stopped and looked around. She was sure there'd be a "T" there, not a four-way option. Shoot. Now she knew it. They were lost.

"Where do you think we should go, Nancy?" Shree asked.

Nancy pushed her glasses closer to her face. "I have no idea. It's tough seeing through the dense walls."

Shree turned and looked at Dave, whose head was cocked to the right. So that was why his head was always in that position—he was listening. Well, that was one mystery solved. Now if only they could find their way in this clammy catacomb.

"Dave," Shree said, not sure asking his opinion was the best idea even now. "I'm not sure which way we should go. What do you think?"

"I'd have to say left. I'm hearing some funky noises coming from the right, and if there's one thing I hate, it's rats."

"Rats!" Eleanor exclaimed. "That is it for me. I vote left."

"How do we know Dave isn't trying to trick us?" Nancy asked. "He could be leading us right into a trap."

"How could he do that? None of us have ever been down here before. We've got to figure this out together," Shree said.

"Okay," Nancy grunted. "Whatever."

After several more minutes of walking, the tunnel got colder and narrower. Shree felt slime on the walls when she accidentally brushed against them. Who knew what kinds of insects lived down here? Dave had already heard rats, and who knew what other creatures lived with them: bugs, worms, maybe even snakes? They'd taken turn after turn until Shree was completely unable to tell where they'd come from, or if they were going in circles.

The only thing that gave her hope was that the path under their feet was still angling downward. If they weren't going in the right direction, wouldn't they be going back up? Shree didn't know. She was beginning to feel tired. She was the one to blame for this mess, too. Eleanor and Nancy had been roped in on her say-so, and now they might not be able to find their way back.

Her last remaining hope vanished when the group reached the end of the highlighted route. Shree stood frozen with the others behind her, staring at the wall in front of her. It was a true dead end. There was nowhere else to go but back.

Shree turned around and addressed the group. "Listen, guys, I'm sorry. I made a mistake somewhere. This should've been where the secret key is buried."

"What do we do now?" Eleanor asked.

"I'm not sure," Shree said. "I guess we should try to retrace our steps and—"

"Shree, say that again," Dave interrupted, leaning his head towards the far wall.

"Say what?" Shree asked.

"Say something. Anything. I think I've noticed something here. Just talk for a while."

"Well, uh," Shree said, "I know I was supposed to be the leader here, but I seem to have gotten us into this mess."

"That's good, Shree. Do you hear that?" Dave asked, straining his neck.

"Hear what? I don't hear anything. Do you Eleanor? Nancy?" Shree asked.

"Nope, but Dave's the one with the big ears," Nancy said. "This is no time for your stupid games, Dave."

Dave said nothing. He knocked repeatedly on the far wall, first along the top, then the middle, and finally the bottom.

"Dave," Nancy insisted. "Tell us what's going on. We're getting tired and we're cold."

"Shree's voice," he said excitedly. "You probably can't hear it, but the echo is different in this section of wall. It has a little vibration. I think we're at the right place."

"Why do you keep knocking?" Eleanor asked.

"Because if the knocking sound I make is different," Dave explained, "then the wall composition is different. The wall seems thinner here. Maybe there's something on the other side, not just earth, but another room."

Nancy pressed her glasses closer to her face. "Point your flashlights up here," she told the others. "Let's see if I can see anything."

Nancy asked Dave to knock again where she was standing. "You know there *is* something different here," she said. "I can't really see anything clearly, but the light is different, too. Everywhere else is completely black, like the earth. Here the light is reflecting off something."

Shree felt her worries ease. Could they have found it? She couldn't see anything different about the wall, and definitely couldn't hear anything other than their hollow, tunnel-bound voices. But if Dave and Nancy thought so, then maybe they had found something.

"Eleanor," Dave said. "Do you think there's any way you can make your hand big enough to break through this wall?"

"I know I can," Eleanor said. "I can shrink them and flatten them, but I can also grow them. How big do you think I should make my fist?"

"Wait a second, we could cause a cave-in or something," Nancy interrupted. "How do we know what will happen?"

"We don't know, Nancy, but what else are we gonna do?" Dave asked. "We've been walking around here forever, and we're either getting nowhere or we've stumbled onto the right place. We need to do something."

"Let's take a vote," Shree said. "Eleanor, what do you think?"

"I think we have to try," Eleanor said. "Sorry, Nancy, but Dave is right. We cannot just stay here or keep walking around in circles."

"I think Dave's onto something," Shree said. "Nancy, what do you want to do?"

"If you guys all think it's a good idea," Nancy said, "then I'm in".

"Okay," Eleanor said. "Here goes nothing."

Eleanor stood a few feet back from the rest of the group. She put her hand out in front of her and took a deep breath. In a few seconds her fist was the size of a volleyball. In another few it was the size of a basketball, then a giant beach ball.

"Whoa," Dave said. "You're not competing with Hellboy, you know. Nancy's right, we don't want the place to fall down around us."

"Sorry, I guess I got carried away," Eleanor said as she shrunk her hand back down to the size of a basketball. "Step back, everyone, it is time to take a swing."

Dave and Nancy spent a minute trying to agree on the best place for Eleanor to take aim. When they finally decided, everyone except for Eleanor stepped back from the wall.

"One, two, *three*," Eleanor said and smashed her fist against the surface of the tunnel's wall.

The result was a small hole with cracks emanating from the center.

"Do it again," Shree said. "But be careful. You've already gotten it started."

Eleanor backed up and repeated the punch. This time there was a hole about ten inches in diameter.

They all crowded around the hole and looked inside. Shree then turned to Eleanor and smiled.

After peeling back a section of the relatively thin wall, Eleanor again did the honors. This time she made her arm long and thin and sent it down through the hole to retrieve a box on the ground. She carried it back up and angled it out into the tunnel again. Then she handed the box, no more than six by eight inches, to Shree.

Shree was speechless. They'd found it. Not that they knew what "it" was yet, but it had to be something important. Or else why would it be sealed up in this tiny room underground?

"Shree, come on, what're you waiting for?" Dave asked.

"Don't be so impatient," she answered. "I'm appreciating the moment."

"Come on, let's open it up and see what's inside." Dave said.

Everyone, Shree included, held their breaths as she tried the latch on the box. The enameled top had an etching of a castle with a labyrinth of hedges in front of it. It was the image on the map, but in vibrant colors— reds, purples, blues, greens, and yellows. Unfortunately, the latch wouldn't budge.

Nancy bent down to have a closer look under the beam of the flashlight. "It should open," she said. "There doesn't seem to be anything in the way. Try it again."

Shree was afraid she'd break it altogether, so she jiggled the latch gently. Suddenly, the spring gave way and the latch separated. The box opened.

Shree lifted the lid slowly. The inside was lined with a thick red velvet cloth. The bottom of the box was built up to make a kind of pedestal. On the pedestal of velvet was a rusted metal key, bigger than most standard keys. It looked worn-out and chipped. It wasn't a key that could fit in a modern lock. It was the kind people used to keep in the doorplates or cabinets, an ornate skeleton key about three-and-a-half inches in length. The top of the key was in the unusual shape of a book.

For a moment, they all stared at the key with puzzled looks on their faces. *This* was the famous secret key? Shree thought. What was so secret about it?

"What the hell's so special about this piece of metal?" Dave said, grabbing for the key and holding it up. "I mean, you really think *this* key is gonna open the treasure? I could've designed a much better key than this junk." He turned away from the girls and looked inside the hole Eleanor had made. Shree had the feeling Dave was searching for something else.

Next to the key was a piece of thin, rolled parchment. Gingerly, Shree unrolled it and looked at the writing.

"Let's see," Nancy turned the flashlight toward the paper. "What does it say?"

Shree read it aloud:

> *Countless treasures you will uncover,*
> *When seeking knowledge, truth, and power,*
> *The secret key shall open doors,*
> *Beyond those built by earthly lords.*
>
> *Under the bridge with the claw of the bear,*
> *Risk your life if you truly care*
> *To gain access to every world,*
> *Without the need of dagger or sword.*
>
> *Once inside the fisherman's wharf,*
> *There will be challenges for giant and dwarf,*
> *Water, Fire, Wind, and Earth,*
> *Things to light your inner hearth.*

The cross shall mark the rightful site,
Where eyes shall feast with all delight.
Uncover the right stone if you are bold,
And you will be granted silver and gold.

The note was signed JH. John Harvard.

"This is it. He's telling us where the treasure is." Shree read the note again as the others high-fived each other.

"Yeah, it must be underneath one of the bridges by the Charles River. All we have to do is figure out which one." Shree was relieved. The letter confirmed the existence of the treasure, which was theirs for the taking.

They had hit the jackpot.

Tired but ecstatic, Shree knew they needed to get up to the surface fast. None of them had brought a watch, but it had to be late. Unfortunately, they had no idea how to get back. They could use Dave's sense of vibration or Nancy's vision to guide them, but that could take forever. Eleanor came up with the only viable option. It would take some time, but she'd run her arms up and down the tunnels and see how far they'd go. When she reached a dead end, she'd have to retract and start again from the last point of reference.

It was long, tedious work, but finally she gave a shout. "Guys, I did it. I feel the air outside. There is a breeze. Follow me, we will be out of here in no time."

Shree pulled up the rear of the group. She needed some rest in a nice, warm place. Her toes had long ago gone numb and her fingers felt like ice. But she had to keep going.

Eleanor went flying out of the tunnel first as her hands snapped back into place. Dave was next, then Nancy, and finally Shree, who gave Eleanor a giant hug. "You did it, El," she said. "You got us back."

With their arms around each other, they followed Nancy and Dave out the stone door with smiles on their faces.

And that's when they saw Ralph.

Chapter 29

Defeat Of The Freaks

Ralph was propped up against the tree closest to the John Harvard statue. His hands were tied behind his back and his mouth was taped shut. He had a black eye and several cuts on his face.

The Demons stood in front of him. Katherine, the Queen Demon, was disguised as a witch, Colleen as a she-devil (if the red leather skirt and long plastic fork were any indication), and Jason and the twins as bikers in the same gang. Totally unoriginal, Shree thought, but decidedly on the mark.

"What's going on?" Shree demanded. "Let him go."

The Demons laughed as if she'd told some kind of a joke.

"I mean it, what's he ever done to you? Ralph, it'll be okay, don't worry," Shree said.

"Yeah," Jason said. "It's gonna be okay, fatty. Shree the bee will take care of you."

Ralph's eyes got bigger, seeming to plead with Shree to get him out in one piece. Behind her, Eleanor and Nancy stood with their arms linked. Dave stood a few feet farther away, appearing unaffected by what was going on.

"What exactly do you want?" Shree asked again, louder this time.

"You didn't think we'd let you keep the treasure all to yourself, did you?" Colleen took a step toward Shree and pointed to the box. "Just hand over the box and we'll let Ralph go." She made a move toward her, but Shree recoiled as if slapped. She'd almost forgotten she was still holding the box with the secret key.

And why hadn't Dave used his powers for that matter? He'd managed to insinuate himself into their band of treasure hunters by saying he'd be able to hear if the Demons were around. He hadn't heard a darn thing. Either that or he knew and hadn't said anything. Shree didn't know which was worse. She didn't like thinking this way, but what if he'd led them straight into this ambush? What if he was in league with them all along? She glanced over at Dave. He stood to the side, still saying—and doing—nothing.

Shree felt her stinger start to itch. But at this point she was afraid she was too weak from the long trip down into the tunnels and from the cold air to successfully transform. What if she tried and could only get halfway there? Would she stay half-bee and half-human forever? Would she be stuck in limbo, unable to get back? No, there had to be another way to get Ralph back and get out of there safely.

"You don't get it, do you?" Katherine emerged from behind Colleen and Jason. She shook her head lightly from side to side, and took a step toward Shree. "I guess you didn't read your book carefully when you had the chance. You know, for someone who's as smart as you are, it's disappointing that you have no idea what you've stumbled onto."

"What are you talking about?" Shree asked. She was starting to feel dizzy.

"You have no concept of what it is you're seeking. This treasure is bigger than you could ever imagine. I guess if you were as smart as you make people believe, you would've figured it out already. But you're too busy trying to outperform me in class." Katherine walked around Shree slowly, shaking her head as she looked at her up and down.

Shree stood frozen in place. She was too confused to concentrate on any one thing. She wanted to save Ralph, she wanted to transform into a bee, she wanted to safeguard the key—but she also wanted to figure out what Katherine was talking about.

"I could care less about outperforming you or being valedictorian. And what're you talking about? How do you know about the treasure?" Shree glanced over at the twins and put two-and-two together. "You stole my book, didn't you? And that's how you know."

"Don't worry about how I know. The point is that you've missed the big picture. But it doesn't really matter, does it? You're going to hand over the key without causing a scene. Otherwise," Katherine paused and stared at Ralph, "the twins will show Ralph what happens when you choose the key over his safety."

While the twins walked over toward Ralph, Shree turned around and looked at Eleanor and Nancy. Neither of them was making any moves, so she had no choice but to concede.

"Okay, Katherine, you win," Shree handed over the box. She felt powerless and defeated.

"Now, that wasn't so hard, was it?" Colleen snatched the box from Shree. She then walked over to Eleanor and Nancy. "Thank you, ladies, for not doing anything stupid." She looked over at Nancy and snatched her glasses off her face. "I always thought you'd look better without these things."

Eleanor made a dash at Colleen, but stopped midway when she saw the twins and Jason approach. Colleen smiled and tossed the glasses to Tom, who caught them and placed them in his front pocket.

With the secret key in their possession, Katherine, Colleen, Jason, and the twins started for the North Gate, the one farthest from the craziness that was now unfolding on campus. It was nearly midnight and dorm parties were overflowing into the middle of Harvard Yard.

As soon as they were gone, Shree went over to Ralph and took out her Swiss army knife. She had to get him loose and get them all out of there. Fast. If they got caught— she didn't even want to think about that possibility. Her parents might be reasonable people (for parents), but they'd never get over this one.

If it were possible, Ralph looked more terrified than before. Shree reached down and ripped off the tape as gently as she could.

"Shree," Ralph said immediately. "I'm s-s-sorry."

"Look, Ralph, we just need to get out of here before the security guards want to know what we're doing. We can't afford to get caught." Shree sliced through the ropes on his wrists. "Head for the South Gate behind Widener Library. That's closest to your house and away from Holworthy."

Ralph stood up shakily.

"Can you walk?" Shree asked.

He nodded uncertainly, shaking out his legs. "Pins and n-n-needles."

"Ralph, you've got to get moving," Shree said urgently. "There's no time to waste."

With tears in his eyes and a last look at Shree, Ralph finally loped off into the shadows of Harvard Yard.

Shree looked at the others. "Well, guys, it's time for us to leave. Dave, you follow Ralph. Make sure he gets home okay. Nancy, Eleanor, and I will go out through the East Gate. We need to get back to my house before my parents do or we're going to be in major trouble."

"I'm nobody's babysitter, especially not Ralph's. He's the reason why we lost the key."

With that, Dave turned and walked slowly toward the North Gate. Shree noticed that after several steps, Dave's ears grew in size and before she knew it, he was gliding several feet above ground, heading at full speed toward the gate. In a few seconds, Dave was gone.

Still in a daze, Shree turned to Nancy. "Are you okay?"

"Yeah, but I can't see a thing," Nancy said.

"Hold onto us. We'll guide you home. Step carefully," Shree said. "We've got a long way to go."

Chapter 30

A Common Dilemma

"Hey," Shree said. "There's Ralph over there, in the corner." Despite the crowd, Shree caught the occasional glimpse of Ralph, who sat by himself on the opposite end of the cafeteria.

Nancy and Eleanor turned around to look. "Why do you think he is over there?" Eleanor asked.

"I can't see," Nancy said. "These glasses are old and my distance vision is terrible, worse than my near."

It was true that Nancy's old pair of glasses, which supposedly she'd found at her house over the weekend, were even thicker and uglier than her usual ones—not that Shree would ever say anything. "I don't know," Shree said. "But I bet he's probably still upset about the other night."

"Well, I do not blame him," Eleanor said. "He was supposed to keep watch, and because of him we lost the key."

"That's true," Shree agreed. "But you know the Demons. They're vicious. Poor Ralph never had a chance. I think what bothers me more is that he could've used his powers to do something. I mean, what good are powers if you just let people run right over you?"

"If you put it like that, though," Nancy said, "none of us really did anything, did we? We let them ambush us, take the secret key, and make fools of us. Now they'll probably get the treasure, too."

"And what was up with Dave?" Eleanor asked. "He stood there like a jerk. I thought he could hear all the way to New Jersey. He sure did not hear the Demons ambushing Ralph, did he?"

"I wondered about that, too. Do you think that maybe Dave—" Shree paused. "Well, do you think he was in on the whole thing?"

Nancy and Eleanor were quiet.

"I know, I know. It's a terrible thing to say," Shree added. "But why wouldn't he have heard them coming?"

"I do not know," Eleanor said, "but you can ask him yourself. Here he comes. As always, he somehow shows up at the right time."

Dave strolled over with his lunch tray and sat down next to Shree. "What's up girls?"

"What's up? *What's up?* You're asking us what's up?" Shree demanded. "After what happened the other night? I think you owe us an explanation."

Eleanor and Nancy nodded.

Dave ripped open a packet of ketchup, spread it on his burger, and then took a huge bite. Shree waited impatiently as he chewed and swallowed.

"Well?" Shree asked again.

"Well, there's not much to say," Dave said.

Nancy exploded. "Not much to say? You told us you could hear a pin drop in New Jersey and that you'd be able to warn us if the Demons were around. What happened? Why didn't you hear anything? Is there something you're not telling us?"

"Look," Dave began. "I didn't know that I wouldn't be able to hear anything when we were underground. I mean, I could pick up different vibrations when we were down there, where we found the key, but I didn't hear anything from up above. I know you guys don't believe me, but honestly I had no idea those guys were waiting for us when we got out."

There was a brief moment of silence. "I'm serious," Dave said. "I usually hear all kinds of conversations—they drive me crazy half the time. But it was so quiet down there. I was just happy to have quiet for once that I forgot all about trying to hear anything else. Plus, I was too focused on finding the key."

Shree didn't know whether to believe him. But when she thought about it, Nancy hadn't been able to see through the dense earth in the tunnels the way she could structures above ground. So maybe it was the same for Dave. If Shree was being honest, even her own powers had been useless because she'd been so cold.

Eleanor spoke first. "All right, let us say for the sake of argument that you are telling the truth. Why did you not do anything when we came out of the tunnel? I mean, you just stood there and did not even make an effort to resist those creeps."

Done with his burger, Dave took a sip of his soda. "It's pretty simple. It would've been pointless to try fighting them then. They had ambushed us. They had Ralph hostage. And they outnumbered us. Fighting them would've been a waste of my time." He looked at Shree. "It's the same reason why none of you guys did anything either."

As Shree was about to defend herself, Ralph had apparently gained enough courage to walk over to their table. He stood for a minute in front of the group, staring at the floor and not saying anything.

"Hi, Ralph," Shree said encouragingly.

"Um, hi, Shree. Hi guys. I, um, I just w-w-wanted to say that I'm, uh, I'm—" he floundered.

"Oh, spit it out," Dave interrupted. "Be a man."

"Cool it, Dave," Shree said. "Go on, Ralph. You were saying?"

"I, um, I am s-s-sorry," Ralph said. "They caught me off-guard. You guys were gone so long and it was boring and cold up there. I guess I n-n-nodded off for a second. The next thing I knew they were t-t-tying me up and putting tape over my mouth."

Ralph paused and cleared his throat. "I'm really, really sorry," he said again. "I know I messed up."

Dave mumbled something under his breath.

"If you have something to say, say it out loud," Shree demanded.

"Okay, I will," Dave said. "Ralph had a simple job to do and he didn't do it. The kid can turn into a whale, for God's sake. But he didn't. He didn't fight back. And now I'll never get my Ferrari."

"Dave, I can't believe you're saying that," Shree said. "You didn't fight back, either. None of us did. We didn't even try. We're all a bunch of pathetic..." she paused, trying to find the right word. "Freaks."

That broke the tension. Suddenly, they were all laughing. "You are right, Shree," Eleanor said. "We are freaks. And freaks have to stick together."

"It's too bad that we gave up that key," Nancy added. "Now the Demons have everything."

"Well," Shree said. "Maybe not *everything*."

The four others eyed her curiously. Shree took out her notebook and opened it carefully. Inside, she had pressed a piece of parchment between two pages. It was John Harvard's note from the box, the one that had held the secret key.

"Shree, how'd you get that?" Dave asked.

"I cannot believe it!" Eleanor exclaimed. "You mean the Demons did not get it after all?"

"What's going on?" Nancy asked as she pressed her old glasses against her face.

"Shree kept the note that came with the key," Eleanor whispered to Nancy, who drew in a breath.

"A note from John Harvard," Shree explained for Ralph's benefit. "We found it with the secret key. I took it out of the box for safekeeping before we came out of the tunnel. I really don't know why I did it. It probably would've been safer in the box since that's where it has been all these years."

Ralph took the note and held it carefully, reading it while the others continued to congratulate Shree.

"That is amazing," Eleanor said. "Do you know what this means?"

"It means that we know where to look for the treasure and the Demons don't," Nancy chimed in.

"Well, not exactly," Shree said. "The note from Harvard is all one giant riddle. It refers to the treasure, but it's written in a cryptic way. I guess he wanted to make sure that the treasure didn't fall in the wrong hands."

"I am sure we can figure out where the treasure is," Eleanor said.

"I don't know about that," Shree said. "How are we supposed to figure out the riddle? And even if we did, it doesn't really matter since the Demons have the key anyway."

Shree glanced over at Katherine's table and saw Colleen leaning toward the twins and Jason, showing them something she held around her neck.

Eleanor gasped. "The key."

Despite the dull color of the metal object that dangled from Colleen's silver necklace, the secret key was easily recognizable from where Shree was seated.

"There's only one thing to do then," Dave muttered in anger. "We need to get that key back." He stood up from his chair and took a step towards the Demons' table.

"Wait, Dave. Do not do anything stupid." Eleanor grabbed Dave by the forearm and forced him to sit back down.

"Eleanor's right, Dave. This isn't the right time or place," Shree said. "We need to get the key back, but it can't be done here."

"I think I know w-w-where the treasure is," Ralph whispered to himself, continuing to stare at the thin, delicate piece of parchment.

"What'd you just say?" Dave asked.

Ralph cleared his throat, looked up, and repeated the statement, this time louder and with more confidence. "I know where the t-t-treasure is. You see, I go swimming in the Charles River a lot, especially by the b-b-boathouse. It's always fun swimming there b-b-because I get to watch the crew team coming out every day for practice and—"

"Get on with it already," Dave said.

"S-s-sorry," Ralph said. "Anyway, on the b-b-bottom of the boathouse there's a sign. I was confused when I first read it because it d-d-didn't make sense to me. But that's what's written in the stone on the f-f-foundation of the boathouse." Ralph pointed to the middle of the poem. "There's a carving of a b-b-bear's claw and underneath it's written:'The cross shall mark the rightful site.'"

There was a brief moment of silence. Finally, Shree said, "Ralph, you're incredible."

He beamed.

"I am sure Ralph is right. It would be the perfect spot to transport treasure, down by the water, with access to boats. You are a genius," Eleanor said.

That set Ralph off so much that he got crimson all the way to the tips of his ears.

"I'd bet anything that John Harvard's treasure is either inside or underneath that boathouse, and we're going to be the ones to find it," Shree added.

"Well, I hate to be a party pooper, Shree, but this brings us back to our original problem. We don't have the key," Nancy said.

Shree glanced back at the Demons' table. Katherine sat calmly reading a book. Colleen, on the other hand, was laughing loudly as the twins took turns putting on Nancy's glasses and making stupid faces.

Shree was angry. "The nerve of those guys."

"What? What are they doing?" Nancy asked.

"Nothing, Nancy. They are just being a bunch of jerks," Eleanor said.

"What should we d-d-do now?" Ralph asked.

"We need to come up with a way to get the key back and go after the treasure. That will show them," Eleanor said.

"You girls leave it up to me," Dave said, staring at the twins. "I'll have to keep my ears extra open this week. But we *will* get that key back."

Chapter 31

A Word Of Advice

Shree rolled out of bed on Thursday morning with a series of moans and groans. It was just after five in the morning. The mid-autumn sun had not made it past the horizon. It was getting harder and harder to get out of bed in the cold. It was getting even harder to sleep more than a few hours each night, which left Shree in a state of limbo: too awake to sleep, and too sleepy to get out of bed. If she was going to control her bee powers, she needed to learn to manage the human part as well. Like staying warm.

She went to her closet and took out a heavy woolen sweater to put over her pajamas. She walked over to her desk, opened the drawer, and took out John Harvard's note for the tenth time that week. Shree was finding it difficult to focus on anything else besides the poem. Assuming they were able to take back the key from Colleen, and that was a big assumption, then what? What would they do after? They couldn't just head to the boathouse without knowing where to look for the treasure. She still didn't know where they'd start their search once they got there.

Shree continued to shiver beneath her sweater. She walked over to the heater with the poem and continued to read it over and over again, trying to figure out exactly what it meant. If there was another set of tunnels underneath the boathouse, then there could be a series of doorways that they'd need to unlock in order to get to the treasure. So that could well be the place where:

> *"The secret key shall open doors,*
> *Beyond those built by earthly lords."*

But what was all the stuff about *"Water, Fire, Wind and Earth"*? For some reason that statement made her feel a little nervous.

And what about what Katherine had said about the key—that it was bigger than Shree could ever imagine? What did that mean?

Finally, tired of trying to interpret a puzzle with too many pieces, Shree set the poem down on a pile of other books and papers. Whether she liked it or not, she still had to finish her math homework before she left for school.

That was when the most incredible thing happened. Shree had been working hard at her last quadratic equation, the hardest problem of her assignment, when she pushed the pile of papers and books aside to make more room to write. Harvard's note fluttered down from the pile and onto the top of the heater. It must've sat there for a minute before Shree looked up, her pencil tip in her mouth, thinking about how to proceed with her calculations. When she saw the thin parchment on the heater, she made a garbled choking sound and grabbed for it, plucking the paper off the heating unit and setting it down on her desk again. It could've burned up, been nothing but ashes in seconds. But thank goodness it was all right—a little warm, though, but undamaged.

At least that's what she thought until she saw the markings. But she'd never seen any markings on the back before. Would the heat have caused that kind of damage?

Shree stared at it. Something was happening. In three seconds more, the markings had morphed into something else entirely. A drawing. It was another map! The discovery was so unexpected that for a minute she was sure she was seeing things. And then suddenly, even as she looked, the map began to fade. Shree almost cried at the sight of the vanishing image.

Then she got an idea. The map had surfaced when the paper fell on the heater. That meant that it must be some kind of invisible ink, something that revealed itself when it came in contact with heat.

With shaking hands, Shree held the parchment over the heater again and held her breath. She didn't want to bring it too close to the heat source or risk burning it. Sure enough, within a couple of seconds, the image began to reappear. Shree saw a couple of lines, then what looked like a swirl, and then a rectangular shape.

Come on, she thought. Couldn't it go any faster?

Soon she'd seen everything. It was another map. There was a different set of tunnels, some small writing etched on the margins, and another "X" that marked the spot where the treasure was hidden. It was the final map that would make them all rich. And, most importantly, it would help her figure out what Katherine meant about the secret key.

Shree couldn't contain her excitement. She grabbed her cell phone and dialed Eleanor. She told her everything.

"El, it was crazy. When the paper got hot it showed where the treasure's buried. John Harvard used invisible ink to make a map on the back of the poem."

"I cannot believe it, Shree. That is amazing. We have the map and we have the clues. Now we really need the key."

"I know. How are we going to get it?" Shree thought for a moment.

"I do not know," Eleanor answered. "I am sure that getting into Katherine's house was hard enough, even when you were a bee, but this? This is impossible. How can we get it off Colleen's neck?"

"Do me a favor. Call Nancy and let her know about the map. She needs something to cheer her up. She's been so depressed since the twins stole her glasses. I'll call Dave. Maybe he's heard something important that could steer us in the right direction."

Shree hung up and dialed Dave's number. She looked at the clock. 6:45. It might be too early to call, but Shree hoped that Dave would pick up the phone anyway.

She tapped her foot impatiently as she dialed. As soon as she marked the last number, there was a voice on the other line.

"Helllllooooo."

"Dave?"

"What's up, Shree?"

"Um, not much, but—" Shree faltered. "Wait a second. The phone didn't even ring. How did you know to pick it up?"

Dave answered slowly, his voice filled with sarcasm. "Now, Shree. Do you *still* have to ask?"

"Oh, yeah, I forgot." Shree then got mad. "You know, that's really getting annoying. Did you hear *everything* I just told Eleanor?"

"Not really. I only heard part of it. I was busy doing something else," Dave said.

"Well, anyway, once we reach the boathouse and find the entrance into the tunnels, we'll be equipped with the map to help us find the treasure. But we still need to get the key," Shree said.

"I think I can help with that," Dave said.

"I'm listening," Shree said warily.

"Well, I heard Colleen telling Katherine that her parents were going away for a few days. She invited Katherine to spend the weekend with her. They have this routine they do anytime Colleen has her over. They spend Friday night doing their nails and watching old 80's movies. Then the next morning they wake up, have breakfast, and go tanning by Colleen's pool."

"What does any of that have to do with the key?"

"You don't get it, do you?" Dave laughed. "I guess you've never been in a tanning booth before. What kind of girl are you?"

Shree was silent, too angered by that statement to say anything.

Dave continued, "You see, when Colleen and Katherine go inside the tanning booth, they have to take everything off, including their jewelry. Otherwise, they'd get a tan line, and I know that Colleen would hate that, especially in a place so exposed by the skimpy shirts she wears."

Shree gasped. "She'll have to take the necklace off."

"Now you're following, genius. All you guys have to do is sneak into her house on Saturday morning, wait until they go tanning, and steal back the key," Dave said.

"What do you mean by you guys? Aren't you and Ralph going with us?" Shree asked.

"Um, well, we can't." Dave cleared his throat. "We have, um, stuff to do this weekend. We'll just have to talk at school next week."

"What? I don't understand you, Dave. This is the perfect opportunity and you don't want to help us out. What's going on?"

"Listen, Shree. You guys can handle this without us. Ralph and I have other stuff to do. Anyway, I gotta go." Dave hung up abruptly.

"But—" Shree heard nothing but a dial tone on the other end.

What could Dave be up to? Shree wondered. And now he was dragging Ralph along with him. She didn't like it one bit. She had to let Nancy and Eleanor know that Dave was up to something.

Unfortunately, this was probably their only chance to take the key back. Sooner or later, the Demons would figure out a way to steal the treasure map from them. Shree was certain that the more time that elapsed, the less chance she had to find the treasure. It was now or never. She'd have to convince Eleanor and Nancy that they needed to do a little breaking and entering at the

O'Connor's on Saturday morning. It was time to take back what was theirs to begin with!

But it was also time to get ready for school. She looked at the clock. Shoot. She needed to get her stuff and leave. Her mom was already complaining to her dad downstairs about her running late for school again.

Five minutes later, Shree ran out of her bedroom, her bag filled with books and papers. She hadn't had time to figure out which she needed, so she stuffed everything that was on top of her desk inside her backpack, put on her uniform, and brushed her teeth. Her dad was waiting outside her door. She nearly ran him over as she slammed the door and turned to run downstairs.

"Oh, hey, Dad."

"Hello, Shree. I think it would be best if I give you a ride to school today. You are running late and probably will not make it on time."

"That's okay, Dad. I'll be fine. I can speed walk to school in under ten minutes. Plenty of time to make it to homeroom." Shree knew she was probably giving herself more credit than she deserved, but she was in no mood to be stuck inside the car with her dad. He had a way of knowing if something strange was going on, and there were too many secrets she was keeping from him: the key, the treasure, her powers, the Demons.

"Okay, then." Her father looked suspicious for a second. But then he smiled. "You have a good day at school." He kissed her forehead.

Shree ran downstairs, relieved that she had dodged a bullet. Another crisis avoided, she thought. Lately, everything was a regular minefield of potential problems.

As she reached the last step, her father called out. "Shree?"

Damn!

She turned around slowly. "Yes, Dad?"

"I know you must be under a lot of stress with school and friends and other things. Your mother and I have noticed that you have been exceedingly preoccupied lately. We know that you are under a lot of pressure at your new school but, just remember, your mother and I love you very much."

Shree was glad to have such a great father and now felt guilty for pushing him away. "I know, Dad."

"And please remember, Shree, that sometimes all you need is what is around you. It is not necessary to search beyond your surroundings to find happiness. Sometimes what we spend our lives looking for is right in front of us."

Shree gave a smile and walked out the door.

On her way to school, her father's words began to play over and over inside her head. Shree remembered her first day of school at Kennedy and her dad's words of advice then, particularly about how our strength lies in our differences.

If *this* was what being different was all about, Shree had to agree with her dad. Different was good. Different was power.

But different was also dangerous.

Chapter 32

Stealing It Back

At nine in the morning, the girls met at Colleen's front gate as planned. What Shree hadn't planned on was feeling so awed by what she saw. Nancy had told her that the house was big, but Shree had assumed that Nancy's sixth-grade memories were larger than real life. Instead, when Shree saw just how massive the Tudor castle was, she was engulfed with a dreadful feeling of doubt, forcing her to rethink her original plan.

To Shree, it looked like something out of King Arthur's court. She expected to see a drawbridge come down any second across the moat—an actual moat filled with water and Japanese koi—right there in the middle of Cambridge.

Shree saw Eleanor gaping, taking in the topiaries and tennis courts and the Olympic-size swimming pool, closed over with a tarp for the winter. Nancy, on the other hand, squinted behind her old glasses, apparently unable to take in her surroundings.

"Maybe this is not such a good idea," Eleanor said. "They probably have an alarm system in the house. One that is connected right to the police station."

"We're not going to break in," Shree said. "We're going to *sneak* in."

"How?" Nancy asked. "Do you have a plan we don't know about?"

"Not yet," Shree said. "But I'm working on it."

"They're probably not even in there," Nancy said.

"But Dave said that they would be," Eleanor said.

"Yeah, but so what? Dave's not perfect. Maybe he made a mistake. Or maybe he's trying to set us up," Nancy added.

"You know, I hate to say it, but he was acting really sketchy on the phone. I mean, this is our only shot at taking the key back and he's *busy*. What's up with that?" Shree asked.

"Yeah, and what's up with Ralph hanging out with Dave all the time now?" Nancy chimed in.

"Well, I think it is good," Eleanor said. "I mean, Ralph never really had any friends. And Dave is so, well, *Dave*. It is probably good for Ralph to have someone smart and funny to be with, don't you think?"

"Maybe you're right and we're just being overly paranoid. But still, Dave is definitely up to something and he's not telling us." Shree stared at the mansion, trying to figure out their next step.

"Hey, Shree. Maybe you should check out whether Katherine and Colleen are really in there. If they are not, we are wasting our time," Eleanor said.

Shree thought about it. Eleanor was right. If Katherine and Colleen weren't there, there was no reason at all to be standing in the cold, taking the risk of going into Colleen's house uninvited, and then having to get out undetected.

"You're right. I'll go in. But I'll need you guys to come closer and warm me up. I can't transform when I'm so cold."

They made a little circle and Nancy and Eleanor rubbed Shree's arms for a minute. Finally, Shree was ready. "Okay, I'm going to fly up there and see what's going on inside. When I get back, we'll work on the next part of the plan."

They gave Shree some room and stepped back.

It was hard to make the change because she was shaking so much from the cold. But eventually the heat from Nancy and Eleanor's bodies paid off and Shree suddenly felt herself shrinking into a tiny insect. And once she turned into a bee, she felt the endless amounts of power and energy that came along with the transformation.

She gave the girls a buzz and flew off in a straight line for the upper story windows. She was betting that Colleen's room was somewhere up there.

In the third group of windows she spotted pink polka-dotted drapes. That had to be it. She zoomed over to take a peek. She was right. Inside, the two girls slept in a king-sized bed, surrounded by a hundred or more stuffed animals. Clothes were everywhere, on every surface, as if they'd been trying on every single outfit Colleen had ever bought. Shree had never seen so many clothes outside a department store.

She took a closer look at Katherine, on her back, arms thrown out to her sides, in skimpy pajamas. Next to her, Colleen suddenly turned over to her side, causing the key on the end of the chain around her neck to catch the light. Shree felt her stinger. Colleen was sleeping, and Shree was a bee. How hard could it be to find her way inside the room, transform back to human, and take the key?

The door to Colleen's room opened and the housekeeper came in. Shree almost fell off her perch on the window ledge in terror. She didn't wait to see any more. She turned around and flew straight back to Eleanor and Nancy.

"You were right," Shree said once she'd transformed into her human self. "They're in there all right. They were still asleep, but probably not for long. We've got to get inside before they get downstairs."

"And we have to find a place to hide so we do not get caught," Eleanor added.

"But how?" Nancy asked.

"Give me a minute," Shree said. "I'll think of something."

Eleanor and Nancy let Shree plan the next step while they stomped their feet to keep warm. A light blanket of snow had fallen the night before and the morning air was downright cold.

Shree watched the house for a while, but the only activity was the housekeeper, a large and muscular Hispanic woman, who was going in and out, carrying a variety of small rugs and an implement that looked like a wire snowshoe.

"I did not know anyone did that anymore," Eleanor remarked. "She is going to beat the rugs to get them clean. It reminds me of back home in the Dominican Republic."

"Hey, that gives me an idea," Shree said. "Look. When she goes in and out through that door—probably into the kitchen—she leaves the door open. We just have to get over there, stick something over the latch, and then when she goes inside, it won't close."

"How do you know that is going to work?" Eleanor asked.

"I don't," Shree answered. "But I saw it in a movie. And it's all we've got."

They waited a while longer until Shree was worried she was freezing to death. Finally, the housekeeper seemed to have all the rugs. One by one, she methodically beat the dust and dirt from each one. Shree's patience was growing thin. She didn't have much time left before she'd be nothing more than a popsicle. She wondered how the housekeeper was able to weather the cold with such indifference.

Just as Shree was going to suggest they try again later, that she'd had it, the housekeeper started piling up the rugs again to bring them in the house. Shree held up a finger to give the signal. When the housekeeper went to take in the first couple, Shree whispered, "Now!" and the girls ran through the yard to hide behind the row of hedges by the door.

Shree stuck her head out and looked inside the big glass window with the gold-plated frames. The door did indeed lead to the kitchen, the biggest kitchen she'd ever seen. It was more like a restaurant, filled with stainless steel appliances, the counters topped with black marble.

Shree took a piece of tape out of her pocket and stuck it on her finger. She'd been keeping a constant supply of things she might need for any occasion in her jacket and backpack since Halloween night; it was definitely paying off.

The housekeeper was humming a catchy Spanish tune as she stepped back out into the yard to get two more rugs. As soon as she was far enough away, Shree leapt out from behind the hedge and headed for the door. She placed the piece of tape over the latch the way she had seen it in the movies. She had no idea if it would hold—or if the housekeeper would see it and rip it off. She didn't want to think about that possibility—what the woman in the white apron with the bulging biceps would do if she thought she had uninvited guests.

Shree took the few feet back to the hedge in a couple of leaps and bounds. The leaves on the trees hadn't even stopped moving when the housekeeper went back inside, passing within inches of Shree's toes. With the rugs in her arms, she hadn't noticed much else.

Shree whispered, "We need to stay here until she leaves the kitchen. Then we'll sneak in and find somewhere to hide. Okay?"

Nancy and Eleanor nodded. Shree prayed it wouldn't take long.

Not more than a couple of minutes had passed when they heard noises in the kitchen. The housekeeper had left, but Colleen and Katherine had come in to get their breakfast

"Shoot," Shree said. "This'll probably take forever." But she hadn't counted on the fact that the two skinny girls weren't much for pancakes and bacon. They grabbed some kind of smoothie from the refrigerator and left not thirty seconds later.

"Yes," Shree said. "Let's go."

Pulling Nancy between them to make sure she didn't falter, the three moved lightly over to the door and pushed it open a tiny bit. The tape had held. Their luck was holding, too. Shree expected the door to creak the way it would in her house, but it was absolutely silent, a solid reminder of the wealth of the O'Connors.

The girls tiptoed into the kitchen and looked around. It was fancier than any kitchen Shree had ever seen, including the ones on the cooking shows of the Food Network. For a minute they stood there, mouths open.

"Um, shouldn't we get out of here?" Nancy asked.

"Yeah, you're right," Shree whispered. "Do you remember which way we should go?"

"Well, when I was here we had the party in the backyard," Nancy said. "We could see the pool through the living room windows. I'm pretty sure the tanning room will be back there. So that means we need to get to the back of the house."

"Okay," Eleanor said. "Keep a hold of my hand, Nancy. We are going to have to walk single file here and try to find our way. It is too bad Dave is not here. If he heard anyone coming he could let us know."

They walked as quietly as they could out of the kitchen and through a swinging door, which opened to the dining room. The table was big enough for fifty people. But there was no time to waste with their mouths hanging open. They might have only seconds before the housekeeper showed up again.

Shree pulled them through the dining room and then out into the living room, again a room so huge her whole house could have fit inside. There were several doors leading from it—where they went, Shree had no idea.

"El, see those doors?" Shree asked.

Eleanor nodded.

"We need to find out where they lead. I'll—" Shree stopped abruptly. "Get down. It's the housekeeper."

Shree yanked Nancy and Nancy yanked Eleanor and all three toppled down behind a big leather sofa. The housekeeper walked within three feet of them, still humming the same catchy tune. Shree held her breath as the woman pulled the drapes shut on one of the windows, dusted a pair of small glass sculptures that stood on a shelf behind the grand piano, and then picked up a stray leaf from the floor.

The housekeeper held the leaf in her hand and looked around. Shree could almost hear her mind clicking, wondering how the leaf had gotten into her clean living room. She strolled around the room slowly, a puzzled look on her face. She stopped humming for a minute, picked up the thick wire that she had used to beat the rugs outside, and walked toward the big sofa.

She held the wire like a weapon as she approached the girls' hiding spot. And, with a burst of energy, the housekeeper leaped to the side of the couch. Her eyes were wild as she lifted the thick metal wire and brought it down with a vengeance, hoping to strike whomever was hiding behind the couch.

Chapter 33

At The Twins' House

Ralph watched Dave as he cocked his head to one side and listened. Ralph was fascinated by Dave. Even though each one of his new friends had their own special powers, he was especially impressed with him. Dave could use his ears to hear distant whispers, *and* he could also use them to glide through the air at bounding speed. He also had a funny comeback for just about anything. Ralph wished he were a little more like Dave. But, at the very least, he was glad that he could call Dave his friend.

"All right, Ralphie. This is it. The twins are on their way to basketball practice. This gives us plenty of time to go in and check out the house."

As soon as Dave had finished speaking, Tom and Tim and their mother walked out the front door. Ralph could see the twins fighting for the front seat of the black Range Rover until Tim finally gave in and sat in the back. Tom turned on the radio as soon as his mother turned on the car. Seconds later, they were gone.

Ralph and Dave waited a minute before coming out of the bushes and walking around to the backyard. Dave tried the patio door, but it was locked.

"Maybe we should just head b-b-back home?" Ralph looked around nervously.

"Come on, Ralph, it was your idea to come along. I was perfectly happy doing this by myself. You're not losing your cool, are you?" Dave asked while scanning the house.

"No, but m-m-maybe we'll get caught and my mom would not be happy if—" Ralph faltered.

Dave pointed to the upstairs window. "Stay here. That window up there looks like it may be open. I'll let myself in and then come get you."

Before Ralph could ask how Dave intended on climbing up to the second floor, Dave's ears grew in size. They flapped repeatedly, gaining speed as they lifted him up from the ground. Dave made his way toward the window and hovered in place as he lifted the glass up.

A minute later, Dave held the door open for Ralph. The two climbed the stairs to the second floor and began their search.

The twins' room was a mess. It was filled with athletic equipment of all types, which was scattered in every corner. There were books and papers on the floor, and *Maxim* and *Playboy* magazines on the bed by the nightstand.

"You start over there," Dave said, pointing to the right. "I'll start on this side."

Ralph nodded. There were two beds, two desks, two dressers; everything looked the same. The only difference was that one of the twins was neat, and the other one liked magazines a lot.

"This must be Tim's," Ralph said, looking at the desk that had a neat pile of books and papers. "His name is on the books."

"Yeah, and this must be Tom's. He's a magazine fanatic. And look at the food on the floor. What a slob," Dave said.

"Are you sure the t-t-treasure book is here?" Ralph asked.

"That's what I heard," Dave looked through Tom's magazines.

"Okay, let's keep searching," Ralph said. "Why d-d-don't we start under the beds?"

"How long do you think that food's been under there?" Dave asked, pointing to a bowl of moldy cereal. "That's disgusting."

"Do you s-s-see anything else?" Ralph asked.

"Nope, nothing so far." Dave tossed the magazines and crawled underneath Tom's bed.

Ralph looked inside Tim's closet, around his desk, and under the bed. He found nothing but books, sports equipment, and a few *Playboys* squirreled away between the mattresses and springs.

"Shoot," Dave said. "Not a damn thing."

"Its g-g-got to be here," Ralph said. "If you were the twins, where would you hide something you d-d-didn't want your mother to find?"

Ralph thought about his own question while Dave walked around the room.

"That's it, dude. It's got to be inside one of their backpacks," Dave said. "I heard Katherine reading one of the entries at lunch yesterday. She gave the book back to Tim right after she was done. She wanted to make sure Shree didn't steal it back."

Dave walked to the desk and, after rummaging through all the paraphernalia, found the backpack. Seconds later, the book was in his hands.

"You d-d-did it, Dave. You got the b-b-book back," Ralph said.

"We did it, buddy. Now let's get outta here. I hear the twins' mom a block away."

Ralph followed Dave downstairs and out the house. The two walked in silence for a minute until Dave suddenly stopped.

"Oops, I almost forgot. I have to go back," Dave turned around and started walking back toward the house. "There's something I gotta do."

"But their mom, she's going to be b-b-back any minute," Ralph pleaded.

"That's all right, buddy. I can take care of myself." Dave's ears went back to their giant size and he started gliding down the street toward the twins' house. He turned and called out from a distance, "Don't worry about me, Ralphie. I'll catch up to you later."

Chapter 34

Resolution 101

When the housekeeper swung down the metal rod, she connected with nothing but air. Shree could see that the woman was stunned. The housekeeper continued to stare behind the couch for a full minute, making sure she hadn't missed anyone. From her place of safety, Shree could see the woman's face getting redder and redder, and her pupils widening.

Thankfully, Shree, Eleanor, and Nancy had managed to crawl around the couch just as the metal rod came down. They sat perfectly still, huddled closely together on the opposite side. Shree knew that it was only a matter of time before the housekeeper walked around and discovered them.

Suddenly, Shree had an idea. She turned to Eleanor, pointed to her hands, and then turned and pointed to the far corner of the room.

Eleanor appeared confused at first, but seconds later she seemed to understand. Shaking her wrists as quietly as possible, Eleanor extended her arms across the room along the floor. When her hands finally reached the two glass statues that were located behind the grand piano, she pushed them off. The sound of shattered glass filled the room almost instantly.

The housekeeper shrieked and ran toward the piano. The girls took the opportunity and headed to the next room. Eleanor held onto Nancy while Shree followed closely.

Once they reached the second dining area, Shree let out a breath and gasped for another.

"That was way too close," Shree said. "Come on, let's go. Eleanor, go check that door over there. I'll take Nancy with me and check these two. Hurry."

Eleanor found the right door first. "It is over here. I can see the pool."

When Shree and the girls got to the double doors leading to the pool area, they could hear a *Northern State* rap song playing loudly. There were huge potted plants everywhere and a long marble bar running the length of the room. Colleen and Katherine, though, were nowhere to be found.

"You guys see anything?" Nancy asked.

"I don't," Shree said. "What about you, El?"

"There," Eleanor pointed out. "See that over there? I think that is the tanning room. Are those not their clothes hanging on the chairs?"

"You're right," Shree said. "And it looks like Dave was right, too. They took their clothes off. Boy, Nancy, I wish you still had your glasses. It'd be great if you could see if the key was there with Katherine's clothes."

"Yeah, me too," Nancy said.

"That is okay, I will find out for us," Eleanor said, shaking her wrist and instantly extending her arm and hand. She stretched until her hand was thin enough to squeeze through the space under the door and then she sent her hand over to the edge of the pool. For a minute it looked as if she was going to let her hand go swimming, but then she turned her arm to the right and extended it around the edge of the big blue water. Slowly, her hand crept along the floor until it got to the red-and-white striped lounge chairs, and then up to the seats where two small piles of clothes sat. One by one she picked up each piece of clothing.

Shree was about to burst with nervous energy. If they didn't find the key soon and get out of there, they might not get another chance. She could hear the housekeeper in the next room talking on the phone. Shree didn't need supernatural hearing to realize that she was calling the police. Now it was a matter of minutes before they needed to leave the house. Being arrested for breaking and entering would probably not go over well with her parents, regardless of whether they were there to steal back what was rightfully theirs.

Suddenly, Eleanor's hand picked up something and held it up. It was the key. She gave a big okay sign with her thumb and forefinger and then pulled back her hand the way it had come, several inches at a time.

Shree could hardly contain her excitement. When Eleanor's hand produced the key, Shree wrapped her arms around her. "You did it, El."

"Yeah, Eleanor. Great job," Nancy said. "Now let's get out of here."

Shree and Nancy turned to leave but were suddenly stopped by Eleanor, who had a last-minute request. "Wait girls, just one more thing." Eleanor shook her wrist again and extended her hand back to where it had just traveled. This time, though, her arm continued past the pile of clothes. Seconds later, her hand had reached its destination.

Shree understood right away what Eleanor was doing. As her friend's fingers wrapped around the tanning booth timer, Shree could see that Eleanor wanted to give Katherine and Colleen a little extra tanning time. Soon, Eleanor had wound the dial back a half-hour. A moment later, her arm was back to its original length.

"What did you just do, Eleanor?" Nancy asked.

"I am just giving the girls what they wanted," Eleanor said. "They wanted a tan, and that is what they are going to get."

Chapter 35

Making Amends

"Oh, good, here they are," Shree said. She put down her spoon and wiped her mouth with a napkin.

Ralph and Dave approached the girls' table, talking and laughing on the way. The school cafeteria was packed. When the boys sat down, Shree noticed a glint in Dave's eye. But what did it mean? What was he up to?

"Hey, guys," she said. "What's going on?"

"Not much. I was just telling Ralphie here that Barnes and Nobles had a sale this weekend. And I picked up a really cool book." Dave opened his backpack and took out the treasure book. "Not sure if it's any good, but I liked the cool maps in the back."

Shree was beyond words. "Dave, how did you find it?" She grabbed the book from Dave's hands. "When did you get it back?"

"Oh, we did some errands this weekend. Right, Ralph?" Dave winked over at Ralph.

"R-r-right," Ralph answered.

Shree flipped the pages to the map in the back and then looked up. "So that was what you were doing this weekend."

"Yup," Ralph said. "What about you? Did you get the k-k-key?"

Shree looked around to make sure none of the Demons were in the cafeteria. Once she was certain the coast was clear, she reached inside her pocket and pulled out the key.

"Great j-j-job, Shree," Ralph exclaimed.

"Well, it wasn't as easy as we'd hoped. Eleanor did most of the work," Shree said.

"Nice work, Eleanor. I wish we were t-t-there with you guys, but we had s-s-something else to do," Ralph said.

Shree wondered what he was talking about, but Dave interrupted her before she could ask any questions.

"Hey, you even kept Colleen's necklace," Dave said. "That's great, Shree. Welcome to burglar-hood."

Shree looked down in shock. "Oh, no. I totally didn't realize." She quickly separated the key from the necklace.

As soon as the key was off, Dave picked up the silver band from the table. "You know how much this is worth? We're not giving this back. If you don't want it, I know someone that does."

Before she could object, Shree noticed a sudden lull in the lunchroom conversation. She looked around and saw that everyone's eyes were fixed on the two figures entering the cafeteria.

Katherine and Colleen hobbled inside in short, slow steps. It was obvious that they were in a lot of pain. They were covered head to toe with a thick white cream. The few spots of skin that were free of lotion were all beet red.

It was difficult to contain her laughter, and yet Shree couldn't help feeling a bit guilty about the whole thing. She looked over at Eleanor and saw that she was feeling just as bad. Eleanor's hands covered her face and she was blushing.

"What the hell happened to them?" Dave asked. "Did someone paint them red, or did they spend the weekend roasting marshmallows too close to the fire?"

Shree answered, still staring. "Let's just say their tanning timer was mistakenly changed."

"You girls are bad, but I love it." Dave smiled and turned to Eleanor. "Don't worry about them, Ellie. It's just a bad sunburn. They'll get over it."

The Freaks looked at each other and then, all at once, they burst out laughing. And for the second time since she started Kennedy Academy, Shree felt like she was part of something bigger than herself.

Seconds later, the bell rang. The group walked together toward the exit. By this time, Katherine and Colleen had gone inside to get food, so the Freaks were in the clear.

Outside the cafeteria they said their goodbyes, splitting into two groups. Eleanor, Shree, and Nancy walked one way down the hall toward history class, while Ralph and Dave headed to their Spanish class on the opposite side.

After taking a couple of steps, Dave ran back to the girls. "Hey, Nance. Wait up."

"What do you want?" Nancy asked. "We're going to be late for class."

Dave opened his book bag and took out a small package gift-wrapped with brightly-colored birthday paper. He handed it to Nancy. "Consider this my way of saying I'm sorry." He then ran back to Ralph and caught up to him as he was turning the corner.

Shree was confused by Dave's gesture. It wasn't Nancy's birthday so Shree wasn't sure what Dave was up to. She watched Nancy carefully unwrap the package, squinting the entire time. When she finally finished opening the box, Nancy let out a sigh of delight.

"My glasses!" she cried, removing the ugly old frames and putting on the special ones: the ones that gave her the super-vision she'd been missing.

Even through the thick lenses, Shree could see tears starting to form on Nancy's face.

Nancy turned around to thank Dave, but he was already gone.

Shree walked home, enjoying the change in weather. A warm front was over Cambridge. She let her sense of smell guide her way. She closed her eyes and thought about how great life was at that particular moment. Things were now where they needed to be: Shree had the key, Nancy had her glasses, and they were once again on their way to finding the treasure.

The Freaks had all met after school, deciding that they needed to go after the treasure that coming weekend. They knew that the longer they waited, the more opportunity it gave the Demons to plan a counter-attack. Shree knew that Saturday night was the best time for them to go to the boathouse. She had done her research. The Harvard Crew team would be at an away meet at Dartmouth, and her parents had another faculty party. It was the perfect time.

Shree was about to open the gate to her house when she got the strangest sensation, like someone was staring at her. She swung around, but saw no one. She immediately looked up at Katherine's house. It was happening a lot lately, the strong feeling that Katherine was up there watching her. It was as if Shree could smell a different pheromone in the air, which somehow altered her current mood. She had convinced herself that she was just being paranoid, but it was worse than ever, that feeling that there were eyes studying her every movement.

Katherine now had every reason to get revenge for what Shree, Nancy and Eleanor had done to her. Shree knew that Katherine wasn't stupid and had probably figured out that the girls were responsible for stealing the key back.

Shree shook it off. Even if Katherine was watching her from her room, there was nothing at all that she'd see that could make any difference.

She lazed around the house after she let herself in. Her mother was out shopping and wouldn't be home for a while. Shree sat at the kitchen table and had a couple of honey granola bars for her snack, then brought a glass of apple juice upstairs with her. She had lots of homework, but was feeling far too excited after the honey granola bars to do much more than prepare for the treasure hunt.

Eleanor called just before dinner to say that Nancy and she had asked their parents about staying at Shree's house for another sleepover. Then Dave called to say that he and Ralph had made plans as well. Dave had told his mother he'd been invited to Ralph's overnight and Ralph had told his mother he'd been invited to Dave's. It was risky, but it was a chance they'd have to take.

Shree was beyond nervous. She knew this was it. This was the weekend the Freaks would find the treasure. But she also knew that there'd be major resistance from the Demons.

Chapter 36

A Sixth Sense

At first, Dave thought it was because he had wax in his ears. But when that turned out not to be the case, he had to wonder why he hadn't been picking up much activity. It had been quiet on the Demon front—much too quiet, if you asked him. The twins were having plenty of stupid conversations about plenty of stupid stuff, but it was all chatter and no substance. And it was all fine and good listening to Jason and Colleen making out every once in a while, but even that got boring fast.

The thing that really bothered Dave was the fact that Katherine had all but disappeared. It was totally suspicious. No more snide remarks, no more whispered conversations with Colleen, no more arguments with her dad. To Dave that meant one thing, and one thing only: the Demons were planning something big.

Having her glasses back on her nose where they belonged made Nancy the happiest girl in the world. Her parents had kept bugging her to get a new pair of glasses instead of wearing her really old ones, the ones with the heavy black frames, but she'd put them off time and time again. They still didn't understand why, of course. Because how could she tell them that the pair she'd "lost" had given her (and *only* her) the ability to see through walls? To see both far away and really close up?

Getting new glasses was never an option. She didn't think so. Not in this lifetime.

The last few days had been very strange, though. There was something that was really bothering her lately. Even though she could see through walls and into buildings—and sometimes, down stairs and around corners, the same as she could in the past—she was having this odd sense that she was missing something. It was almost like the people she was looking for knew she was looking, and they were staying out of her range of vision. Which was ridiculous, of course, because no one knew about her powers—except for the other Freaks. And they wouldn't say anything to anyone.

On the days Ralph's mother couldn't pick him up from school, Ralph walked home using the exact same route—past the Longy School of Music, past the Cambridge Commons, and through Harvard Square, where he often stopped for a piece of baklava at The Pita Shoppe.

The last few times he'd walked home, though, he'd felt his fin tickle. It only did that when it was trying to alert him to something, to let him know that something wasn't right. The problem was that he hadn't figured out what that was. There had been no more Demon attacks, which in and of itself was unusual.

So, what was it that made him feel so itchy, as if something was going to happen and Ralph could do nothing to stop it?

It was Eleanor's turn to do the chores, so when her parents went to sleep and her brothers went upstairs to play, she shook her wrists, extended both hands and, with one fell swoop, carried all the dishes from the dining room table to the dishwasher. She placed each dish in its rightful slot within seconds and then extended her forearm around the corner to grab the dishwasher detergent. After placing some in the tray, she turned the dishwasher on and walked back to the dining room.

She looked around the house and, again, with the skill of someone who'd had powers her entire life, cleaned the entire dining room table with a single stroke of her gigantic hand. She then placed all the leftover waste inside the trash bin. It was garbage day. On her way out the door, she thought it odd how the wind had finally died down despite it howling all throughout dinner. The night had suddenly grown quiet. When she dropped the garbage off at the corner and turned around to head back home, Eleanor stopped suddenly in the middle of her driveway. She didn't have secret hearing or powerful vision, but she did have the strange sensation that there was someone spying on her. She looked around, but it was cold and dark and she knew that part of the problem was the butterflies she felt in her stomach over the upcoming weekend's adventure.

Eleanor went back inside, completely oblivious to the two figures that hid on the other side of the fence, watching and waiting.

Chapter 37

Treasure Hunt

Finally, Saturday was upon her. For Shree it was one of the longest days of her entire life. She was so nervous she thought she'd jump right out of her skin. By the time her parents finally left for their faculty dinner, Shree was ready to push them out the door.

As soon as the door was closed, she rushed up to her room for her backpack and her Swiss army knife. When she got back to the kitchen, she added two flashlights, some rope, some duct tape, and several freshly-made honey granola bars from the jar on the counter. Then she went into the living room to wait for the others.

Shree reread the last journal entry of the treasure book. Sir Malcolm Winthrop had written about a series of challenges hidden deep inside the recesses of the boathouse. He kept on referring to the "four elements," but Shree still had no idea what this meant. She assumed that Winthrop was alluding to the "water, wind, fire, and earth" in John Harvard's poem, but what did it all mean? She was fairly certain that she'd find out once they got to the labyrinth underneath the boathouse; she just hoped that it wouldn't catch them by surprise.

She looked out the window. It was still light, but dusk was falling fast and Shree wanted to get ready. When six o'clock rolled around and the rest of the Freaks hadn't arrived, Shree started to pace. Where were they? Had something happened? Had Dave or Ralph's parents found out what they were planning to do? Ralph could be so easily scared. What if he told his mother?

By 6:15, Shree was a wreck, and thinking about calling Eleanor.

Then the bell rang.

Shree ran to the door and swung it open. Eleanor and Nancy were there, both of them in black jeans and black hooded sweatshirts, looking like cat burglars. Shree laughed and laughed, as much from relief as from the sight of them in their matching outfits. Mrs. Martinez gave the horn of her car two short beeps, waved, backed out of the driveway, and was gone.

"I was about to call you," Shree said. "What took you so long?"

"My brothers," Eleanor said. "We had to wait until my father got home to take care of them before we could leave."

"Where are Dave and Ralph?" Nancy asked.

"I have no idea," Shree said. "But if they don't get here soon, we're done for. We can't do this without them."

"I am sure they will be here," Eleanor said.

They were just turning to go back in the house when the boys arrived at the gate. Ralph looked guilty.

"He almost chickened out," Dave said pointing to Ralph. "I had to physically drag him out of his house."

"That's not t-t-true," Ralph protested. "It's just that I feel kind of b-b-bad lying like this."

"Ralph," Nancy said. "Desperate times call for desperate measures. When we find the treasure, I promise you'll feel better than you've ever felt in your life."

Shree couldn't have agreed more. "Come on in, everyone. Let's make sure we've got everything we need and then let's get going. There's no time to waste."

The quickest way down to the boathouse was a shortcut behind Harvard Square. The side streets in Cambridge were always pretty dark, but Dave knew the way and each held a flashlight in case they needed it. They had to walk in pairs because the sidewalks were so narrow. Shree was in front with Nancy, then Eleanor in the middle, and Dave and Ralph pulled up the rear. Shree wondered if the others were all as excited as she was. Her heart was beating much faster than usual and her stinger was acting up, as if it wanted to get in on the action. She looked over at Nancy, who was walking next to her, not saying a word, the streetlights reflecting off her huge glasses. Even Dave had gone quiet. It was unnerving to have the five of them together with no one talking.

Shree felt her chest for the hundredth time to make sure the secret key was still hanging on the chain around her neck. Ever since she had gotten it back from Colleen's house, she was afraid to let it out of her sight. It was old and rusty, and not the most comfortable thing to wear, but keeping it hidden was critical. Now the trick was finding what it opened. That is, if they ever figured out how to get into the boathouse, and then found where to go from there.

An owl hooted in a tree above Shree's head and she jumped a mile. They all laughed nervously. Ralph stopped in his tracks and didn't move until Dave took his arm and pulled him along.

As they moved down Eliot Street to Massachusetts Avenue, there was more light, and plenty of cars and pedestrians. One by one they switched off their flashlights and let out a big sigh of relief. Shree imagined all of them were pretty spooked, but nobody wanted to admit it.

"Dave?" Shree asked.

"Yeah?"

"Do you hear anything?"

"It's funny you ask," Dave said. "Lately I've heard nothing at all. I don't get it. I mean, the twins are talking about stupid stuff all the time, but, like, right now, they're really quiet. It doesn't make sense."

"What about Colleen and Katherine?" Eleanor asked.

"Same thing. Maybe they got into a fight or something," Dave said.

"I don't know," Nancy said. "It seems fishy to me."

"I agree. I guess all we can do is keep our ears open," Shree paused, smiled, and turned to Dave. "I mean *you* need to keep your ears open."

Dave wiggled his ears and smiled back.

As they waited for the light to change, Ralph moved closer to Shree.

"Shree?" His voice was almost a whisper.

"Yeah?"

"What's it like to b-b-be a bee?" Ralph asked.

"Well, I don't know how to describe it," Shree said. "I guess mostly it's just really cool. I get to fly around and see things I wouldn't ordinarily see. Plus, it's really heightened my senses. Why do you ask?"

"Well, d-d-do you ever not want to come back? You know, be human again?"

Shree almost tripped on the curb as the light changed and they started to cross the street. Why was Ralph talking about this now? What should she say? Should she tell him that she thought about that kind of thing all the time?

"Well, if you really want to know," Shree began.

Ralph nodded.

"I guess the answer is yes. Sometimes I just wish I could go on flying around and stay a bee forever. It'd be easier than some of this real-life stuff we have to deal with, you know what I mean?"

Ralph nodded again.

"But then I remember how much I really want to go home. I'd miss my family too much." Shree looked at Ralph. "And besides, bees aren't like whales. We have very short life spans."

Ralph didn't say anything the rest of the way, which left Shree wondering what was going on in his head.

Chapter 38

The Boathouse

Black knit hats pulled firmly down on their heads, the Freaks stepped off the sidewalk and onto the grass behind the boathouse. Suddenly, it was dark again, although the traffic whizzing by was a reminder of just how close to civilization they really were. Shree had looked over her shoulder the whole way; she had seen nothing out of the ordinary, but her nerves were still frayed.

Shree knew she wasn't the only one feeling edgy. At one point, Nancy had whipped her head around as if she'd seen something, but then shook her head no. Then Dave had done the same thing a couple of times, as if he had antennae that were picking up on some unknown frequency. It was disconcerting, and by the time they reached the vicinity of the boathouse, Shree was as tense as a bee under a swinging flyswatter. She forced herself to take a couple of deep breaths and told herself to stay calm. If she didn't, she might transform when she didn't want to, and that wasn't part of the plan.

Slowly, in single file, Shree and the others made their way down the right side of the Weld Boathouse facing the river. They stuck pretty close together, except for the spots where bushes and rocks got in the way. As they approached the water Shree could hear the sound of the Charles River lapping against the shore.

Shree felt Ralph tense behind her. Was it the proximity to the water? She turned around to ask if he was okay, but all of a sudden he was peeling off from the group.

"Hey, Ralph," Shree said in a loud whisper. "Where are you going?"

"I'll b-b-be right back." Seconds later, Ralph had disappeared into the darkness of the night.

Shree looked at the others. "Where'd he go?"

"I am not sure," Eleanor answered. "He has been acting very strange."

"Dave? Do you think Ralph's okay?" Shree asked.

Dave shrugged. "He's fine. He was nervous, I know that. But he also likes the water. Maybe he went for a dip."

Shree started feeling dizzy and nauseous. Her sense of smell was telling her something bad was about to happen, but she didn't know what. She was picking up a different pheromone in the air that didn't quite agree with her. And now Ralph had disappeared.

"Anyway," Dave continued. "We're almost there."

Sure enough, they had reached the corner of the building. There was a long ramp that led to the front doors. Still in single file, Shree and the remaining Freaks plastered themselves against the side of the wall and moved towards the doors at a snail's pace.

Dave reached out and stretched his hand across Shree's shoulder before she could walk any further.

"What's the matter?" Shree asked.

"I think I hear something," Dave said. "Wait a minute."

Shree stood in place for a moment, listening to the creaking of the wooden boards and the lapping of the water, until Dave finally said, "I could've sworn I heard something."

Nancy and Eleanor both let out a collective breath, and continued onward following Dave and Shree. Finally, they all reached the main door.

"Nancy? Can you see anything in there?" Shree asked. The moon was about half full and it was a partly cloudy night. If they were lucky, there'd be some light shining through the windows of the boathouse.

Nancy approached the thick, wooden double doors, and placed her face close to them. "All I can see is a big, empty space—except for a bunch of boats hanging on the walls."

"Do you see the doors to the other rooms?" Shree asked.

"Well, it's hard to make anything out, but I think so. In the back," Nancy answered.

"Come on," Dave said. "Shree, try the door already."

"Okay, okay," Shree said. But she put her hand on the solid wooden handle and gave it a little shake. "It's locked."

Of course she knew it would be, but still it made her slump with disappointment.

"What are we going to do now?" Eleanor asked.

"I brought some stuff," Shree said. "We're going to have to—"

She stopped speaking when she heard a loud noise from inside the boathouse. Shree's hand went to her heart, which was pounding so hard she swore it had left her chest. "What was that?"

"I don't know," Dave said, "but whatever it was made a huge splash."

For a minute Shree stood listening, but an eerie quiet had fallen. The waves continued to lap at the shore and the groans of the old building in the water were the only sounds she heard.

Shree was closest to the entrance, so she was almost hit in the chest when the wooden doors suddenly swung open. Crying out, she dodged the door by jumping back. She stumbled to the edge of the pier and then lost her footing.

Eleanor quickly reached her arm out just in time to keep Shree from falling into the water.

Then a voice came out of the darkness.

"Hi, guys. What t-t-took you so long?"

Chapter 39

A Shaky Foundation

It was Ralph. He appeared from the darkness drenched in water, and beaming with pride.

"Ralph, how'd you get in there?" Nancy asked.

"I swam under the b-b-boathouse."

Shree stared at Ralph as if he'd appeared from thin air.

"But why didn't you tell us?" Nancy demanded.

Ralph's smile disappeared. He looked apologetic. "It's just that w-w-when I get near the water I get so excited. I can't help it. It's been so long, with the c-c-cold weather and all. I just couldn't stop myself."

"Well, I have to say, Ralph, that was an amazing trick. But next time, please let us know what's going on. We didn't know where you were," Shree said.

Ralph nodded, and looked down.

"But for now," Shree said, "thanks to Ralph, we're in."

Ralph looked up and smiled again. He held the doors open while Shree and the rest of the group filed into the boathouse. It was pitch black until they closed the doors and turned on their flashlights.

"Careful," Ralph said, pointing down. "You have to w-w-walk up the middle on this ramp, or else you'll fall into the water on either side."

Ralph was right. A narrow ramp about two feet in width was the only thing keeping their feet—and the rest of them—from the water below.

Shree shivered. She knew how to swim, but the Bronx pool was the closest she'd come to the water in a long, long time, and she didn't intend on testing her abilities any time soon, especially not in the cold black depths beneath her feet.

As if on cue, they all began to move forward and up the ramp. At the other end, the beams of their flashlights showed rowboats, kayaks, and sculls hanging from the ceiling and along the walls. Shree aimed her light against the back wall. Two doors were barely visible in the relative dimness.

"There," she said. "Let's try the one on the right first."

"I think we should split up," Dave said. "Try them both at the same time."

Shree hated the idea of splitting up, even for something so apparently easy as this. But Dave was right. They'd wasted enough time already.

Shree nodded, and moved off to the door on the right with Nancy and Ralph at her side. She turned the knob, and the door opened with a loud creak. Shree walked in first, placing her feet carefully on the ramp with each step.

Soon she realized that the room was a continuation of the first. Again, there was water on either side to bring the boats in.

Shree called out. "Dave, did you find anything?"

In a minute a whisper came back. "Nothing yet. It's like the other room. You?"

"Yeah, the same thing. We're moving to the back."

Shree stepped over the ramp carefully, with Nancy and Ralph following closely behind her. Life jackets of all sizes were hanging on the walls in long columns. There had to be hundreds of them. It smelled musty, like old sofas.

Shree had just remarked on that to the others when they heard Dave calling to them. "It smells like old sofas in here."

Shree, Nancy and Ralph had to laugh.

"We are moving to the back. There are oars and paddles everywhere," Eleanor said. "Piles of canvas, too."

"Same here," Shree said, shining her light into a corner that revealed a ten-foot-high stack of white canvas sheets, probably sails for the sailboats.

They walked a little farther down. The ramp finally gave way to a larger room with solid flooring and no water underneath. Shree was relieved to be away from the water, even if she could still hear the lapping sound nearby.

"Look," Nancy said pointing to the back of the room. "The floor is different over there. I can't see anything underneath it."

"That doesn't make sense," Shree said. "There has to be ground under there. We've walked all the way to the back of the building."

"I'm telling you, there's nothing." Nancy said.

"Guys, can you hear me?"

It was Eleanor from the other room.

"Yeah, we hear you," Shree replied.

"We found something—or, well, Dave found something. The floor in here is funny. It does not sound the same when you walk on it."

"That's amazing," Shree said. "It's the same in here."

"I'm not sure, but I think this must be where we enter the tunnels underground," Nancy said. "The flooring in that corner of the room looks hollow. There's got to be a cave or hole or something that will lead us down."

"What do you think, Dave?" Shree asked.

"I can't hear anything coming from under here—not even water. And it doesn't sound as dense as solid ground. I think Nancy's right," Dave said.

"Well," Shree said. "There's only one way to find out."

After ten minutes of searching, the Freaks were frustrated and dirty. Shree and the others hadn't found a way to gain entrance into the tunnel—not through a loose floorboard nor through a secret hatch.

"Nothing," Shree said. "What should we do now?"

"I don't know," Dave said. "There's nothing here either."

Shree kneeled on the floor. She was in dire need of energy if she was going to continue. She reached into her backpack and took out a honey granola bar. Ralph and Nancy split one in half and started chewing. Eleanor and Dave kept searching the flooring and the walls for clues.

Shree pulled out a second granola bar. Stuck to it was Harvard's note, which she had wrapped in plastic to keep it from getting ruined. After eating the bar quickly, Shree read the note to herself.

"Listen, you guys. There's got to be a hint in here somewhere." She reread the poem. When she finished the fourth stanza, she looked up and spoke: "The cross shall mark the rightful site." She paused a moment. "That's it." Shree jumped up.

"What is it?" Eleanor asked.

"The cross shall mark the rightful site, where eyes shall feast with all delight." She looked up from the note. "That has to mean under this ramp—or the one in the other room—between the water and the wood. It's the physical barrier that divides two of the four elements."

When Shree looked up, she saw four puzzled faces staring at her. "You see, Harvard's note talks about water, fire, wind and earth. Do you guys remember learning about the ancient Greeks in middle school? To them, all matter was composed of these four elements. In fact, they considered these elements more than just physical things. The Greeks thought each element also had some kind of spiritual power."

"What does that have to do with anything?" Dave asked.

"I'm not sure, but I think the entrance to the tunnels has to be somewhere between water and earth. It's got to be somewhere that either divides or crosses these two elements." Shree paused and turned back to the ramp. "Ralph, shine your light over there. Let's see if we can see anything, any kind of writing or drawing. Dave, you and Eleanor do the same on the opposite side. Nancy, focus your glasses on the wall dividing the two rooms."

Working their way backwards, Shree and Ralph moved their flashlights back and forth across the planks of old wood on the opposite wall. Although the boathouse was old, it had been kept in immaculate condition, and the wood was shiny from layers of shellac.

"Look," Shree said pointing to the far wall. She was about a foot from the end of the ramp, right where it met the water. "It's some kind of reddish paint." She shifted her flashlight from right to left, lighting different sections of the wall at a time. The largest of the two-person sculls hung in perfect symmetry on the wall, suspended firmly by two wooden planks.

"Yeah, you can tell that a section of that wall is painted a different color. From above and below, and from right and left," Nancy said.

Eleanor and Dave came running.

"What is it?" Eleanor asked.

"What's going on?" Dave asked.

"I think, well, yes, it could be." Nancy continued to stare at the wall. Shree could see thousands of images flashing at lightning speed from Nancy's glasses, again giving Shree the impression that she was fast-forwarding a movie.

"W-w-what is it?" Ralph asked.

"It's a crimson cross," Nancy exclaimed. "Look, the red paint is in the form of a cross. You guys can't see it because that boat is right in the center of the cross, and all the life jackets on the wall block the four corners. But…" Nancy paused and pressed her glasses closer to her face. "It's definitely a cross."

"Shine your flashlights at the same spot in the middle of the wall. Nancy, see if there's anything behind that scull. Maybe in the middle of the cross," Shree said.

At her request, Ralph, Eleanor and Dave pointed their flashlights at the same spot on the opposite wall. The Freaks were huddled together. Only the narrow stream of water, about two feet wide, stood between them and the wall.

Minutes passed before Shree heard anything from Nancy. She noticed that Nancy was having a hard time seeing through the wall. She held onto her glasses tightly and squinted.

Shree was deep in thought, wondering if she had missed something. They had found the cross, so now she figured they'd find a door or some kind of portal that would lead them underground. But there was nothing. Not a door nor entry into the next labyrinth.

And that's when Shree figured it out. She shifted her own beam of light from the wall to the water below. "Ralph, didn't you say you saw a statue of a bear's claw underwater?"

"Yeah, it's right under the b-b-boathouse. Actually, it's right under that wall. I just swam b-b-by it," Ralph said.

"Nancy, look underwater," Shree said. "I bet you the portal is right under that wall with the cross. That's where you and Dave think it's hollow. I bet you we'll find something there."

Soon, Nancy found the entryway, hidden behind a marble arch that was covered in algae. She pointed to a dark blue mass somewhere in the murkiness of water.

"It's right there. I can see a large portal with a lock and everything."

"So what d-d-do we do now?" Ralph asked.

Shree removed her necklace and detached the secret key. "Well, there's only one thing to do. Let's open that portal and see what happens." Shree turned to Eleanor. "Care to do the honors?"

Eleanor grabbed the key and smiled. "It would be my pleasure."

Shaking her hand at the wrist, Eleanor attempted to extend one of her arms towards the marble portal, but stopped as soon as her fingers touched the water. "Brrr, it is freezing."

She pulled back instantly, took a deep breath, and then sent her hand underwater again, aiming toward the direction where Nancy was pointing. Eleanor struggled to locate the lock, but when she finally found it, she let out a huge sigh of relief.

"Okay, here goes nothing. I am going to put the key inside. Is everybody ready?" Eleanor asked.

"Ready," Shree replied and crossed her fingers tightly.

"Okay, here I go," and Eleanor turned the key.

Nothing happened at first.

But seconds later, the Freaks were fighting for their lives.

Chapter 40

A Subterranean World

All at once there was chaos. A plank of wood began to slide out from under Shree, retracting into the floor and separating the ramp from its wooden fittings on either side. A huge wrenching sound could be heard, as if the world were tearing in two. Then Shree heard the sound of wood splitting apart, and doors being ripped from their hinges. It came from all around the Freaks, from behind them, beneath them, and at their feet.

Shree began to slide down as the floor gave way. Trying to hang on, she let go of her flashlight, which fell into the water with a splash.

When the plank had receded all the way into the flooring, the ramp had nothing to keep it in place. For one surreal moment, it hung suspended in the air above the water, as if it had been levitated there, as if it didn't realize there was nothing to hold it up anymore. And then, it fell straight down into the dark water, and along went Shree with it.

She tried taking a breath before being engulfed in the coldness of the water, but she dropped too quickly. Instead of air, she inhaled a cupful of saltwater. She coughed and struggled to come back up for air, but she kept getting knocked against the wall and dragged down by a strong current from underneath.

As she slid into the moat of water and wood, Shree frantically attempted to grab hold of something—anything—with her arms and legs. But it was too late.

Plunging ever deeper into the abyss, the icy coldness of the water paralyzed Shree's muscles, preventing her from out-swimming the force that pulled her from below. As she was dragged, she suddenly realized what had happened: when the underwater portal opened, water had rushed inside the underground room, exerting downward pressure on the ramp she was standing on and causing her to fall in.

Shree stopped fighting and allowed herself to be dragged by the current. The exertion was too much for her; there was nothing she could do. She drifted into unconsciousness as the oxygen reaching her brain slowly dwindled to nothing.

Moments later, Shree felt another force, this one pulling her from the opposite direction. She felt something smooth gliding underneath and then lifting her quickly back up to the surface.

It was Ralph. He had transformed into a small humpback whale. Despite his orcan features, Shree could recognize his smile. Ralph placed her carefully onto the wooden floor, and then disappeared.

"Quick, we need to warm her up. She's freezing," Nancy called.

Eleanor shook her hands and sent them across the boathouse. Seconds later, they brought back a pile of canvas. Soon Shree was wrapped tightly in several makeshift blankets.

Shree thought she'd never get warm. "What do you think happened?" Shree asked, shivering uncontrollably.

"I think that when Eleanor turned the key, the whole place fell apart," Nancy said.

"I wonder if that is what was supposed to happen," Eleanor said.

Dave pointed to the opposite corner. "It looks like that's exactly what was supposed to happen. Check it out."

Shree turned and saw what Dave was talking about. Part of the wall had opened up. It revealed a narrow passageway.

At that moment, Ralph showed up. He was drenched from head to toe.

"Ralph, are you okay?" Nancy asked.

"I'm f-f-fine. Are you okay, Shree?"

"Yeah," Shree smiled. "Thanks for saving me."

Ralph blushed. "No p-p-problem."

Shree felt a sudden jolt of energy. Ignoring the muscle cramps in her arms and legs, she unwrapped herself from the canvas and stood up. "Let's get that treasure, guys."

Despite the pain, Shree led the group inside the entrance. Eleanor had to bend down and walk awkwardly, crouching to prevent her head from hitting the low ceiling.

Dave, Ralph, and Nancy walked closely behind her. After making it a short distance down the narrow path, Shree hit a dead end. In the ground, though, was a large hole.

"Nancy, can you check out what's underneath?" Shree asked.

Nancy walked over and stared down. "It's deep, but it's totally do-able. We can definitely climb down."

"Well, I can't see as well as Nancy, but I do know one thing. There are rats in there. Dozens of them. And, as you guys know, if there's one thing I hate, it's rats," Dave said.

Shree took out the rope from her bag and started tying it around a wooden column nearby. "Well, Dave, you're just going to have to be a man and suck it up. You're not scared of a few furry rats, are you?"

"I didn't say I was scared. I just hate them." Dave walked up to Shree and took the rope from her.

"Ladies first," Shree said, grabbing the rope back from Dave. "I'll go down first with Nancy and Eleanor, and yell out to you when we hit bottom."

Not waiting for Dave to agree, Shree plunged down into the darkness.

Chapter 41

Unlocking Doors

"Shree? Nancy? Eleanor? W-w-where are you?" Ralph called out from a short distance away.

"We're over here," Shree answered. "Keep walking. Just hang onto the rope and follow it. You'll never believe what we found."

"Wait, wait, we're coming. Ouch, Ralph," Dave said. "Back off, dude. You just stepped on my heel."

"Oh, s-s-sorry, Dave," Ralph said.

"We're almost there. Stay cool," Dave said. "Hey, Shree, shine your light so we can see where you are."

Shree waved her flashlight in their direction.

"We see it," Dave said. "We're coming."

Shree saw Dave and Ralph turn the corner. She stood with Eleanor and Nancy just past a small space, a cave of sorts, lined with stones. Once they walked through the narrow passage, Dave and Ralph joined the girls inside a larger cave. Shree stood at the far end. In front of her was a door.

"What's going on?" Dave asked.

"We found one of the doors from Harvard's note," Shree said. "It's marked with a Roman numeral I."

"So what's the problem? Let's get going." Dave grabbed the door handle.

"Stop!" Eleanor exclaimed.

"Why? What's wrong?" Dave asked.

"Harvard's note specifically said that we need to be careful," Shree said.

Dave took a couple of steps back. "So what do we do now?"

"Nancy was trying to see behind the door before you guys got here," Shree explained.

"Yeah," Nancy said. "But it's pretty dark inside. It just looks like an empty room."

"All right, let's open the door then," Dave said.

Shree looked at Eleanor. "Do you still have the key?"

Eleanor pulled it out of her pocket and handed it to Shree.

"But what if something else happens? We almost lost you, Shree, when we unlocked the underwater portal," Eleanor said.

"Well, we came here for the treasure, so we'll just have to be careful." Shree turned and faced the door. "Okay, then. Let's see what's behind Door I."

The door was about four feet high, its latch a large rectangle of wood with a big keyhole. Shree placed the key inside the lock.

Suddenly, the latch shifted down where Shree's hand had been leaning. The crossbar swung upwards. Behind her, the rest of the Freaks gasped.

But nothing happened. The silence was deafening.

Shree waited until her heart stopped pounding before addressing the group. "No problems so far. What do you guys say we go in?"

"Wait, Shree. I have a bad feeling about this," Eleanor said. She looked more frightened than Shree had ever seen her.

"Don't worry about it, Ellie. We're together and we got powers. Nothing's gonna happen," Dave started for the door.

"Wait, Dave. If Eleanor's concerned, we should at least take a vote." Shree turned to Nancy and Ralph. "Who thinks we should go in, and who thinks we should wait and try to figure out what may be waiting for us?"

"I vote for going in," Nancy said, turning to Dave and smiling.

"Ralph? How about you?" Shree asked.

"Well, I guess, um, I—" Ralph faltered.

"Ralph, make a decision. We don't have all day," Dave said.

"Okay, I'm s-s-sorry. I say, we w-w-wait."

"Well, Shree, I guess it's up to you, then," Dave said. "What's your vote?"

Shree felt pulled in both directions. She desperately wanted to see what was behind the door, but she also felt her back aching, almost as if her stinger was trying to warn her about something.

She looked at her friends. They were all waiting for her decision. If she chose right, they could be rich in a minute. More importantly, she'd find out what Katherine meant about the treasure being bigger than she could imagine. If she chose wrong, though, they could wind up dead. She shook her head, as if to expel any uncertainty. She'd made up her mind.

"Well, I guess if we stay together, we could always run back if something happens, right?" Shree looked at the others.

"Right," Dave said. "Okay, here we go."

There was a collective drawing in of breaths as Shree put both hands on the door handle and started to pull. She heard an eerie creak and saw some tiny pebbles raining down from the inch-wide opening. A puff of dirt landed at Shree's feet. She stopped pulling and the movement ceased.

Shree raised her eyebrows and gave another little pull. More dirt and pebbles came tumbling down, but again stopped after a few seconds. She waited and then gave a third pull until the door was about six inches open. At that point pebbles and dirt began to pour out through the crevice, as if it had all been pushed up against the back of the door and couldn't wait to get out. Then they heard a faint sound. It was far away and vague, like something heard inside a seashell.

Dave cocked his head. Then his eyes got huge.

Shree might have ignored him if the expression on his face wasn't so terrifying.

"Dave. What is it? What's that noise?" Shree asked.

It was getting louder.

Dave opened his mouth to speak, but nothing came out.

Nancy said, "It's water. Dave, it's water, right? We're about to be—"

That's when Shree knew she'd made the wrong decision.

Chapter 42

Water

Water rushed through the opening so fast that the door flung open and hit Dave straight in the chest, propelling him across the room. He hit his head on a boulder on the opposite wall, making him moan in agony. Blood began to trickle from a small cut just below his eyebrow.

"Dave," Shree ran over to him. He looked dazed, kneeling on the floor and holding his head with his hand. The water was filling the little cavity around them at an alarming rate. It wouldn't be long before the tunnels flooded and they'd be nothing more than fish food.

Shree turned to run back the way they'd come in. "We have to get out of here," she yelled over the sound of rushing water. "Nancy, come on, take my hand. Ralph and Eleanor, go help Dave. Hurry."

Dave was shaken up, but luckily he hadn't lost consciousness. Ralph took one arm and Eleanor took the other, and together they attempted to steer him out of the room and back into the passageway.

Nancy reached out to take Shree's hand, but tripped over the backpack Dave had left on the ground. She landed in the mud, her glasses flying off her face.

Shree reached for the glasses, but as she went to grab them, she saw Eleanor's long hand jutting out past hers at lightning speed. Eleanor caught Nancy's glasses right before they hit the stone floor.

With the water now up to their calves, the Freaks waded into the passageway, following the rope Dave had left as a guide. Unfortunately, after only a few steps, Shree noticed that the rope was now floating in the water and useless to lead them anywhere. They'd have to find their own way back—and if they didn't do it fast, they'd be in big trouble.

Shree turned around and saw that Ralph had disappeared. Eleanor was having a hard time dragging Dave through the muck and water. Shree ran over to help her. Dave felt incredibly heavy.

Where had Ralph gone? He was supposed to be helping. She looked back, but they'd turned the corner and Ralph was nowhere to be seen. Shree called out to Nancy, who was a few feet in front of her. "Nancy? Do you know where Ralph is?"

"No, isn't he with you?" Nancy's voice sounded compacted and small, as if she were in a coffin.

Shree was about to yell for Ralph when she noticed that the water level was no longer rising.

"Hey. Nancy, El, check it out. The water stopped flowing," Shree said.

"You are right," Eleanor said. "But why?"

"I don't know. Listen, I'm going back to see what's going on with Ralph," Shree said. "Nancy, come back here and stay with Dave."

Nancy waded back and stood with Dave, propping him up in her arms. Shree turned and headed back through the tunnels toward Door I. Moments later, she was standing with her mouth gaping. There, blocking the doorway to the room she had just unlocked, was Ralph. He'd transformed into a whale and was blocking the doorway with his massive body. All on his own, he was keeping the water from flooding the tunnels.

"Ralph, are you okay?" Shree asked, feeling odd that she was speaking to a whale.

Ralph squealed and nodded his giant head repeatedly. Shree stared at Ralph in amazement before heading back.

When she reached the others, Dave was already awake and talking.

"Okay, guys. I totally understand if you want to stop searching and head back," Shree said.

"No way we're stopping now," Dave said, forcing himself to sit up.

"I agree. We've come too far." Nancy stared at the far end of the tunnels. She pushed her glasses closer to her face. "And I know exactly where Door II is."

"Are you sure?" Shree asked.

"Yes, it's right around the corner," Nancy said.

"Well, what're we waiting for?" Dave expanded his ears and flapped them repeatedly. Seconds later, his body hovered above ground. He shook the water from his pant legs, and glided straight down the tunnel at full speed toward the direction where Nancy was pointing.

Shree followed Dave, with Nancy and Eleanor close behind her. While she walked, she considered their current situation. She was lucky to be alive after almost drowning twice. And now they were heading to another door, likely leading to another life-threatening trap. Was the treasure worth her life and that of her friends?

This was not the first time the thought had crossed her mind. She was not materialistic, so whatever jewels and gold they discovered were certainly not worth the risk. Neither was the challenge of uncovering this legendary treasure, Shree grasped that now. Maybe it took nearly dying to realize it, but Shree finally understood the true source of her motivation. Something had been nagging her ever since Halloween night. What had Katherine meant about the treasure being bigger than Shree imagined? This was plaguing Shree, and she knew she wouldn't be able to rest until she found out.

"Hey, I hear Ralph. It sounds like he's using his blowhole to expel the water from the tunnel. That guy is awesome," Dave smiled and turned back to the girls. He stood in front of Door II.

Shree was brought back to the present. She needed to be focused if they were going to survive. She looked down at the floor and realized that Dave was right—the water level was now down to her ankle and was steadily falling.

"All right, let's do it." Dave tried opening the door, but it was locked. "You'll have to use the key, Shree. Hopefully, our boy Harvard used the same lock."

Shree had placed the key back around her neck, so she took her necklace off and gave it to Dave.

Dave turned the key slowly. With a high-pitched creaking sound, the ancient lock released its hold and the door opened.

Shree hesitated before walking inside. The room looked empty and ordinary—apart from the walls. These were oddly smooth, except for dozens of very thin horizontal lines etched onto the stone surface. The lines were in random batches on all four-walls. On closer inspection, they were arranged in groups of four, and each was parallel to the other. The walls they were etched on were shiny, and Shree noticed that she could see her own reflection on the rock surface.

She couldn't imagine the treasure being hidden in that room. There was nothing inside; it looked completely deserted. Shree started to second-guess herself about the existence of the treasure. Then, again, they had survived what was behind Door I and were still alive to tell about it.

The air crackled with a new scent and Shree felt goose bumps running all the way up her arms.

Nancy scanned the room and repeated aloud what Shree was thinking. "The walls look very peculiar. They're pretty uniform, but the markings are so strange."

Shree turned to Dave, who wasn't saying anything. He had his head cocked to one side, a puzzled look on his face. "What about you, Dave? Do you hear anything?"

"I'm not sure." Dave spoke slowly and wrapped one hand around his ear, as if he were attempting to catch every audible tone inside the small room. "I hear a low frequency hum, almost a whistle. It's coming from that corner. It's weird, but whatever it is, it's getting more and more intense."

Suddenly, the door slammed shut behind them.

Shree turned around and tried to figure out what had made the door close by itself.

In a matter of seconds, she knew.

At first, it was a light breeze that made Shree and the others shiver. Soon the wind picked up and before long, Shree and her friends were being elevated above the ground by an invisible force. And then, one by one, they were thrown against the opposite wall with a sudden thrust.

Shree felt her body being forced to spin in circles as the wind intensified inside the small chamber.

It was like the room had suddenly been hit by a tornado, and the Freaks were in the middle of a terrifying and unpredictable storm.

Chapter 43

Wind

"Whaaaaaaat's goooooooing oooooooon?" Shree yelled. She was pinned up against the wall by the vacuum created from the indoor tornado. The others were stuck in opposite corners, each Freak grabbing a wall on either side for stability. But it was no use. The walls were too smooth to provide support. Soon Shree was using her hands to try and steady herself against the winds' force. In a moment of terror, she figured out how the deep parallel lines along the walls had been made—gouged out by who knows how many people's fingernails.

As the wind picked up, Shree was forced to travel counterclockwise around the room. Despite her effort to stand in place in the corner, she was no match for the wind that originated from somewhere above the chamber. None of them were.

"It's a wind tunnel. When we walked in we must've triggered the opening of a vent on the ceiling," Shree shouted, pointing up and trying to make herself heard over the roar of the wind. "That's what's creating the vacuum that we're experiencing. I don't see a way out of this."

"You mean we're going to die," Nancy yelled as she was tossed around the room at an alarming speed. As the smallest and lightest among them, the wind was flinging Nancy about as if she were a crumpled leaf on a winter's day.

The third time Nancy flew around the room, Eleanor extended her hand and caught her in mid-air. She then recoiled her arm quickly, bringing Nancy tightly toward her and away from the wind.

"Nancy," Shree asked. "Can you see which corner of the room the wind's coming from? Maybe Eleanor could try to plug it by extending her hands and covering the hole." It was a long shot, Shree thought, but Ralph had been able to block the water with his body. This could be their only hope.

Nancy held on to her glasses with both hands as Eleanor's arm wrapped around her tiny frame several times. Shree wondered how Nancy could possibly see anything inside the room. The wind was causing dust to pick up. Shree had to squint and put her hands in front of her in order to see anything.

"It's that one over there." Nancy pointed to the farthest corner of the room.

A sudden gust tore Shree from the corner and spun her rapidly around. The room vanished from Shree's sight as she circled the chamber at lightning speed. She bounced from corner to corner, the blurred image of her three friends whizzing past her.

But just as suddenly, Shree found herself enveloped in what felt like a sheet or membrane of thin skin. She could feel the wind vibrating over her, but she was safe. When she opened her eyes, Dave was next to her. She looked around and realized what that membrane was; Dave had grown and expanded his ears to cover both their bodies. Shree could see small arteries pulsing their bright red blood as Dave struggled to use his ears as refuge for both of them.

Through a sliver of open space between Dave's ears, Shree saw that one of Eleanor's arms wrapped around Nancy and held the doorknob as an anchor, while the other extended toward the ceiling along the wall. It traveled with the wind, lengthening and stretching like a rubber band under tension.

It seemed like forever until Eleanor's hand reached the vent. But when it did, Shree no longer felt the wind. Dave's ears rose and Shree came out of her skin shelter, happy to be alive. Dave held his ears with his hands and rubbed them repeatedly. Slowly, his ears shrank back to their original size.

The room was quiet. On the opposite side of Shree stood Eleanor, holding onto Nancy. One of her arms was stretched to the ceiling. Shree followed it until she saw Eleanor's left hand plugging the hole where the wind had originated. Shree could tell that her friend was struggling hard to keep her hand in place.

On the adjacent corner of the ceiling, there was a large opening. This must be where they would've ended up if it wasn't for Eleanor.

"Quick, let's get out of here," Shree said, taking hold of Nancy and racing to the door.

"I will keep my hand in place to cover the hole," Eleanor said. "Let us all leave the room. When we are a safe distance away, I will pull back my arm quickly. Dave, you close the door as soon as you see my hand come out."

Eleanor opened the door and allowed Shree, Dave, and Nancy to step out first before she ran out herself. Once they were all a safe distance away, she pulled her arm back to her body. Dave closed the door just as Eleanor's fingers slipped by.

Shree heard the wind picking up again and saw the door shaking violently. The Freaks had narrowly escaped the trap, unharmed once again.

Chapter 44

Fire

"That was way too close," Shree gasped, still trying to catch her breath.

"Yes, and if there are any more surprises like this, I have a feeling we may not be as lucky," Eleanor said, rubbing her arms.

"What's next?" Dave asked.

"Well, we've encountered water and wind," Nancy said, "so the next element we'll face is—"

"Fire," Shree said. "And unless one of you guys has the ability to put flames out, I think we should stop here and cut our losses." Shree was now rethinking everything. Finding out what Katherine meant about the treasure was no longer worth the risk.

"Well, I'm going on with or without you guys. Come on, we can do this," Dave said.

Shree could tell that he wasn't planning on backing down. He started to walk down the narrow passage, compelling Shree and the rest of the girls to follow. Shree didn't want to admit it, but she was glad that Dave was the one rallying the group to continue.

Several minutes later, Shree, Dave, Nancy and Eleanor stood in front of Door III.

"Shree, hand over the key," Dave said.

Shree stared at the door. "I'm not sure if the key will help us open this one. Check it out. This lock looks completely different from the other two."

"Skeleton keys aren't as lock-specific as regular keys, so it should work," Dave said.

Shree gave the key to Dave. He was persistent, and she *did* want to find the treasure, despite having had second thoughts about it.

Dave placed the metal inside the lock and turned it. To Shree's surprise, the key fit perfectly.

Dave opened the door a crack and turned around. "Are you guys gonna stand there, or are you coming with me?"

Shree took a few steps, but then stopped. The pungent odor from inside the room hit her almost instantly. She felt nauseated. She couldn't tell exactly what it was that made her feel the way she did. For some reason, though, the others didn't seem to notice the fumes emanating from the chamber.

"Guys, don't take another step. There's got to be a reason why this next challenge is fire. I smell something funny, and I don't like it one bit." Shree felt a series of sharp pangs in her lower back, almost as if the bee inside was trying to warn her of potential trouble.

Nancy walked back to where Shree was standing and scanned the room. "Dave, shine your flashlight over there." Nancy pointed to a spot on the floor inside the chamber.

Shree and the others stood behind as Nancy adjusted her glasses and stared into the darkness. Shree couldn't see a thing until Dave aimed his flashlight at an unidentified mass located in the middle of the room.

Nancy gasped right away, but didn't say anything. At once, Dave ran inside with the flashlight. Even with the light shining, it was difficult for Shree to make sense of what was inside the room. It wasn't until Dave picked up one of the objects on the floor and held it up in the air that Shree realized what they'd encountered.

"What is that?" Eleanor asked, hiding her face behind her hands after seeing the grotesque-looking thing Dave was holding.

Dave brought the object close to his face for a better look. "It's a human skull."

"What is it doing here?" Eleanor spread her fingers slightly and peeked through before shutting her eyes again in horror.

Shree was deep in thought. It was a distinct smell that permeated the room. She closed her eyes and concentrated on the uniqueness of the odor she was now attempting to identify.

"That's it," she exclaimed. "It's kerosene." Shree aimed her flashlight at the other objects in the middle of the room. "And those are the remains of past treasure hunters. It makes total sense now. Back then these guys didn't have flashlights. They used flaming torches. When they walked inside this room, the torches must've started a fire because

John Harvard had covered the entire room with kerosene. And that's how these guys died: they were consumed by their own light."

Nancy focused her eyesight at the pile again, then turned and stared at the skull Dave held in his hands. "I think you're right. I'm glad we brought flashlights and not torches."

Shree and the others left the room in a hurry and gathered just outside the door.

"So, what do we do now?" Eleanor asked.

"Well, we've gone through three rooms and have encountered three of the four elements: water, wind, fire," Shree paused.

"That leaves earth," Nancy said, turning to Shree. "That's it, isn't it?"

"Yeah, but what does that mean?" Shree asked, looking around and trying to figure out the last piece of the puzzle before it was too late.

Chapter 45

Earth

"Maybe the t-t-treasure is buried in this room," Ralph said.

Everyone glanced over at Ralph, who stood by Door I looking exhausted.

Upon seeing him, Shree realized that the Freaks had made a complete circle through the labyrinth of tunnels, and were now back in the main room where they'd started. In the meantime, Ralph had managed to empty the water from the cave using his blowhole and had transformed back to his human form.

"We've already seen what's behind the three doors," Shree said, glancing around the room. "Maybe Ralph's right. Maybe the treasure's hidden here."

Shree grew excited. They'd originally neglected the main room. Instead, they had focused on the doors and the series of passageways that led to them.

"Nancy, take a look at that side of the room," Shree said. "Dave, use the flashlight to help Nancy. Eleanor, you take the other side and see if you find anything out of the ordinary. I'll take this wall. Ralph, you stay near the door and make sure it doesn't break down on us," Shree paused, and then added. "It looks awfully shaky."

She could see water trickling from underneath; the door itself looked like it was bulging slightly outwards.

The Freaks took their assignments and started working desperately to find the treasure. Eleanor extended her arms along the surface and felt every crevice of the stone wall. Nancy and Dave stood in front of the adjacent wall. Dave held the flashlight with one hand and knocked on the wall with the other. Shree guessed he was trying to see if he could sense a difference in the wall's composition like he'd done before.

Shree walked to the opposite side of the room, but after a few minutes of aimless search, she went back to the middle of the room and stood there, watching her friends at work.

"Do you guys see anything?" Shree asked.

"Nothing here. Do you, Nancy?" Eleanor's arms extended to the top and her long fingers continued to feel around each stone.

"Not a thing. The walls all look the same," Nancy answered.

Ralph hung out in the corner, his back to the others, staring at Door I. Shree could smell the salty sweat that filled his hands. She could tell he was nervous, but she was confident that if the door broke down, Ralph would save the group by turning back into a whale.

Shree smiled. She was starting to realize that they might not find the treasure. And, surprisingly, she was okay with that. As she looked around the room and saw the others at work, Shree was happy she'd found a good group of people she could call her friends.

The year had been one long emotional roller coaster ride. She had been abused by the Demons and forced to feel ashamed about who she was. But somehow, through it all, she had survived. She had discovered her new powers. And she had made great friends. It was as her dad had told her a few days before: *"Sometimes what we spend our lives looking for is right in front of us."*

And suddenly, it came to her.

Shree ran over to where Ralph was standing. She stared at the door, which looked like it was bulging out farther and on the verge of destruction. A lone Roman numeral "I" was the only thing written on it. She ran her index finger over the letter, which was carved deeply onto the wooden frame. She then glanced over at the dark corridor that had led the Freaks to the other two doors. In all, there were three different Roman numerals and, behind each of them, they'd encountered three different challenges mentioned in John Harvard's note. She looked around the room. They had to find the fourth Roman numeral because behind *it* they'd find the fourth and final challenge.

What had Harvard's poem said?

The cross shall mark the rightful site.

And it had. The crimson cross inside the boathouse had provided the entrance into the tunnels. But what did the poem say afterwards?

Shree ran over to her book bag and took out Harvard's note. Thanks to the plastic covering, it was still dry and readable. Gently, she took it out of her bag, opened it up, and read the last paragraph.

The cross shall mark the rightful site,
Where eyes shall feast with all delight.
Uncover the right stone if you are bold,
And you will be granted silver and gold.

Shree looked down at her feet. She took a few steps back and then made a small circle around the room. Shree's mind started to crowd with thoughts, mostly from her father: "*Things are always clearer when you step back from your problems.*"

And then, with the little energy she had left, Shree ran to the far corner and pointed to the middle of the room. It was now plainly obvious where the treasure was hidden. She could see from where she was standing that the floor was made up of two different colored rocks: a dark red and a light gray. It was difficult to tell from where the others stood, but from Shree's perspective in the corner, looking straight toward the middle of the room, it was a bit more obvious. Depending on where you stood, the dark red rocks made a distinct pattern against the lighter gray ones.

Shree grew excited. "I guess in this case, 'X' does mark the spot." She pointed to the center. One by one, Nancy, Dave, Eleanor and Ralph saw what Shree was referring to. Each smiled when they figured out the pattern made by the stones. It was an "x" if you looked at it from one side of the room, and a "+" if you looked at it from one of the four corners of the chamber. A crimson cross!

The treasure was hidden underneath the rocks—somewhere deep down, in the earth.

Chapter 46

Gold, Silver and Jewels

Almost an hour later, Shree dragged yet another stone from the middle of the giant hole the Freaks had made. Dave, Nancy, and Ralph stood next to her, lifting the surrounding boulders and dragging them out of the way. Eleanor cupped her expanded hand and made a makeshift shovel, which she used to dig through the earth.

Shree and the others had removed a pile of stones and had finally hit dirt. Unfortunately, there was nothing at all to show for their hard work. Shree looked on as Eleanor scooped a large amount of earth, hoping she'd found something. But there was nothing but more dirt and pebbles.

Suddenly, Eleanor stopped digging.

"I think it is another large boulder. I am going to need the help of everyone. It is pretty heavy," Eleanor called out.

Shree knew that if there wasn't anything under that stone, it was all over.

"Okay," Eleanor said. "On three. One, two, three!"

With the five sets of hands, the rock moved easily. As it did, instead of the slurpy sound of stone oozing up from the muck, there was the sound of something scraping a hard surface. Shree reached down through the mud to feel around.

"What is it?" Dave asked.

"There's something down here, but I can't quite…" Shree paused. "Wait a minute. I think I feel something hard." Her hand was elbow deep in dirt.

Each Freak started scraping the earth around the large object Shree had found. Finally, they could see that it was a wooden chest with a thick metal lock. Ralph took one handle while Dave took the other, and together they lifted the chest onto the stone floor.

Shree held the old, rusty key in her hand and brought it towards the lock. The secret key had opened four other locks before this one. She prayed that it'd open this last one too.

Shree slid the key inside the lock. She took a deep breath and gave it a turn. Nothing stopped it. She gave another turn to the left. Suddenly there was a big click, and the lock opened.

"This is it, guys," Shree said. "It's time to put our hands on our treasure." And as the lid of the chest was lifted up, Shree gasped.

A steady torrent of gold and silver coins, gemstones, and jewels gushed out all at once from the wooden box. Despite the dark surroundings, the room came to life with the bright light that emanated from inside the treasure chest. Shree knelt on the floor and picked up a few of the coins. The gold was brighter than anything she had ever seen. The silver sparkled like a newly-cleaned mirror. The jewels had stones of a dozen different colors, each one richer and more brilliant than the other.

Shree's heart beat a mile a minute. There was no nausea, no weird sensation in her back, no nagging fear. There was just happiness—complete and utter happiness over having found the lost treasure of John Harvard.

Shree looked at her friends. Eleanor had grown her hand the size of a baseball glove and used it to cup large portions of the treasure. Ralph grabbed a single coin and studied the back with interest, while Nancy tried on a deep blue sapphire necklace. Dave tossed a bunch of gold coins up in the air and watched them sparkle, lighting up the cave that had sheltered them for centuries.

But all at once and without warning, the happiness Shree had felt only moments earlier vanished. She sensed that there was something missing. Even though each one of her friends celebrated with renewed energy, she couldn't help feeling a little disappointed. The treasure was theirs. They had survived multiple life-threatening challenges. Eleanor, Dave, Nancy and Ralph bathed in several million-dollars worth of coins and jewels. So what was it that was bothering her so much?

Shree realized this was an incredible accomplishment, and yet all she could think about was Katherine. Shree expected to uncover the reason for Katherine's cryptic comment about the treasure, but seeing the wooden chest in front of her now made Shree realize that she wasn't going to get the answer she was looking for. There was nothing among the gold or silver coins, or the expensive jewels, that was going to provide Shree with the knowledge she sought.

And to make matters worse, she began to sense something was different in the air. The nausea and dizziness started up again and she felt a sharp pain pulsating through her entire back.

"This is awesome," Dave exclaimed, breaking Shree's train of thought. "I can't believe we did it, guys. We're rich—" Dave stopped speaking abruptly. He cocked his head to the side.

Shree noticed Dave's face growing strangely pale. While the others continued to celebrate, Shree stared intently at the opposite end of the room. "What is it, Dave? What's wrong?"

Dave spoke through clenched teeth. "It sounds like we've got company."

Chapter 47

A Celebration's End

Why hadn't she noticed their presence in the tunnels, Shree wondered. Her body's warning had come too late. Was it because she was too preoccupied with the treasure? Is that also why Nancy hadn't seen them coming?

"What are we going to do?" Eleanor asked.

"I'm not sure. The only Demons I hear are the twins. They got their own rope and they're heading our way," Dave said.

"Maybe we should just confront them. There are five of us and we have powers. Let's just take them on." Nancy was angrier than Shree had ever seen her.

"I don't think that's a good idea," Shree said. "There's no telling what these guys will do without teachers around. They could've brought weapons, or worse."

"So what do we do?" Eleanor asked again.

Shree thought for a moment. "I think we need to split up. We can then figure out what we're up against." She looked around the room. She remembered passing other sets of tunnels that gave way to smaller-sized caves.

Suddenly, she got an idea.

"Okay, this is what we'll do. Ralph, you stay here and guard the treasure. Dave, I think that it's time for you to show the twins what happens when they mess with the Freaks. Maybe you could show them why Dumbo's ears are his strongest features?"

Dave didn't say anything, and then Shree saw what she had hoped for: a giant smile of understanding crossing his face. "Okay, now we're talking," he said. "I know exactly how to keep them entertained."

"I'll head back up to the boathouse with Nancy and Eleanor," Shree said. "We'll sneak past the twins while you distract them. You can then go back and help Ralph with the treasure. We'll meet you guys back at the boathouse." Shree was ecstatic. It was the perfect plan.

"But Dave, you can't deal with the twins by yourself. Maybe one of us can go with you," Nancy said.

"Don't worry about me," Dave replied. "I can handle these clowns." He winked and expanded his ears. He turned from the group and took a few running steps before gliding through the air at full speed toward the twins.

Chapter 48

Hear No Evil

"Dude, will you get your foot off my face? When the hell are we gonna—" Tim stopped speaking when he finally hit solid ground. He took a few steps past the rope and looked around.

Tom followed shortly, holding onto the army-sized flashlight. They walked together down the narrow passage as Tom shifted his light back and forth to guide them through the dark abyss that swallowed them.

"We should've just waited for them up there. What were we thinking?" Tom asked as he looked around the deserted tunnels.

"Who cares? We're here now. So let's get those Freaks." Tim studied his surroundings. They had entered a small room with a bunch of different tunnels to choose from. They stood in front of the entry, confused as to which way to go.

Suddenly, they saw something moving from above.

"What the hell was that, Tim?" Tom pointed to the far corner.

"I have no idea," his brother answered.

Again, there was movement at the opposite wall, this time near the ceiling. When Tom pointed the flashlight, there was nothing there. The twins could hear the sound of pebbles hitting the ground next to them.

Then, out of nowhere, Tom was hit at the center of his chest, tossing him across the narrow cave. The flashlight went flying out of his hands, landing several feet away. As the beam of light moved in rapid circles around the room, the twins caught sight of what looked like a large animal flying high above them.

"What the hell was that?" Tim yelled out as he ran to retrieve the flashlight.

Tom picked himself up from the ground and ran toward his brother. He stood right next to him, scared beyond words. Tim pointed the flashlight at the ceiling and started waving it back and forth. His hands shook as he scanned the room.

From a distance, they heard laughter. And then, they heard a whooshing sound coming at them. But this time both twins found themselves propelled in mid-air, landing several feet further from the entrance. Their bodies ached from the blow.

Again, they heard the sound of someone laughing from a distance.

"Tim, what the hell's going on?"

"I don't know, Tom. But I say we get the hell outta here."

From inside one of the tunnels, a voice mocking the twins could be heard. "Now, I think it's a little too late for that, isn't it?"

Tom pointed the flashlight at the voice. To his surprise, he found Dave leaning against the stone wall, smiling.

"Dumbo, you son of a—" Tim said.

"You're gonna pay for this." Tom ran at him.

Dave held his ground, not budging an inch. Seconds before Tom threw a fist, Dave leaned back, grew his ears, and disappeared.

Tom's hand landed on the boulder Dave had been leaning against moments earlier. The sound of bones smashing rock echoed throughout the cave. He let out a loud curse.

Tim ran over to his brother. "Where the hell did that little punk go?"

"I'm in here, you dummies," Dave said.

Dazed from the blows and too angry to notice anything but Dave, the twins moved further inside the tunnels. Unbeknownst to them, Shree and the girls sneaked right past them.

Dave heard the three sets of footsteps crossing the adjacent room and heading straight for the rope the twins had left. He smiled when he heard Shree whisper, "Thanks, Dave," before she and the other girls climbed up the rope.

He turned to the twins. Now for a little revenge, Dave thought. He flew at full speed and landed another swift kick to the chests of both twins. Because he could glide quickly past their range of vision, Dave continued the game of flying, kicking, and hiding without fear of getting caught. He continued doing this until he'd given the girls enough time to get safely up to the boathouse.

After several more minutes, the twins stood at the far end of the cave, looking hurt and scared. Dave made one last loop around the cave, throwing pebbles at them from the ceiling. He then landed on the ground, several feet from the twins.

"So, what do you say boys? Ready to give up?" Dave asked playfully.

"Yeah, Dave. We give up, man. We're sorry. We shouldn't have followed you." Tim put his hands up, apparently conceding defeat.

"Yeah, don't hit us again, man. We're sorry." Tom got on his knees.

The twins' pleading voices sounded strange. Dave guessed it was probably because this was the twins' first experience at being bullied. They'd finally lost at their own game.

Dave continued to stare them down, wondering what to do next.

Before he'd made a decision, a shovel hit him in the back of the head.

Chapter 49

Showdown At The Boathouse

Shree made her way up through the narrow passage as quickly as she could. Eleanor followed closely and, as soon as they'd pulled themselves out of the hole, Shree and Eleanor gave Nancy a hand. Once inside the boathouse and onto solid ground, the three girls hugged each other and celebrated over making it out of the tunnel in one piece.

Unfortunately, the laughing and high-fiving was cut short by a familiar voice.

"What are we celebrating, girls?"

Shree couldn't believe her eyes. It was Katherine. Inside the boathouse. Standing with Colleen at her side.

But how had they found them? This couldn't be real. It had to be a nightmare.

Shree felt ill. It couldn't end like this. It just couldn't.

"What do you want?" Shree asked. "You guys have no business here."

"Did you hear that, Katherine?" Colleen laughed and looked at Shree. "I'll tell you what business we have, you little Indian twerp. We're here to take the treasure that you've so kindly found for us. It's ours now. You and your little friends are going to hand it over."

"Yes, and you'll also hand over the secret key," Katherine said. She stared at Shree, shook her head and smiled. "It's amazing what the power of suggestion can get you. I plant a little seed in your head and you run off and find me the treasure." She laughed quietly, adding, "Who's smarter now?"

Shree looked at Katherine. She saw herself and her friends through Katherine's eyes—filthy, tired, scratched up, and wet—clearly, not all that much of a threat. Shree snuck a glance beyond Katherine and Colleen to the entrance of the boathouse. But there was no escape. Not that way.

Shree shifted her attention back to Katherine and Colleen. They were blocking the only door out of the boathouse—which was feeling more and more precarious. Debris was still falling from the ceiling and the foundation was shaking intermittently. Shree was sure that down below, Door I was on the verge of breaking any minute. With it, the tunnels would flood with water and the boathouse above them would collapse. Shree didn't know if Katherine had any idea just how much danger they were in—or what would happen if she told her.

"How did you find us?" Shree asked. She had to keep Katherine and Colleen talking. At least until she thought of something. Anything. She couldn't let them get away with taking back the key and stealing the treasure.

Colleen took the bait. Obviously, talking about herself was an opportunity too good to pass up. "You were all so busy making plans that you had no idea what was going on around you. All we had to do was follow you—from a distance, of course. And we made sure we didn't say anything aloud. It was easy," Colleen said. She shook her head and added, "I don't know how you guys do those things you do. You guys are freaks. You're nothing but a bunch of mutants."

Shree thought about all those times when she'd sensed that she was being watched. Then she remembered how Ralph, Eleanor, and Dave had felt the same way. Even Nancy had said something about not being able to see what she felt was there. It had all been right in front of their faces. The Demons had been following them all along. The Freaks had led them to the boathouse.

Shree's chin fell a little closer to her chest. They'd been stupid, totally stupid. And now look where it had gotten them. The treasure was about to be stolen from under them and they were going to end up with nothing more than bruises for their efforts. Still, she had to do something.

That got her thinking. Whatever happened, she was responsible. She had dragged her friends down to the boathouse. She had organized the expedition that had put all their lives at risk. And now Katherine and Colleen had ambushed them.

But Shree also knew that she could find the power to change the outcome. Her father had always said that it was all up to her, right?

Shree's stinger began to itch. She was going to have to take matters into her own hands.

Shree scooted a little closer to Eleanor. She tried getting her attention, but Eleanor's mind seemed to be elsewhere. What was wrong with her? Didn't she appreciate how critical the situation was?

Then Shree saw that her friend was standing incredibly still. And that her arms were slowly growing longer and longer, sliding down her side, coursing down the back of her legs, and making their way towards Katherine and Colleen.

"Hey, get away from her," Colleen yelled at Shree.

But why should Shree listen to Colleen? And what could Katherine do? If they all fought back, there was no reason they couldn't get out of there. Why should they just stand there and do what they were told? With the twins somewhere deep inside the tunnels under the boathouse and Jason nowhere in sight, it was three against two: and they had powers. The odds were in their favor.

Shree's stinger started to itch. She could feel it growing. She'd be a bee in another minute. She could do it. *They* could do it.

As Shree began her transformation, Katherine reached into her backpack, removing the biggest can of *Raid Insect Repellent* that Shree had ever seen. And when Katherine aimed it at her and pressed down on the spray can, Shree was instantly in a cloud of insecticide: lethal while she was in bee form. It not only reversed the transformation, but also left Shree momentarily paralyzed. The deadly poison hit her immediately, making her body feel like it'd been stung by a thousand daggers. Shree fell to the ground writhing in pain, curled up in a ball on the floor, moaning in agony.

Katherine looked down at Shree. "You think that just because I'm blond and beautiful that I have to be stupid. I knew about you turning into a bee and breaking into my house. Believe it or not, Shree, I'm a lot smarter than you. I'm walking away with the treasure, while you might not walk out of here at all."

Shree continued to moan. She caught a glimpse of Eleanor's hand jutting out towards Katherine and, for a split second, Shree forgot all about how much pain she was in.

But then, to Shree's dismay, Colleen intercepted Eleanor's hand with a metal wire contraption. It looked like some kind of Middle Age torture gadget. Barbed wire encircled Eleanor's thin, elongated hands, which were now trapped inside the chamber as Colleen quickly closed the frame. She turned a small bolt to secure it.

Shree could see Eleanor trying to withdraw her hand, but it was no use. Her fingers were caught between the sharp teeth of the metal. Eleanor's attempt to make her fingers thinner to escape the trap was met with more pain. And with each one of Eleanor's feeble attempts, Colleen laughed harder and harder.

Shree looked at Nancy. Despite her small size, Shree saw her friend lunging at Colleen. It was a valiant effort, but she was not surprised that Nancy's attack ended in defeat. Nancy lay helpless on the ground next to her, fresh bruises having been inflicted by Colleen.

With Shree, Eleanor, and Nancy out of commission, Colleen proceeded to tie them up. She told the girls to sit down by the big floor-to-ceiling post. Colleen started with Shree, binding her wrists tightly with rope and then tying her to one of the wooden bars at the far end of the boathouse. Once she was done tying Nancy up against the post next to Shree, Colleen led Eleanor to the opposite wall and placed the metal contraption above a high beam, securing it with rope and making sure the bolt that locked the barbed wires in place was screwed tight.

Shree saw that Colleen did all the work while Katherine stood by, keeping her eyes fixed on Shree and smiling. She's enjoying this far too much, thought Shree.

But how did Katherine and Colleen know about their powers? It didn't make sense. Even if they were spying on Shree and the others, how did they know *exactly* what weapons to bring? There had to be something else she was missing.

Shree had noticed her body's warnings, but ignored them. She should've paid attention to the signs. She should've listened to the voice inside telling her that something was wrong. Now it was too late.

As the rope bit into her wrists, Shree wished she could transform into her animal form. If she could turn into a bee, there'd be no ropes to hold her. She could sting the girls, transform back, and help her friends. But she couldn't. She was too weak, her body ached too much, and she still had the fumes of insecticide in her system.

Nancy glared while Colleen readjusted the rope behind her back. "You're stupid if you think you're getting away with the treasure," Nancy said, spitting her words out with renewed anger. "Pretty soon Dave's going to be here and there'll be nothing you can do to stop him."

"I wouldn't bet on Dave helping you out." Jason appeared from the tunnel, carrying something over his shoulder. He dropped Dave's limp body on the floor.

"Dave," Nancy exclaimed, struggling to free herself.

Jason looked at Nancy. "Oh, Dumbo can't hear you, Four Eyes. He's going to be out of commission for a long time."

Colleen came around Nancy and slapped her across the face. Shree could see Nancy's cheek turning red. A drop of bright red blood formed on her lips, and her eyes filled with tears.

"You're gonna be here for a while, so get comfortable," Colleen said. "By the time help arrives, we'll be long gone with the treasure."

Just then Shree saw the twins coming out of the tunnel with the treasure. Suddenly, she panicked. Where was Ralph?

Katherine walked over to Shree. "Oh, and I wouldn't rely on Ralph to come save you either," she said. "Thanks to the twins, he's, how shall we say, indisposed?"

"Yeah, and just in time. The tunnel started flooding just as we were coming up. We heard the door break. So I'm sorry to tell you guys that you won't be seeing Ralphie anytime soon," Tim laughed and gave Tom a high-five.

Shree watched in despair as the treasure chest was carried by the twins out of the boathouse. And any hope of freedom went along with it.

Chapter 50

Saying Goodbye

The boathouse continued to creak and moan as the twins hoisted the treasure chest onto their shoulders and transported it out of the boathouse, and then onto the boat they had anchored right outside the main doors.

Shree listened to the Demons celebrate. She looked at Nancy and Eleanor and figured they were thinking the same thing she was: Ralph was trapped below, Dave was badly hurt, and none of them could do anything about it.

The door closed and something big and solid was pushed through the latch. The Demons had locked them in.

"What are they doing outside?" Eleanor asked.

Before Shree could answer, she heard a new sound. It reminded her of something. Something she'd heard earlier, but she couldn't hold onto the memory. It was too vague.

Eleanor shook her head at Shree and then pointed her chin up at the ceiling. The whole boathouse was shifting. Tiny pieces of wood and debris were floating down, as if they were splintering off from above.

The entire structure was coming apart at the seams. But that sound, what was that other sound? A kind of low, faint whooshing sound, like being inside a shell.

That was it. Just like when Dave opened Door I and water started gushing out.

Water was flooding the tunnels.

And the Demons knew it.

Shree and her friends were tied to the posts and water was going to start pouring in from below at any second. Soon the boathouse would flood and it'd be nothing more than matchsticks. And they'd disappear along with it.

For several minutes the floors continued to creak and whole pieces of wood fell around Shree. Water suddenly started pouring in from the tunnel entrance and before Shree knew it, it was up to her waist and rising quickly.

With renewed energy, Shree struggled to free herself from the tight rope, ignoring the sharp bolts of pain she felt with any movement of her wrists.

Next to her, Shree saw the others fighting just as unsuccessfully to get free. Eleanor tried to extend her hand through the metal cage, but Shree saw the pain in her eyes as she failed to dislodge herself from the trap. Nancy struggled against the post, water rising up to her chin. Dave hadn't moved an inch since he'd been plopped next to Eleanor. And Ralph was still nowhere to be seen.

Shree closed her eyes. She let herself relax against the post and repeated over and over the words that'd started her first transformation.

Nothing happened. Shree knew she was tired and she hadn't eaten in far too long. But a little while ago she'd been so mad that the transformation had begun on its own. She'd have to try to feel that anger again, and see if it would help her find the strength she needed.

"Embrace your differences, embrace your differences, Shree," she chanted again and again.

But again, nothing. What was happening? Why couldn't she transform?

She looked across at Eleanor and saw her neck stretched to keep her head above water. Her teeth were holding onto the back of Dave's shirt. Eleanor struggled to keep his inert body above water. Her forehead was drenched in sweat and all her veins were popping out of her neck.

Shree looked for Nancy, and that's when panic took over. She was nowhere in sight. Instead, Shree saw only bubbles and a torrent of water where Nancy's head used to be.

Shree was neck deep in water herself and knew it was only a matter of time before she succumbed to Nancy's fate. She struggled harder, but still couldn't break free from the rope.

She had to try to transform again. She closed her eyes tightly.

By this time, she couldn't smell the insecticide anymore. There was no more nauseous feeling when she thought about being a bee. She felt the water around her and realized that the insecticide had been fully washed off from her body.

She was now free to transform.

Shree closed her eyes even tighter, letting the fear, panic, anger, sadness, and every other emotion take hold of her.

And when she opened her eyes seconds later, she was no longer Shree. She was a bee.

She felt her energy growing as she expanded her wings and flew high above the water. The ropes were no longer a concern. Shree was free.

She reached the ceiling and then started to fly in circles, dodging debris that dropped from above as she tried to get her bearings. She could see Nancy underwater continuing to struggle for air and Eleanor in the corner holding on to Dave with her teeth. What could Shree do to help?

Shree circled the room again, and continued to dodge pieces of sheetrock and wood that fell from the ceiling. She buzzed around, frantically trying to figure out how she could call for help.

That was it. It was her only chance.

Shree flew straight for Dave's ear. She pushed her way inside his ear canal and inched her way close to his eardrum. She hoped that what she was about to do would wake Dave up from his unconscious, but it'd also likely leave him deaf in that ear for a very long time. It might even permanently damage his powers. But she had no other choice.

She inhaled and then let out the loudest buzzing sound she could manage. Shree could feel the vibration within Dave's eardrum. And then she felt his head shaking back and forth. Shree flew out just in time. Eleanor couldn't hold onto Dave anymore and he dropped in the water. Seconds later, though, his face emerged from the murky darkness, drenched but awake—and alive.

"Dave, go help Nancy. She is drowning," Eleanor called out.

Shree sat perched on a ceiling beam and rested her wings.

A minute later, Shree had transformed back into human form. The first thing she did was to loosen the bolt that held Eleanor's hands together.

Once she was free, Eleanor sent her arms straight across the room. Shree could barely breathe as she watched Eleanor's arm emerge from underwater, wrapped around two bodies. Were they dead?

Dave held onto Nancy tightly as she coughed up water.

Shree drew a sigh of relief. They were both alive.

Eleanor dragged Nancy and Dave through the water a fair distance with her until they all reached the adjacent room. Shree overturned a long kayak and they all sat on top to rest.

Shree saw Dave holding one of his ears with his hand and looking around the room with a puzzled expression.

"We're still in the boathouse, Dave," Shree explained. "The Demons took all the treasure and tied us up. But we're all okay. We need to get out of here, though, before the place caves in on us. Do you think you can make it?"

"I don't know. My head's pounding and this ear's ringing," Dave answered.

"Yeah, Jason must've ambushed you when you were dealing with the twins. As for the ringing in your ear, I'll take full responsibility. I kind of had to act like an alarm clock to wake you up from your unconsciousness."

Dave nodded weakly.

"Look out," Nancy screamed.

The beam above Shree's head came crashing down, missing her by inches. The boathouse was finally about to collapse.

"Eleanor, can you get us out of here?" Shree asked.

"The place is about to crush us," Nancy added.

As if it had heard Nancy, the boathouse started falling in on itself. Another beam let go and swung from the rafters. Dirt rained down. Loud creaking could be heard from every corner of the building.

Shree looked around the room. "Eleanor, can you send your arms outside and get rid of whatever they put over the door?"

"I do not think so," Eleanor answered. "There is not enough room under the door for my hands. But I can try to break it open." She stared at the door, and then at Dave.

"Don't worry about him," Shree said. "We'll take care of Dave. We'll be right behind you."

Shree grabbed one of Dave's arms and Nancy grabbed the other. They slowly pulled him up, but Dave was so weak he could barely stay upright. Treading through water and stumbling, they all headed towards the door.

As soon as they got there, Eleanor grew her fist to the size of a basketball and tore the wooden door open with one swift punch. She then turned to the others, shrinking her hand and stretching her arm at the same time.

Eleanor's long limbs reached in and surrounded Nancy, Shree, and Dave in one big hug. She gave a yank and drew them out onto firm land just as the Weld Boathouse gave a final lurch and began its descent into the depths of the Charles River.

Shree stood back in the dark with the others and watched the boathouse as it seemed to implode, board by board. First, the rafters and roof, then the walls, then the floor vanished beneath the surface. When it was all over, the only thing left was the ramp that led from the street along the side of the huge building.

But Ralph was still nowhere to be found.

And with that thought in mind, Shree fell to her knees in tears.

Chapter 51

Massachusetts General

"What's going on now, Nancy?" Shree asked, eager for an update. From where she was standing, Shree could barely catch a glimpse of Dave, and that was only when a nurse or doctor opened the double doors leading to the Neurological Intensive Care Unit.

"Dave is still asleep. His mother is next to him and she's talking to the doctor." Nancy paused, and shifted her glasses forward. Then she turned to Eleanor and Shree. "She's crying. I'm not sure why, but she's crying."

There was a moment of silence as Shree considered what to do next. She wished she could turn into a bee, sneak inside, and get more information. But she couldn't stand the thought of transforming. Not again. Not for a long time. She was too exhausted, physically and emotionally, to summon enough energy to make the transformation into a bee.

And she was still too distraught to focus on anything other than Ralph. The thought of Ralph dying underneath the boathouse was too much for Shree to endure. How could she have let it happen? What was she going to tell Mrs. Snodgrass? That Ralph died searching for a hidden treasure underneath Harvard University property?

Shree closed her eyes and thought about the treasure. It had been stupid to chase after it to begin with. Shree wished she'd never met Mrs. Twichett, she wished she'd never found the book that started the whole treasure hunt, and she wished, above all, that she hadn't talked Ralph and the others into pursuing the treasure. She had put her friends' lives in danger, and now Ralph was dead and Dave was in critical condition.

For what? Shree wondered. She had risked everything for shiny metal and stones. Because that's what the treasure amounted to in the end. It was worthless to her. Just a bunch of junk.

Deep down inside, though, Shree knew that it had never been about the treasure. It was about proving to herself that she could find it when others before her had failed. And, if she was really being honest with herself, it was mostly about figuring out what Katherine had implied about the treasure. It hadn't sat well with Shree what Katherine had said to her on Halloween night; she had insulted her intelligence and that had irritated Shree beyond words.

"What are we going to tell the police when they get here?" Eleanor asked.

"I'm not sure, El. I guess we have to tell them the truth," Shree said.

"Yeah, but who's going to believe us?" Nancy asked. She continued staring at the doors leading to the Neurological ICU.

"And what are we going to tell Ralph's mom?" Shree was on the verge of fresh tears when the doors of the waiting room suddenly slammed open.

"Ralph!" Shree screamed as she ran over to him.

Eleanor followed, then Nancy.

"Ralph, where have you been?" Eleanor asked, wrapping her arms around him.

"We're so glad you're here," Nancy added, squeezing her way inside the circle.

They hugged for a minute, leaving Ralph blushing and speechless. When Eleanor finally released her hold, Ralph looked up and smiled. "Hi, girls. I'm so g-g-glad to see you."

"Ralph, we're so happy you're alive," Shree said, wiping tears from her eyes.

"What happened to you? How did you get out of the boathouse?" Eleanor asked.

"Yeah, how'd you do it? The twins said that they'd put you out of commission. We were worried sick thinking that they'd hurt you and that you were dead," Shree added.

"Well, they did rough me up a b-b-bit, and then tied me up so I couldn't fight them. I waited until they left with the t-t-treasure chest before I changed into a whale. By that time, the d-d-door had busted open and the tunnel was flooding."

Shree noticed for the first time that Ralph was still drenched. His face was filled with scratches and bruises. His clothes had stretch marks and the bottoms of his jeans were in tatters. Shree knew that Ralph must have suffered more than he led on, but she wasn't going to bring it up.

"How is Dave d-d-doing?" Ralph asked.

"We're not sure. He's unconscious. We're waiting to hear from the doctors, but nobody's speaking to us since we're not close family." Shree turned her attention back to the hallway leading to Dave's room.

"Do you think that he's going to b-b-be okay?" Ralph asked, walking to the main doors and trying to get a glimpse inside.

"Let's hope so," Nancy answered. She resumed staring at Dave's room.

"It is too bad that the Demons got the treasure," Eleanor said.

"Who cares about the treasure? We're just glad that Ralph's alive." Shree smiled and put an arm around him.

"The Demons d-d-didn't get the treasure," Ralph whispered, almost to himself. He continued to gaze at the entrance, standing on tiptoes and straining his neck every time the double doors opened.

Shree turned to Ralph slowly, sporting a puzzled look on her face. "What did you just say?"

to"When you g-g-girls left, I dumped the t-t-treasure inside the hole we dug and covered it up," Ralph said. "Then I filled the t-t-treasure chest with rats. It was easy. The rats were more afraid of me than I was of t-t-them."

Neither Shree, Eleanor, nor Nancy said a word. Then, all at once, they hugged Ralph again, this time harder. Shree was certain that Ralph was blushing brighter than ever. He was her hero; Ralph had proved himself once again.

A minute later, the doors to the ICU opened and Dave's mom came out.

"Dave's going to be all right," Mrs. Jackson exclaimed, running over to the group.

Before they hugged, Shree closed her eyes and let the last remaining tears fall to the floor.

Epilogue

Six months later, on a sunny afternoon in May, Shree and her parents drove down to the Charles River for a picnic. A lot had happened since the night at the boathouse, but things were slowly getting back to normal. At least as normal as Shree expected they'd ever be, given the circumstances.

Her family's brand new yellow Toyota Prius held four huge baskets of fruit, bread, cheeses, and other goodies—everything her friends and their parents would need at their picnic. Shree got out of the car and looked around. The Weld Boathouse was no more, but a new boathouse was being erected in its place. It made Shree sad to think that all the underground tunnels, and all the hard work that had gone into building them, would never be seen by anyone else. On the other hand, the Freaks would've never found the treasure if they hadn't happened on the booby-trapped obstacles, which ultimately destroyed the old building.

Shree lay down on the soft, green grass, sniffed the sweet smell of flowers in bloom, and closed her eyes, thinking about the ceremony that she had just attended at Harvard Yard.

Blue-tailed robins flew over the yard searching for worms, and woodpeckers busied themselves in the trees above. Shree had listened with half an ear to President Eli Bicer's speech. She had been looking forward to the picnic afterwards.

The president had droned on and on about the history of the treasure and its significance to Harvard University. "The fact that this treasure, hidden for almost four hundred years and part of the original Spanish Armada, is comprised of gold, silver, and jewels worth almost $25 million does not for a moment speak to the real value of the relics that came from an age when—"

Shree's back straightened. She couldn't believe her ears. Twenty-five million dollars? That was a lot of money. Even though none of her friends would ever get anywhere near that amount, they each had been guaranteed a full scholarship to Harvard University once they graduated from high school (as long as they kept up their grades).

The glorious day had continued without a hitch. Shree and the others were asked to go up on the platform to receive their awards for returning the treasure. Shree had to admit she'd been a little disappointed at first. It would've been nice to keep some of it for herself. But she kept her mouth shut and smiled all the way through the end of the ceremony.

Then the guest speaker got up to talk. It was none other than a distant relative of Sir Malcolm Winthrop. A hush fell over the crowd as the eighty-seven-year-old scholar began to speak. "I would personally like to thank Ms. Shree Mandvi, Mr. David Jackson, Mr. Ralph Snodgrass, Ms. Nancy Yoon, and Ms. Eleanor Martinez, for their bravery, skill, fortitude, scholarly prowess, and, above all, generosity. Without them we would never have known that the stories my parents told, the ones that were passed down to them through the generations, were true. I'm sure that Sir Malcolm would have been very, very proud."

Shree blushed and went up with the others to accept the plaque from the kindly old man. When he shook her hand and she saw the tears in his eyes, she knew they'd done the right thing.

After Mr. Winthrop had handed out all the plaques, he stepped back up to the microphone. "I have one more announcement to make. It was tradition, back when my ancestors were still alive, that the mayor of the city would grant those citizens whose bravery contributed to the betterment of society with a key to the city."

He paused to clear his throat, then smiled. "Well, I am not the mayor nor do I possess such a key. But in honor of a good deed that will never go unappreciated, I would personally like to reward each of these students with $50,000."

And that's when Shree Mandvi—girl, treasure hunter, and bee—fainted dead away.

The picnic was a big success. As Shree lay with her eyes closed, she heard rowers in the water, Eleanor's brothers playing volleyball and arguing about who was out of bounds, and Dave telling Ralph that he was his "number one man."

Shree smiled as she reached for the secret key around her neck. The rusty piece of metal had become a permanent fixture since that night at the boathouse. She held onto it to remind herself of all the things that had happened that year. The list was short but incredible. She'd made four fantastic new friends, she'd found a treasure that had been buried for nearly four hundred years, and she'd even had a few minutes of fame and fortune. But the most amazing thing of all was learning that she had the power to be and do anything. She owed that as much to her father as to her adventures, and she'd never forget it.

Shree thought back to the diner in Salem, where she'd discovered the treasure book in the old library. She wondered if Mrs. Twichett had seen her on the news and knew they'd found the treasure. That day at Mrs. Twichett's was really the start of everything. What was it she'd said to Shree that day? Something about not doing it alone? Well, she'd sure been right about that. Without the League of Freaks, Shree would've never found the treasure.

But what else did Mrs. Twichett say about the treasure? Something about there being more than one? Didn't the book also mention the possibility of finding other treasures?

No, that wasn't quite it. Shree prodded her memory. Suddenly, she remembered with a start. The book had specifically said something about "countless" treasures. How could she have overlooked that? Were there really more treasures out there, waiting to be discovered by Shree and her friends?

But what did that mean exactly? Had she skipped a chapter in the book showing where those treasures were hidden? No, that couldn't be it. She had read every word of that book a dozen times.

The treasure book had said that the secret key—the one now in her hand—would open the door to "countless" treasures. But there were lots of kinds of treasures, weren't there? What about the other stuff, things that money couldn't buy?

Shree felt the key and rubbed the rough metal.

Then it came to her.

What if the key was not only meant to open the doors beneath the boathouse, but other doors as well? What if it could open *any* door?

Sir Malcolm Winthrop had mentioned something about "a key to the city" in his speech. Shree remembered reading about that somewhere. Back in Colonial times, it was a custom for the mayor of a city to give such a key to an elite few; a master key that would allow its owner to open any door of the city.

What if the secret key now in Shree's possession was such a key—a key that could open any lock, anywhere, at any time?

It was a crazy theory. But she had to test it.

Shree looked around. Nothing but cars. No buildings at all.

But cars had locks, right?

As inconspicuously as possible, Shree got up and moved towards her parents' car. If they asked where she was going, she'd just say she needed something from the trunk. But her parents were smiling and laughing with the Yoons, not even looking in Shree's direction.

At the new Prius, Shree held her breath. If the secret key truly held magical powers, then it could open any car door. She told herself she was nuts again, but it wasn't going to stop her from investigating. Shree drew the key from her pocket. It was too big for the lock, too big, and not at all the right shape.

Shree put the key up to the lock anyway. She touched the key to the circle of metal. The key gave a little jump, as if it were magnetized to the lock.

And then, the door opened.

Shree spent the rest of the day fantasizing about all the things she would do with the secret key.

She'd start out by going to the bookstore after closing hours and "borrowing" all the books she'd ever wanted to read.

She'd take her friends from the Bronx to Great Adventure Theme Park and turn on all the rides in the middle of the night.

She'd also go to—

Shree interrupted her daydream and looked over at her father, who was chatting with Nancy's dad, most likely about something science-related. At that exact moment, her father caught Shree looking at him and smiled.

Shree smiled back and waved.

Yes, she knew what she had to do. The list of things Shree could use the secret key for was endless, but there was something she needed to do for her father. It would take a lot of planning and it'd probably end up being much more dangerous than hunting for treasure in Cambridge.

Shree looked over at her friends and wondered if they'd be up for more adventures. She knew that she'd be hearing from the Demons in the near future. She was certain that they were planning their revenge. She'd just have to be prepared for them.

But for now, though, the secret key would stay right where it belonged—firmly attached around her neck—until the right time came.

Shree went back over to her friends and family, picked up the biggest honey granola bar on the platter, and joined the party.

A Big Thanks

To my family and friends
       for your love,

To Heidi Connolly and Nancy Butts
       for the editing,

To Kim Wagner
       for the cover and website,

To John Rizzo at BookSurge
       for the publishing advice,

To Jack Johnson and David Berkeley
       for your music,

To Jon Stewart and Stephen Colbert
       for your comedy,

And to Shree
       for your inspiration.

Made in the USA
Charleston, SC
12 July 2010